The Auctioneer

CHRISTINE MASTERSON

H 21377798

LIBRARY
SERVICE

Copyright © 2015 by Christine Masterson

All rights reserved. This book or any portion thereof may not be reproduced or used in any manner whatsoever without the express written permission of the publisher.

Standard Copyright License

Christine Masterson has asserted her right under the Copyright, Designs and Patents Act 1988 to be identified as the author of this work.

This is a work of fiction and, any resemblance to actual persons, living or dead, is purely coincidental.

First Printing: 2015

ISBN: 978-0-9930915-7-5

Published by: Christine Masterson, Wexford, Ireland

Book cover: Concept and Design Christine Masterson.
Painted by Liberty Henwick. Photographed by Colette Ward.

email: info@christinemasterson.ie

Available on www.lulu.com

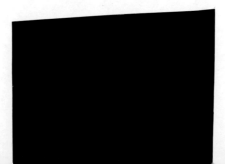

For my parents

Christopher and Lena

Many thanks to my children Ryan and Carolyn. Thanks also to my family in Dublin and The Netherlands, especially my sister Jean for all her encouragement and my brother Stephen for all his support. Thanks to Margaret Galvin who helped me in the very early stages of this book. I would also like to acknowledge Mary Devine, Paul Valette-Devine, Laura Morgan, Liberty Henwick, Colette Ward, Gillian Spurway, Celine Murphy, Gillian Doyle, Carmel Harrington and Ciara Doran for their advice and support in bringing this book to fruition.

This book is also dedicated to my cousin and friend, Ursula Weston (1960-2009) to whom I first spoke about writing a book when I was eleven.

THE AUCTIONEER

I am driving along country roads listening to the radio, it's one of those programmes on how to fulfill your dream and I think of the dream I've always had which is to be a writer. I ask myself, since I always wanted to be a writer, how come I ended up being an auctioneer?

I like to think there is a connection between the two. To me buying and selling houses is a backdrop to the stories and dramas of people's lives. People selling their home, leaving one chapter of their lives behind. People buying, hoping to start a new, better one. Each client to me is interesting. I look at them and wonder what is their individual story?

I work in an auctioneering practice in Wexford, a small seaside town. My boss is nearly seventy and he never married, so at this stage the business is just a pastime to him. He is happy to just let me get on with it. "Tim," he often says. "Only phone me if you have a problem, otherwise deal with it yourself."

So, to my delight I can use my power to bring about what I believe to be the best for people. When, for example, there are a number of people interested in the same property, I literally conspire to sell it to the person I think most deserves it. Call me arrogant; call me unprofessional, I don't mind. I feel it is my only chance to manoeuvre the fates, to put a sense of fairness into an unfair world. In a way I'm an idealist. You see, I like to do good.

Take the property I am selling today. It's a cottage on an acre of land with lots of potential. Everyone's dream. There are three parties interested in it and I have already met one. Her name is Maureen and I showed her the cottage earlier at noon today.

She arrived at the property looking slightly disheveled and stressed. She was a small plump woman in her early fifties and she got out of the car and slammed the door with such a sense of purpose that I knew she was a woman with a mission. She walked quickly up to me and we introduced ourselves.

Her hurry could have been the simple fact that she had to collect her grandchildren within the hour or she was about to make some major changes in her life. Which would it be? It didn't take long to find out.

It's a gift I've got you know. People talk to me; tell me things about their lives. I think because my face is round and soft looking it gives me a personable aura which they find unthreatening. If I had sharp features with lots of hard angles it may give the impression that my view of them was sharp and unsympathetic and stop them from confiding in me.

I showed her into the cottage and she stood breathless in the living room clasping her hands against her chest. "It's perfect, I love it," she said and then she listed off its attractions. "Plenty of light for painting, an open fireplace and the view!" she exclaimed. She flung her arms wide, embracing the room. "I want it cleared out," she said, "pared back with nothing in it except the essentials, my easel, couch and small table. It's so calming. I want calm," she said emphatically, "I *must* have calm," she said again, emphasizing the must.

Her cheeks were red with excitement and she almost squealed with delight. She turned and must have caught the bemused look on my face when she said. "Oh, don't mind me; I am just so delighted to have found the place of my dreams. The only trouble is Harry," she said in a low voice as if talking to herself, "he can come or he can stay in Dublin and preferably I hope he stays," she continued. "I'll just tell him that there are no golf clubs here. That will keep him at home."

My own mind was full of questions now. Who was Harry? Was she moving here for good? I decided to pick a question to ask which would reveal me in the least inquisitive light yet give me the most information. I gently rubbed my forehead with my middle finger and asked quizzically, "Who is Harry?"

"Harry," she replied in exasperation, "is my husband, the man who is driving me to distraction – well only partly. My whole family is. Harry retired six months ago from the bank and far from the lovely relaxing life I thought we would lead, it's turned into a nightmare. I am like a secretary to him for his golf. He's never there. My two daughters have children whom they dump on me at a moment's notice. The only saving grace in my life is my son. He is lovely; he gives me no trouble at all. I can talk to him. He told me to start doing what I want with my life. 'Take up painting again,' he suggested, so I started looking at cottages in the country and when I saw this one I told Harry that I wanted to buy it. We are not short of funds you know," she said, averting her eyes, "although I'm sure I shouldn't be telling you that," she said glancing back at me. "Well what really made my mind up was Harry's reaction to my saying I wanted to buy a place. He laughed and said, "You! imagine you living in the country," "That's it," I thought, "I'm going to leave them all and live here for six months to a year and paint to my heart's content."

I liked this woman. In many ways her frustration reminded me of my own mother's and I resolved to try and turn her dream into a reality. I am a man who has a great affinity with women, especially when they are downtrodden. I was the only boy in a house with an older sister and my mother and father. Their marriage was not good. I watched with dismay as my mother struggled to bring harmony into a relationship where the pair were so obviously mismatched. He was the type of man who, when her heart soared to the sound of a song and she began to sing, his voice grew grumpy with the noise. Because of my background, my antennae are very finely tuned into any woman's distress. And they were finely tuned to Maureen.

We said our goodbyes and she promised to ring me later. She shook my hand firmly and said, "I want it; I really, really, want it."

Buyers number two is a couple and are just coming in the gate. They introduce themselves to me as Rory and Jane. I lead them in to the house. He has a protective arm around her as if for some reason she needs protecting. He is tall and my sister would describe him as very handsome. As I look at her I find myself confronted by a sea of beige. Everything about her is beige. Her coat is beige, her hair is beige, even her skin is pale beige. Her appearance exudes the attributes of a dull, boring woman. Colour must be anathema to her. They look around the room and my instant impression of her as she opens her mouth is of a whinger. Her voice is high in pitch and while sentences come out they are really a series of complaints.

"It's too small and it smells damp," she whines in her baby voice. "I couldn't move into it like this. Could you build an extension for me?" Rory smiles reassuringly. Yes, yes, he will do exactly as she wants. She is not to worry he says. I look at them and wonder. I have seen this sort of relationship before. A good man coupled with a spoilt moan, being crucified by his own goodness and sense of duty. It always mystified me how two people like this, so opposite, could end up together. His character so openly optimistic and energetic, hers so weak and despondent yet with, I suspected, a well masked domineering streak in her nature. The reasons he is with her, must go back to his childhood, I thought dismissively. He must have issues with his own mother.

He loved the house and kept emphasizing every positive point. She was still unsure when they left. Moments later he came back into the cottage and said to me with a wink, "I think I'll be able to persuade her. I know she will love it." He had the demeanour of a little boy trying to please one of his parents. I looked at him trying to conceal any trace of contempt that I knew threatened to settle on my face. "You have my number," I say with false cheerfulness. "Ring me when you decide." But I had decided – they were definitely not getting this house.

They have only just gone when the third couple walk up the path. They look so young. They couldn't be any older than twenty two. They bound into the cottage. The girl speaks first, "Hi I'm Cathy, this is Paul," she says in a friendly voice. "Tim isn't it?" she asks, gesturing towards me. "I'm Tim Brady," I reply smiling. They are full of enthusiasm as they look around "Great isn't it" Paul says. "It is," I reply evenly. "How much do you think it would take to make it fairly habitable, comfortable even?" Cathy asks. "€20,000" I say. Their faces grimace. They look crestfallen. I know they can't afford it. I want to say to them wait, you have loads of time. "Well, we'll think about it," they say heading towards the door. I sensed I wouldn't be hearing from them again. I knew from experience that this particular dream of theirs was gone.

Later, as promised, Maureen phones me. "I'm offering the asking price," she says, "I am sending you a deposit today and I can have the rest of the funds available in three days."

Great! I thought. I got back to the vendor. She was delighted, but wanted to wait to hear from Rory and Jane. When I told Rory of the previous offer he then offered more and went on to say that they were fully mortgaged approved. "Shit," I thought. "Alright, I'll inform the vendor," I reply dully. This is where I know I am going to have to use my formidable skills of persuasion.

"Hi Ann," I begin, "there has been a higher offer from Rory, but in my experience it is not as solid as Maureen's. As they will have to organise a mortgage there could be delays with life assurance, etc." I rattle on. "I personally think they will have problems getting life assurance because, to be honest, she doesn't look the healthiest woman to me, very pale you know. God knows what she might have wrong with her. I know you want a quick sale and the quickest sale will be with Maureen."

"Are you sure she has the money?" Ann asks.

"Yes, I'm sure," I reply. "It's a rock solid offer."

"Alright," Ann says wearily, "go with Maureen."

Recently when I drove past the cottage on a summer's day it had been transformed. It's painted white with a welcoming red door. There's a new conservatory added to the side full of colourful plants and flowers. I slowed the car down and out came Maureen, slimmer with her hair tied up in a scarf, wearing a loose shirt and trousers, looking every inch the artist. She gave me a huge wave and big smile and I knew that she was happy. I wondered how the rest of her story will pan out. I probably will never know, but I was just glad that, for a short while, I had been part of it.

TIM

Lyn's voice calls through from the outer office, "Tim there's a call on the line; it's your sister, Clare."

I pick up the phone.

"Hi Tim," she says in her cheery voice.

"Hi Clare," I reply, trying to sound enthusiastic.

"I haven't heard from you in ages," she says, "you never ring, we miss you."

"I've been too busy," I reply.

"How's life?" she asks.

"It's great," I reply.

"Any new romances then?"

I want to tell her to mind her own business, but she hurts easily so I say nothing. She believes in the boy meets girl, girl meets boy happy ever after stories. It worked out well for her. I can hear her three boys in the background.

"Did you know that Helen's home?"

I pause.

"Tim are you there?"

"Yes," I say coldly.

"If you like," she continues "I can arrange a …."

I've had enough of this I decide. "Clare I've got to go, I'll call you. Bye."

I put down the phone and place my head in my hands. Suddenly I feel tired. Helen's back, I wonder why. I did love her, a little, but she is one of those creative types and uses it as an excuse for everything. All her emotion, her self-expression got on my nerves eventually. That's why I left. I need someone more self-contained.

After London, Dublin didn't attract so I came to Wexford for a change. It's nice, the people are friendly, especially the girls.

There are disadvantages though. I find it very disconcerting, when I walk into a bar and bump into someone I've slept with. I prefer the city where a goodbye in the morning means goodbye forever.

I usually stand at the bar and we get talking and have a laugh. To be honest, I find it boring, the way it's put up to me so easily. There is no mystery, no hint of the chase.

I bring them out for meals, nice places. Sometimes I don't mind what we talk about. At other times, I would love a decent conversation, but they mostly want to talk about houses. My eyes glaze over as it's the last thing I want to do after a hard day at the office. When I try to initiate a conversation about politics or books, their eyes glaze over so we continue our conversation through a mutual blur, discussing irrelevancies. Once I got a veiled marriage proposal. She said to me excitedly: "I've got an acre with full planning permission, ready to go." I thought I'd never get out of there fast enough.

We may or we may not go back to my place, but if we do I always drive them home the next day. I used to utter the useless phrase; I'll ring you, until I said it to one woman recently. She laughed and said, "You don't even have my number," as if it didn't matter to her either way. Since then I don't bother saying it. It's not even expected anymore. We go our separate ways, both happy with what we've got.

I'm not usually in the pub at this time on a Saturday. I'm not long in when I notice someone new in the corner. She is stunningly beautiful with that unusual combination of auburn hair and creamy skin. I haven't seen her before. A few people greet her, she must be local. She comes over to the bar to order a drink. I do my best to engage her, but she avoids me. I am surprised, she completely ignores me. The bar is practically empty yet I can feel the warm heat of her body as she brushes by me. I glance over at her with a questioning look. She raises her glass slightly and smiles at me. I take that as a maybe and sense the unfamiliar thrill of a challenge as I head her way.

. . .

It's three months since I've met Kate and I am totally and absolutely in love with this woman. She is everything I have always wanted; confident, intelligent, witty, with a razor sharp mind. Somehow though we are off kilter. I know I am ready for the greatest love affair in my life and I see a wonderful journey ahead, yet when I try to make plans for the future her answer is a dispiriting "whatever." I am completely thrown.

7

The sexual chemistry between us is amazing, but for once it is not enough for me. I want more of her. I want to explore all these new emotions. To celebrate my love for her, but she'll go so far and no further.

Sometimes, when in sparkling form, she'll pull me close and be warm and loving and then just as quick, she'll change tack, and I'm left floundering again. I find myself reaching for her, seeking reassurance only to feel worse when she pulls away.

The strong confidence I once admired so much in her seems more and more like an impenetrable sheet of armour. The emotion is just not there. I think of Helen and whisper quietly, "I'm sorry." It's those fates again paying me back for being so callous.

There is no solid ground with her, everything keeps shifting. The uncertainty is driving me crazy. There is a tightening in my chest that is becoming more and more familiar with each passing day.

I keep thinking I'm missing something. Anything that will help me get a handle on Kate. I am desperate for clues. Outside I meet her young cousin. He is a funny kid with bright red hair. I buy him a few bars of chocolate and ask, "Do you know Kate well?"

"No," he replies and in between bites he tells me, "my mam says no one will ever really know Kate Tiernan. She is a dark horse."

I say goodbye and walk away.

I realize there is no great mystery to Kate, no complicated puzzle to solve. She is just a mass of contradictions. I misread her totally, mistook her lack of interest for a natural reserve. How can I trust my own judgment again? I feel so unsure, a completely new feeling to me.

I keep walking along the street and slip into a church for a few minutes. I begin to feel a comforting sense of peace. I am not moving from here - I know I have been running for years. I want to get back in touch with my family. That seems important right now. I don't even know my nephews. I think I'll ask them down and spend time with them; we'll have some fun together. I feel light and free as I step back out into the sunshine. I decide to go for a walk by the sea and luxuriate in these new found feelings of relief and be thankful for, what I see now, as my lucky escape.

KATE

They think I have no insight into myself in this town; that I plough through life unaware. They're wrong. I know exactly who I am. I know I hate my job at the Post Office and seek excitement in my abuse of men.

I was brilliant at school. In the last few years I just got lazy and gave up. I decided then I would do it the easy way. I would marry into it. Because I was a beautiful child things came easy to me. I always got extra sweets in the shop and busy people found time to talk to me. My motto now is, "Why bother? I'm all for an easy life."

My father was sad when I refused to aspire to college. Sad for what could have been.

I love to watch those courtroom dramas on television. I see myself as a prosecuting lawyer, tearing strips off the accused. I'd be an excellent lawyer if I could learn to control my prejudices.

I go for men who are well educated and polished. The truth is I am jealous of their education and aim to bring them down.
Although I am not a fool, I want the comfort all their education can bring eventually. In the meantime, I am just having a bit of fun.

When Tim finished with me Dad was sad again. "Kate," he said, "you are twenty seven years of age, don't you think you should be settling down?"

"Don't worry Dad," I said reassuringly. "There's a doctor and a dentist interested in me. I still have time."

He looked appalled. "Kate…" he began. I hushed him quiet and rushed out the door, late again for work.

He often stares at me and shakes his head. I baffle him. I know he blames himself. My mother died young through his neglect. Well, not really, but it's the accusation I hurl at him when I'm in a temper or not getting my own way.

She woke one night in terrible pain and begged him to call a doctor. He had a few drinks on him, which was unusual and roughly told her to go back to sleep, that she'd be alright in the morning. The morning came and through the stillness I heard his piercing scream. I ran into their room and saw him lying helplessly across her lifeless body. She had died during the night from appendicitis. He was never the same again. In all their years together his one act of carelessness led to such a catastrophic outcome. Still the power it's given me, living with a guilty man. I only have to mention her name to get what I want.

I love to walk along the quay watching the boats. It's where Paddy and I spent a lot of time in our childhoods. Paddy's my friend. He's easy to be with. I can read him like a book and he takes everything I say at face value. Here he is coming along the quay waving ecstatically. God it's disgusting how happy he is to see me. His face is beaming. "Let's go out tonight," I say. "I'm sorry Kate, I can't," he replies apologetically. "I've got great news," he continues. "I've just heard I've got the job in Dublin and if I do well they'll train me up. They want me there tomorrow." I am standing beside him, feeling slightly stunned. "You never told me any of this," I say rather too sharply. "I haven't seen you in ages," he answers. "You never returned any of my calls." "I hope it keeps fine for you," I snap back, unable to hide the begrudging tone in my voice and I'm not sorry when he walks away looking forlorn.

Paddy's going. I can't believe it. This must have happened when I was in the throes of my affair with Tim. Tim, his name repeats in my brain. I can see him clearly extolling my virtues, declaring I was the love of his life…speaking about this journey he wanted to share with me. The journey towards the vision he had for his life. Children eventually, a happy home, friends calling and mutual interests together. He asked was that what I wanted too? I didn't know what to say so I said a compliant, "Yes." He said he always hoped to meet someone with whom he could connect with on a deeper level. Someone he could share all his deepest thoughts with, bare his soul to. Soul? I asked and then to myself I answered bleakly, I don't want your soul, it's your sexuality I'm interested in. To hide my face I pulled him close and like a chameleon spoke words of love and devotion.

He wasn't my type anyway. His fussy words of sentiment in bed, the slow declarations of love, I saw as unnecessary delay. On our final night my patience snapped and in the intense peak of desire I pleaded, "Oh just get on with it will you." His face looked stricken, frozen in disbelief. He let out a soft moan and turned on his side, his back towards me. No amount of coaxing could win him round. He lay motionless, barely breathing, like a statue beside me. At least that's how he was when I fell asleep, moments later. The next day he was quiet and I left early thinking he'll get over it.

The following Tuesday he rang and asked me to see him. I was curious. I didn't normally see him on Tuesdays. He probably wants to give me another useless present I thought as I headed over there. Does he not know I have a drawer full of toiletries already and two boxes full of jewellery.

He asked me in. At first his voice gave nothing away. Then he looked at me with his brown eyes, with that penetrating look of his and said simply, "Kate we're finished." Well, I really was stunned. It had never happened to me before.

"Why?" I asked and continued insisting, "I think I deserve an honest answer from you."

"Honesty?" he scoffed. "What would you know about honesty?" Then he said wearily, "Kate you are the most dishonest person I have ever met. You are choked full of aggression."

"You must be joking," I shot back. "I never hit anyone in my life. How dare you!"

"No?" he queried quietly turning to face me fully. "You don't understand. It comes through you passively." he finished.

It did hurt and I hated the way I felt as I slunked away from his house. I felt disappointed with myself. I thought I would have had more time on Tim. I didn't get the chance to work on him properly, to play my psychological games. I like that. It's the part I most enjoy, watching the slow destruction of the personality, the breaking down piece by piece until at last, on the final onslaught, total doubt and uncertainty creeps into their psyche. It's then I walk away, satisfied.

It's seven o'clock on a summer evening and I am walking along the quays again alone. It's one of those easy Saturday evenings when the oncoming night holds all sorts of promise. I can see Jill Jacob with her husband Mark walking along their two young children running ahead of them. Jill gives me a wary look and instinctively links her husband's arm and moves closer to him. I want to say to her don't be concerned, your husband is safe from me that I don't go there, not yet anyway.

Pamela Rowe, so big and awkward in school, jogs assuredly in a pink tracksuit, her thick blond hair tied up in a ponytail which bounces from side to side with each step. I don't know what she is doing with her life, but I can see she is slim. That says everything to me. She must be happy and in control, I construe.

One of the shops along the quay front is a new boutique. It's been recently opened by another classmate of mine. I have the feeling that everyone is moving on, everyone except me. I feel huge resentment well up inside me. This terrible restlessness keeps tearing at me. If I had something in front of me to kick, I'd kick it. A stone obligingly appears in my path. I kick it hard in the direction of the sea and it soars high and free. I wish I could unleash myself up and out of this place, but I know I won't, the ever present inertia always preventing me.

I think of Paddy again. I can't imagine this place without him. He was just always there, part of the landscape of my life. I can feel the tears sting my eyes and hate him for making me feel this way – weak. Rallying, the thought occurs to me - Paddy in management? The idea is ludicrous. He'll be back within three months. He needn't appear to me. He knows sympathy is not one of my strong points.

Passing around the corner of the main street, I see Dr. Cleary coming out of Maeve Wynn's house. They look happy, as if they are going on a date. I'm astonished. Ordinary Maeve Wynn? What's he doing with her? I head home feeling exasperated, like my world doesn't make sense anymore. I don't know which is worse, seeing those two together or the first fine lines on my face this morning.

MAUREEN

On the fourth Sunday after moving in Maureen stood in the living room and happily surveyed the work done on the cottage. She had painters in; they had painted all the rooms white, except the bedroom which was toned a warm yellow. In her living room/studio she had just one couch coloured turquoise with lilac cushions, a small table and lamp for reading and her easel. She filled the conservatory with plants and flowers and one easy chair. When the light was poor she planned to bring the easel out and paint there.

Maureen reflected on her new independence. She had never felt so free in her life. Housework was minimal, a flip of a duster and a quick sweep were all that were needed. No big evening dinner either. She prepared simple meals for herself whenever the fancy took her. Maureen couldn't get over how buoyant she felt. Few possessions suited her. She enjoyed travelling lightly through her world.

Later that day, Maureen decided to take a walk towards the sea. Coming out of the cottage she saw a recognisable face pass by in a car. That's the nice auctioneer, Tim Brady, she thought and gave him a big wave. She felt happy and relaxed and full of enthusiasm for this new way of life.

She had just finished her walk and was approaching the cottage when she saw a familiar car in the driveway. Her heart dropped. Oh no, she thought, it's Harry. He was standing at the front door looking angry and bewildered. "Where the hell have you been?" he roared. "I'm an hour here waiting on you."

"Well if I'd known you were coming, I'd have been here for you," she said, in a don't-get-angry-with-me-tone.

She led him in.

"What kind of a set up is this?" he asked looking around incredulously. "It's like a church in here with all those candles. And what's that water I hear."

"It's a water fountain," Maureen answered. "It's what I need to promote calm," she continued nonchalantly. "I use it for my meditation exercises. This is all part of my personal development, my search for spiritual growth. I want to feel more grounded, at one with myself." she explained sanguinely, knowing, yet not caring that this sort of talk would drive him crazy.

"Your spiritual what?" he asked. "I never heard such rubbish in all my life. Listen, I haven't got time for this. Are you coming home or what? I need to know."

"No," she replied coolly. "I am not coming home, for the time being anyway. I came here to paint and I haven't had time to paint yet, what with getting the cottage ready and everything. I intend to start this week and I'll see how it goes from there."

"Well can I stay?" he asked.

"No," she replied, turning away from him and dismissing him with a gesture of her hands. "I've only a single bed, it would be uncomfortable for me, my hot flushes you know."

"Well when are you getting a double bed?" he asked. "You are my wife. I've a right to know."

"There, there, relax," she cooed. "Stop making such a fuss about nothing. Sit down. I'll go about it tomorrow. Would you like a cup of tea or a drink?" she asked, changing the subject.

"I'll have a drink," he replied sullenly.

After he had his drink he got up to leave. "I better head back," he said. "The traffic will be excruciating."

"Oh that's a pity," she replied, without a hint of emotion in her voice.

At the doorway he turned towards her. He looked defeated, in a state of total incomprehension. "You will see about that bed tomorrow," he asked hopefully.

"Yes, yes, of course I will," she said reassuringly.

"When will I see you?" he asked again.

"Sure, don't worry," Maureen replied. I'll see you when I see you."

The next day Maureen, true to her word, drove to Wexford to see about buying a double bed. In the furniture shop on the main street she surveyed the beds on view for some minutes. The shop assistant came towards her and asked, "Can I help you?"

"Yes you can," Maureen replied. "When can you have that yellow coloured bed delivered?

"That will take approximately three weeks," he politely replied.

"And this blue one?" she queried.

"The blue one is Italian and it will take longer, up to 11 weeks."

"I'll take the Italian one," Maureen replied firmly.

"I can try and get it delivered quicker for you if you like," he offered.

"No, no," Maureen hedged. "I'm in no hurry. Eleven weeks suits me fine."

She spent the rest of the day stocking up on the art materials she needed. Back in the cottage she decided to draw some preparatory pencil sketches to get started.

Two days later whilst expanding on one of these earlier drawings she heard a knock on the door. It was her son Shay. He came straight in. He looked flustered and irate. He got to the point of his visit quickly. "Mother," he began, "what do you think you are doing to the man? He is up there crying every night and has even taken to the odd shot of whiskey. I'm finding it very hard to handle. You've left it all to me. The girls keep away. And while I have every sympathy with you, don't you think you should have tackled this problem years ago? Done something about it then?" The words flowed from him in a flood of frustration. Maureen tried to placate him.

"Ah Shay, I didn't mean to upset anybody. I'll be properly set up in a few weeks and he can come down then. Look just do me a favour will you? Take him out for a few drinks. He knows some men in the local. You can plonk him amongst them and keep with your own friends. Please do that for me?" she implored.

"O.K. mam," he replied, "but I am not happy with this situation. I will be running away myself if things don't improve."

"Sit down; I'll make you some dinner. You look entirely wrung out," she said, anxiously observing him and looked relieved when he eventually sat down.

"Have a look at these sketches and tell me what you think of them," she asked.

He left at seven. His head full of promises from his mother.

The next day the sketching wasn't going too well for her. Maureen decided to water some of her plants in their boxes on the garden wall. She walked down the small path holding her watering can and purposefully proceeded to water the abundant plants. If she could have seen herself she would have been delighted at how pretty she looked. Her blond hair was freshly washed and hung in soft curls around her face. Her skin had a healthy glow which made the blue of her eyes appear more vivid and sparkling. Her lips looked full and soft looking.

She was startled when she heard a man's voice above her say: "Good afternoon, what delightful flowers. Would you mind giving me their names?" The sun was shining directly into her face. She put her hand up to shade her eyes and found herself looking into the most beautiful face she had ever seen. She found herself becoming flustered and embarrassed and began to speak rapidly from nerves. Her mind was going blank.

"Oh well," she began. "I'm not sure if I have any packets of seeds left. Maybe I do have some left over," she said backtracking indecisively.

He kept looking at her with an even stare and did not seem to want to move away. Maureen longed desperately to retreat to more familiar ground. The helpful side of her nature stirred and came to her rescue.

"I will look for them for you," she said, gladly turning to go back to the cottage.

She faltered, unsure what to do. A dilemma faced her. Would it look rude to leave him there and not ask him in or even ruder to ask him in? Instantaneously inspiration struck and she felt she had the more correct form of words to use which would solve the problem.

"Would you like to *step in* for a moment?" she asked.

He followed her through to the cottage and immediately Maureen rushed through the rooms excitedly looking for the extra packages. "Calm down," she ordered herself. It didn't help that he stood in the very centre of the living room able to survey her every move.

"You can sit down," she said hurriedly through a strained smile. Returning to the kitchen she flung open every press and drawer she could find. At last, in the bottom drawer she found them. Her face felt warm and she blew cool air through her mouth blowing the stray wispy strands of hair from her face. She told herself to count to ten and in a hopelessly exaggerated manner, sauntered back into the living room. He kept smiling at her. Maureen shopped short. She hoped that wasn't a sympathetic, teasing look she glimpsed in his eyes and the idea that he could be making fun of her suddenly made her feel cross. Her nervousness vanished. She handed him the packages and said curtly, her voice cold: "These are what you are looking for."

Sensing her change of mood he stood up to go. At the door he turned and said politely: "Thank you very much for your help."

"Not at all," she replied loftily.

"Goodbye," they said simultaneously and Maureen closed the door firmly behind him.

The next evening Maureen was in top form. She had started working with oils and they mixed beautifully releasing the exact tint of colour she required. At eight, she stopped and decided to read. She heard a tap at the window. She looked out and saw the stranger from yesterday giving her an uneasy salute. Maureen opened the door to him. He stood looking slightly sheepish at the doorway. Pushing a bottle of wine towards her he said, "Just a little something to say thank you again."

"Oh, why that's very nice of you." she exclaimed. Feeling positive she said, "Please come in. I'll get some wine glasses."

He sat at one end of the couch and she sat at the other. She took a few sips of wine, studying his face. It was striking. He was so dark. He wore a beard which had flecks of grey through it and his hair replicated it. His eyes were deep set, dark brown almost black in colour. Up closer she could see they held a kindly expression. His face was wide and his mouth generous.

"Your accent," she began, "it's not from around here."

"No it's not," he proffered. "I'm from Wales."

"Really?" she exclaimed. "I've noticed that," she continued, "there is an affinity between Wales and Wexford. A lot of Wexford people go to live and work there and vice versa."

"That's true," he said. "I've been coming here for years. I bought a place last year; it's just up the road. I love it here, it's so close to home," he said, "yet I can experience a totally different country. I find that very interesting."

"I can understand that," Maureen said. "I'm not from here either," she explained.

"I'm from Dublin. I came here to paint, to uncover my creative side again."

"I'm a musician myself," he said.

"Oh how lovely," Maureen thought.

"I specialize in jazz."

"What a coincidence!" Maureen exclaimed. "I love jazz too. My father introduced me to it. I have all of his records at home."

"There's a jazz session in the Talbot Hotel next Sunday morning, would you like to accompany me?" he asked.

"I would be delighted to," Maureen answered, genuinely pleased. "I'll call for you at eleven then. I better head home," he said. "I've left the doors unlocked. Stay where you are. I'll let myself out," he volunteered.

"Alright so, I'll see you on Sunday," Maureen said.

They saw each other regularly after that. That summer Wexford basked in glorious weather. There was a multitude of places to see. They visited the fishing village of Kilmore Quay with its quaint thatch cottages and pretty harbour, took walks on the beaches at St. Helen's Bay and Rosslare Strand and in the evenings had drinks in the Riverbank Hotel which was situated on the opposite side of the river. They enjoyed the wide vista of the town's twinkling lights sparkling on the water before them.

In the town they walked the narrow streets calling in to all the different art galleries, stopping for coffee along the way. The first time they went into a coffee shop Maureen watched as he ordered a slice of cake. Oh joy of joys she thought affectionately as she watched him devour the cake; how wonderful, he has a sweet tooth!

He talked of his vulnerability, the issue it was for him in his life.

Who hurt you she wondered, not able to bear the thought of it. It must have been his wife whom he'd left. That would explain the no wedding ring. He just had to be free, he just had to be free for her, she couldn't countenance anything else.

Why does he feel vulnerable? Maureen pondered later. This man who was so accomplished. This man with the wonderful mind.

He asked insightful questions of her. Questions like,

"Why do you want to paint?" and when she answered,

"Because I won't be happy unless I do."

"You want to honour yourself," he said.

"Yes, yes," she replied delightedly, beginning to believe the most seductive quality between two people was a shared understanding.

His character was formal and very well mannered. As she grew more comfortable with him she felt brave enough to tease him.

"Come out from behind your manners," she said, almost laughing, one evening.

"What do you mean?" he asked unsure of how to take it.

"I mean," Maureen expanded, "I want to know who's in there, who you are."

From then on he let his guard down and became more informal showing the more playful side of his nature. They shared the same sense of humour and often went into peals of laughter over simple, ridiculous things.

She never asked how he lived since he wasn't working, – he never asked her either. She didn't quiz him about previous women in his life and he never queried her. They avoided talk of the future. It was a relationship of the present, all the richer for these constraints.

He did like to elaborate on his youth in Wales, playing music, as the time he felt most alive. She loved listening to him tell her stories about important musicians, their lives, their loves, victories and defeats. She drank in the information, an enraptured listener.

In the evening when John left, Maureen never felt lonely. His presence seemed to remain in the cottage after his departure and his huge energy infused her whole being. Her work output was prolific. She painted energetic, vividly coloured pictures pouring her heart and soul into them. Her vibrancy radiated from them.

Her daughters on their regular phone calls often asked, "Are you lonely?"

"Not a bit," she told them. "I am painting, painting, painting, that's all I do all day." Her sister Pauline (Pol) who was a widow, her husband Peter having died years before, did come to visit and they took turns sleeping on the couch.

Three weeks after they'd met, John returned to Wales for a few days. He had some business he needed to attend to. On the night of his departure Maureen lay in bed thinking of him. She could feel his spirit like liquid swooshing all around her releasing a moist heat at the top of her legs, light pressure, like fingertips all over her body. Were his fantasies somehow transferring to her or merely mirroring her own?

On his return, Maureen stood with her back to the kitchen cupboards drinking tea. John was sitting at the table explaining about his trip, what he'd done in Wales. Her concentration was broken by the sight of his collar, it was standing up on one side of his shirt. It annoyed her. What a pity to spoil its classic line she thought. Moving towards him she reached out to fix it. So close she couldn't resist letting her fingers move slowly down his neck.

"I love you," she said as if it was the most natural thing in the world to say.

He pulled her down on his knee and kissed her. At first, Maureen thought it wasn't like kissing. It was more like melting in. His tongue flicked searching. She found him. It had been lips only with Harry for so long, she had forgotten the raw explosion of it. It's exquisite intimacy.

He took her by the hand and led her into the bedroom. They quickly undressed and he lay on top of her, both embracing the delicious sensations of skin on skin. Her breath was ragged, so strong was her desire for him. Holding her face in his hands he commanded, "Let it go," and she breathed out all the pain and disappointment of her life and breathing him in she whispered, "I'm ready." On the first thrust she came. Only then recognising she was ready from the first moment she laid eyes on him.

The summer months passed quickly. Calls from Dublin stopped. Maureen lived out her life in a cocoon of warmth, love, fun and happiness. She loved this man so much. Her more rational mind knew there was a danger of being completely engulfed by him. At times she wanted to say to him, please turn down the dial on the intensity of your personality, but she knew that would hurt him. She ignored her concerns and gladly relinquished herself to him.

He took such care of her. The little thoughtful acts he did. Once when she had a bad cold he brought her two cold preparations and even made them up for her and insisted she take them. If she had a pain in her shoulder from painting, he didn't mind rubbing it for ages until the ache eased. She loved his kindness. It was an inherent part of him, not forced or false, it came naturally to him. He made her feel special, valued. Maureen was good to him too and loved to surprise him with small gifts.

One evening in the early autumn Maureen thought it was strange. It was a quarter past seven and John was due since seven. It wasn't like him to be late. His punctuality was faultless. Maureen was expecting her sister the next morning, so she busied herself with jobs in the kitchen. By eight she became worried and taking her coat from the stand at the door, made her way up the road to his house. The autumnal air was cool and an easterly wind was beginning to stir. When she reached the house she was surprised to find it in darkness. She went to see if she could look through the windows. Frustratingly all the blinds were pulled down. She began to panic. What had happened to him? He could be lying in there ill from the previous night. She ran towards the next door neighbour, as John was friendly with the old man who lived there, Toss Doyle. He answered the door calmly to her excited knock.

"Toss," she exclaimed. "I'm worried about John. There is no sign of life at the house. Have you a key?"

"No, little lady friend," he replied, without any trace of malice in his voice. "John took the key off me this morning. He's gone back to Wales. He said his wife wants him home."

Maureen stared open mouthed. A gust of wind caught in her throat and she gasped. Her lungs felt as if they were drowning in air. Coughing and spluttering she said goodbye to Toss and closing her coat tightly around her she ran towards the safety of her home. Inside she clambered for the phone. Shay answered.

"Is you father there?" Maureen asked, trying not to make it sound like a demand.

"No, he's gone out."

"Gone out?"

"Yes," he continued, "with Mai Donnelly."

"Mai Donnelly?" Maureen repeated.

Shay spoke gently. "He met her in the pub. Things move on mam," he explained.

"Oh, I know love, I know," she said. Slowly she replaced the phone. Her eyes were drawn to her paintings on the floor, on the walls. What once seemed such rich jewel like colours now glared back at her accusingly, seeming cheap and vulgar. A heavy blackness descended upon her. Her last thought before she blacked out was, Oh God, please don't let this be a stroke.

H 2137798

LIBRARY
SERVICE

Pauline found her and rang the doctor. Together they prepared her for bed.

"Extreme emotional distress," the doctor said and then in a jaunty voice added, "She needs bed rest. In a few days she will be fine. She needs someone to look after her. Can you stay?" "I can," Pauline replied, and added to herself. This will take longer than a few days.

Maureen slept for hours. When she woke and her consciousness filtered through, her body felt heavy, as if it was entombed. Her heart seemed to beat slow and weak as if its only function was too much for it. Sharp dart like pains stabbed at its core. Her hand reached up towards it and she let it rest there, willing it to fight on. She had absolutely no energy. Life seemed to have drained from her. When Pauline came into the room Maureen looked at her beseechingly and said weakly, "Please get rid of the paintings."

"I promise I will," Pauline reassured her.

"Pol, it's my heart," Maureen spoke in a hushed tone, "I have pains in my heart."

"Your heart is broken," Pauline replied. Don't mind what that doctor said. Straightening the bed, she pulled the covers up under Maureen's chin and looking into her eyes said firmly, her voice full of concern

"Rest Maureen, that's all you can do. I'm here. You just rest now."

Maureen let herself sink back into unconsciousness and was grateful for the peaceful oblivion it offered.

The next day Maureen made to get up. "This is silly," she said to her sister. "All this lying around. It's so unlike me."

"Hop back into that bed," her sister ordered. "There's no reason to get up. The weather is awful. It's lashing rain outside. I'll be in with your breakfast in a few minutes."

Maureen gratefully climbed back into bed. She lay there listening to the rain on the window. How could she ever get over him? All the pulsating life they'd shared together, just gone, vanished. It was like she'd been hollowed out and he'd made off with the best part of her. All she'd left of herself was an empty shell.

Pauline came in with her breakfast. She placed the tray on the bed and left. Maureen took one sip of tea and one bite of toast and the rest remained untouched. Her mind felt as if it was going down deeper, turning in on itself. She stared ahead, her expression vacant. She knew she could go mad yet the thought didn't frighten her. Should she let go, embrace it, she pondered? Madness seemed easy, a perfect excuse for dealing with life. Her children now came into her mind. What would they say? How could she leave them the legacy of an insane mother? Her grandchildren, could she fight back for them? She turned her face to the wall and great sobs of grief poured from her. Her body vibrated with their violence. Wails of sorrow rose from her. She cried and cried until she felt physically wrecked. Then a strange calmness settled on her. The unavoidable agony seemed to rest effortlessly on her. Her acceptance was now complete.

Over the next few days high winds and rain lashed the cottage. Pauline went to the shop and stocked up. The weather was conducive to their mood. They lit the fire and sat either reading or talking for hours on end.

After some time Maureen felt particularly hemmed in.

"I've always felt crushed by people in my life," she cried, her voice full of belligerence.

"I have such a huge amount of love and passion in me that people find me too much. They just don't believe it. The only one who didn't try to compress me was my father and he died when I needed him. We shared the same spirit. Harry doesn't need what I have. John celebrated it, my life-force, my being, my exuberance."

Pol wasn't going to indulge Maureen's theatrics. "Your intensity used to annoy me when you were a child." Pauline said quietly.

"Yes and your logic always annoyed me." Maureen retorted hotly.

"Why didn't you ask him if he was married?"

"I was afraid of the answer," Maureen replied.

"So you avoided it?"

"Yes."

"Not very clever," Pol said.

"Don't judge me," Maureen snapped. Her eyes flashed moist with fury.

"I am not judging you," Pol replied. "I just can't help forming the opinion that you should have finished one mess before you started another."

"My marriage was well finished," Maureen replied.

"Yes, but did Harry know?"

"He knew, but was quite happy to accept the status quo."

"The one thing I didn't like about John was the attraction he had to the dark. Some of those books he read were cuckoo."

"No, no, he was good," Maureen insisted. "I refuse to believe anything else about him. He brought out all my creativity. I never would have done any of those paintings without him."

"That's nonsense," Pauline said. "He unleashed it, that's all, but it had to be there first. It was in you Maureen. Give yourself credit for that."

"I loved his way with words. The things he said to me were pure poetry. I will never forget them."

"Maureen," Pauline interjected, you are fifty-two years of age, unhappily married for years. It wouldn't take Einstein to work out what to say to you."

"Oh for God's sake leave me something will you?" Maureen lashed at her sister. "He was sincere. You go too far with the big sister act. Of course this would never happen to you," she sneered sourly. "You being so sensible."

"How do you know?" Pauline responded quietly. Maureen looking puzzled said, "I didn't know you had men friends."

"I just never told you," Pauline answered. "I never gave my all Maureen, not like you. I always held myself back. I think living with Peter for so long, I never knew where I stood with him, not like you and Harry." There was a hint of regret in her tone. Maureen searched her face, a new awareness falling on her. Breaking the pause she continued. "You always liked Harry didn't you? she asked.

"I used to envy you," Pauline replied. "Harry was so steady."

They sat still together marvelling at the irony of their lives. Maureen spoke first.

"Why can't there be a five or ten year contract on marriage and after that time we can look around, see if someone else suits us better and then freely swap and live happily ever after. I know children complicate things, but this is an ideal world I am talking about."

A week later the letter came. Pauline stood at the end of Maureen's bed early that morning. "It's for you," she said, gently handing the letter to her.

"No, you read it please," Maureen begged. "You know everything anyway."

"If you're sure," Pauline said.

Maureen stared out through the cottage window at the mainly flatness of Wexford, towards the faraway hills in the distance as his words poured over her.

"I'm sorry.... My wife is patron of ... .comfortable life...... need security for my creativity.....we have an open arrangement....and finally; I do and always will love you. Your beauty and innocence brought me great joy and happiness. Your ever loving, John."

Maureen stayed looking out the window and let what she thought must be the final tears that were in her begin to flow. Pauline left the room, gently closing the door behind her.

Maureen didn't get up that day or in the evening either. At dusk the room took on an unreal feel, the warm hues of yellow and orange comforting and soothing her. When night-time came and she felt certain that all the world was locked away she came out to Pauline who was reading in their small living room.

"I think it's done now," she said resignedly, "most of my grieving is done. Will you come out with me tomorrow?" she asked her sister. "We'll go somewhere, do something."

"I will," Pauline said, her eyes full of compassion.

"Thanks," Maureen replied and they squeezed hands together in a joint conspiracy of consolation.

The next day, at Our Lady's island, a place of pilgrimage in Wexford, Maureen stood looking towards the outdoor alter, at the small cross placed at its side.

"He warned against this," she said quietly. "These agonizing human dramas people find themselves in. More than anything I think He is a great psychologist." Maureen said a quiet prayer willing it to join in with the prayers of previous generations, becoming strengthened and hopefully bringing what she most longed for, some semblance of peace.

"Come on," Pauline said ruefully, "there's a nice pub across the road, I think we deserve an early drink."

Peace did not come easy to Maureen. Pounding the sands of Rosslare beach she felt she had never hated a woman so much in her life. How could his wife be so cavalier and let him go for months on end? How could he settle for so little? She hoped she was rake thin with a hard face and that during lovemaking his hips were destined to grate against pure bone. She must be thin. John was always in raptures about Maureen's softness, her fabulous fullness he called it. Once he said to her, "You never use the word should." Obviously his wife used it endlessly and in her more vengeful moments Maureen hoped he heard it a million times a day from now on.

Rosslare port was situated at the end of the bay where twice daily ferries made the fifty mile journey across the Irish Sea to Wales. Once in a mad moment she considered jumping on the ferry. She knew she'd be in Wales within three hours. She imagined herself running through Welsh streets, grabbing people by the arm and demanding of them, "Do you know John Edwards? Where's John Edwards?" She rallied between vengefulness and a claustrophobic overwhelming sense of despair. As the days went by, turning into weeks, Maureen knew she couldn't continue like this.

She came to a decision. Taking every petal off the late summer rose bushes in her garden, she put them into her pockets until they could hold no more and drove down the laneway towards the sea. Parking the car, she made her way through the small opening onto the sandy beach. She walked for some minutes until she was well clear from the restaurants and hotels.

The sea was calm and still that late September morning as if the Universe, understanding the importance of the ceremony she was about to perform, had arranged all its elements in such a way as to create the perfect backdrop for it. The sky out towards the horizon was streaked with coral cirrus clouds, the sun shining through them casting a pinky hue. Absorbed in the task, Maureen raised her hand and let the rose petals drop softly onto the water. Watching them fall she said out loud, "John I forgive you and anyone else who loves you."

At first the water seemed to play with the petals as if they were being tickled on the surface. Then the drag of the current brought them further out to sea.

The deep connection between her and John was so strong, she knew, at some level, he would sense her forgiveness, his being released.

"I love you John," she said and began walking slowly back down the beach.

The following day whilst packing up, Maureen decided to place two paintings strategically on each side of the car window. The idea of a moving exhibition appealed to the show off in her. She hoped that there would be lots of traffic in Dublin so that when stopped she could gauge what the passing motorists thought of her work. Beside her was the one painting she would keep. The one with the subtle colours which she would place on whatever wall she ended up in as a testimony to her survival instincts.

Turning into the main street in Wexford, cars were stopped to a crawl, inching their way by. Oh an autumnal wedding, how lovely Maureen thought. There's Tim Brady standing on the steps of the church looking so handsome in his brown pin stripe suit and crisp white shirt. Who is that gorgeous dark haired girl standing beside him? she wondered.

Heading out onto the open road she turned on the radio and heard one of her favourite happy tunes from the early 70's. It reminded her of when she was young and free.

"I am free," she said, the implications dawning on her.

A surge of happiness flooded through her as she pressed her foot on the accelerator. She opened the window; the wind blowing through her hair, suffused her whole being with the giddy thrill of new hope, a new life, a second chance.

KATE

The early summer weeks trudged on for Kate. Each week passed as uneventfully as the last. By late July she had spent the previous four Saturday nights on her own. Even her father had noticed, making tentative enquiries about her social life, her staying in.

After being on a high of male adulation for most for her life Kate couldn't comprehend the fact that there was no man on the scene. Not one, or the hope of one either. All of a sudden the town seemed to be full of either young boys or old men. She even visited the dentist hoping to ignite some interest and was shocked when she couldn't raise a smidgen of lust from him.

Kate was incensed. I am the beauty, I am the prize she reminded herself and felt indignant at how her life was shaping up.

Thinking of Tim she felt a twinge of regret. Trust him to be so sensitive. Could he not even take a joke? Dismissing him from her thoughts she felt she was well rid of him. She wasn't going to waste her life tip toeing around him, watching every word she uttered.

In early August scorching heat descended on Wexford. On her days off Kate roamed the beaches, the sight of happy families heightening her loneliness. There was a sense of exhilaration in the air which she didn't share.

Kate came to hate the intense sun. The bright cheery weather was in sharp contrast to her humour. She felt pressure to be outdoors and happy which only served to accentuate her unhappiness. She longed for dull weather when it was more acceptable to stay indoors and nurse her maudlin mood. As the days passed she reduced her outings to the late evening wearing a cotton shirt, jeans, hat and glasses. She didn't want to meet anyone. She just wanted to be left alone in her misery.

"Hi Kate, beautiful weather isn't it?" a neighbour asked.

"Yes," she replied, preparing to move away.

"Are you going on any holidays?"

"No," she responded sourly.

Tess Codd was insignificant. Kate didn't bother trying to make excuses as to why she wasn't going away. The truth was she had no one to go away with. If she heard any more details of other people's holidays, she'd scream.

Restless and agitated, she roamed the house more irritable and snappy towards her father than usual.

A few days later Kate celebrated her 28th birthday. If celebrate was the word. Her father invited her out for a meal to the most expensive restaurant he could afford.

"Pick whatever you want from the menu Kate, you can have whatever you want," he said, beaming proudly at her.

Kate sat scowling. "Am I supposed to be grateful?" she asked, undoing the folds of her napkin with a sharp snap of her wrist.

"I want you to have a nice evening Kate," he said softly, weary from the familiar rebuke.

Nice? Kate wondered. How can I have a nice evening sitting opposite a 70 year old? I should be out with the man of my dreams, not with an old man like him.

The waiter appeared and they ordered.

Kate felt completely locked in, the back of her chair was hedged against the wall with only a narrow table between herself and her father. She had to face a whole two hours sitting opposite him. At least at home she could excuse herself after her dinner and abscond to some other room. Now she is forced to really see her father and she didn't like what she saw. Noticing how shrunken his face had become, Kate watched in disgust as he attacked his food with gusto, his jaws having to work harder because of badly fitting teeth.

"Is Paddy coming home this weekend?" he asked brightly.

"Yes," Kate replied.

"I'm sure he'll have a lovely present for you," her father said, trying to humour her.

"Have you nothing else to talk about only Paddy?" Kate scoffed. "You never stop talking about him."

"It's just that he is such a nice boy. You could do worse."

"No, I couldn't," Kate said with exasperation, annoyed at his pointed reference to Paddy as a marriage proposition.

"I can't believe you're 28," her father said. "Time flies."

It was the wrong thing to say. I can't believe I'm 28 either Kate mused in amazement, the reality of her single state inducing an unfamiliar feeling of depression. How would she ever achieve her dream of marriage and kids by thirty? She'd wanted her future wrapped up and mapped out again then. She'd have to put that forward to at least 31 or, in the worst case scenario, 32.

Walking home that night Kate had the sense her life was hurling towards some awful emptiness, nearing some terrible dead end. There was something in the air, an uncertainty about her future which she'd never felt before. Kate sensed imminent change. She wasn't sure if it was her imaginings or just the early autumnal chill.

The next day Kate lay on her bed reading. God I'm bored, so bloody bored she thought, flinging the book to the end of the bed. I need a man she asserted lying back on her pillow. Her desire, she knew, was the problem - what to do with it. It had nowhere to go. She couldn't put her mind to anything, all her focus was on the ultimate release. She wished the weather would break. The tension of thunder in the air was almost unbearable. A dog next door kept barking, short rasping barks, heightening the strain on her nerves.

But in this heat the house feels oppressive. Although the small house is over fifty years old, it is decorated in a modern way. Kate has bullied her father into allowing her to decorate a number of times over the years. Cool blues and soft greys are the colours that permeate the house.

In the shower Kate turns the water to cool and stands under it. Washing over her skin she reflects on how no man had touched her since Tim. Look at what they're missing she muses smiling to herself, dreamily lathering soap all over her full breasts and curves.

In the bedroom a drawer full of her itsy bitsy pieces of underwear only serve to remind her of the sex she is not having so she firmly closes it and picks cotton pyjamas from a shelf instead.

Downstairs Kate moves from the kitchen to the living room carrying her indolence from one room to another. She takes a magazine and sprawls herself on the couch. Hearing the key turning in the door, her father comes into the hallway laden down with grocery bags.

"Pops make me a coffee will you?"

Within minutes her father dutifully brings in a mug of coffee.

"Look at you Kate. You're barely dressed. Go and put some clothes on. Your aunt Nina is coming for a visit tonight. She rang late this afternoon. Rouse yourself and give me a hand."

Kate stands in the kitchen avoiding as much work as possible. She is not in the humour to make the effort and lets her father do most of the preparations.

"Is the gorgeous Gareth coming?" she asks.

"No he isn't and don't speak about Nina's new husband like that."

"Well, he is rather dashing."

"He's a nice man," her father replies firmly. "I'm glad Nina has found happiness at last."

Although this visit is putting Kate out, she is glad of the company. She likes Nina and admires her sense of style. Nina is the much younger sister of her father, an intelligent, serene woman. For years she worked as an air hostess when air hostessing was considered glamorous and her sense of grooming was impeccable. Kate has always been a little fascinated with Nina, revering her almost regal carriage.

Suddenly it now seems important to Kate to look well and make a good impression. In her bedroom she chooses an outfit which will determinedly emphasize her youth. She picks a gold top with thin straps which she knows will show off her shoulders and young skin, matching it with a full cream skirt falling just below the knee with lace detailing dipping beneath the hem. Her gold espadrille sandals make the best of her legs. She applies her make-up expertly paying particular attention to her eyes and lips. Pleased with her reflection in the full length mirror she hears her father call her name.

Downstairs she carries the plates of snacks her father has prepared out to the table in the garden. The plates are full of attractively displayed sandwiches and delicious cakes and biscuits.

Outside Kate casts her eyes over the garden checking its appearance. This garden planned by Kate and executed by her father. It has borders at its sides full of plants and shrubs. Pale wood decking has been built near the house where the table and chairs are placed. It's most interesting feature is the wall at the very back, which at one time had been part of the old granite wall which once surrounded the town of Wexford. Kate has embedded plants in its rocky crevices and these have begun to flower, their dainty colors adding a light prettiness to the garden.

She hears voices in the kitchen. Nina and her father come out towards her.

"Kate how are you?" Nina asks warmly. "You look wonderful."

"Great to see you," Kate says, kissing her aunt on both cheeks.

"I thought we'd sit out here for a change," Kate explains. "It's such a warm evening."

"It's lovely here Kate. You've kept it lovely," Nina says, looking around.

"I do my best," Kate replies. "I have wine chilling for you. I know white is your favourite," Kate adds.

"Have one with us Matthew," Nina says, noticing the double wine glasses poured.

"I just have to check something in the oven," he says, getting flustered and runs back into the kitchen.

Kate studies Nina. She has the same colouring as herself. Her hair, caught in a loose chignon at the nap of her neck, is expertly highlighted with tints of russet which accentuated her peachy complexion. She wears an elegant satin blouse and straight cut skirt, her long legs crossed gracefully, her skin silky through the sheen of her stockings. She is so pleasant to look at Kate finds herself warming to her. She watches as her aunt takes a cigarette from the packet and lights it with a slim gold lighter.

"Are you not out with a boyfriend on a Saturday night?" Nina asks.

"No, I'm in a fallow period."

They both laugh.

"There are only old men and young boys in this bloody town." Kate asserts.

For a few moments Kate wonders whether to confide in her and then dying to be rid of the burden of her feelings she begins: "Nina, you were single for a long time. How did you eh,… I mean, well …how did you cope?" she asks, keeping her eyes cast down toying with the heel of her sandal.

"Cope?" Her aunt repeats.

"I mean, when you didn't have a boyfriend."

A slight smile plays on her aunts lips. She won't be drawn. Kate feels she is getting nowhere. Exasperated she expands.

"Oh come now Nina, you're not that delicate. I think you know what I mean. If you want I'll spell it out. How did you survive without sex?"

32

Her aunt pulls on her cigarette and exhales slowly she seems deep in thought. After a few moments she speaks in a measured way. "Sex can be a woman's trap," she says softly. "It can lead you to places that maybe you shouldn't go."

"To be pulverized with pleasure is exactly the place I want to go to," says Kate in a rush reaching for the box of cigarettes.

Nina seeing her agitation calmly places her hand over hers.

"Or even worse it can make you stay in places that maybe you should leave."

"I've always held the key in relationships Nina. No one has ever locked me in."

"Not yet perhaps," her aunt warns. "Coping with frustration is all part of being an adult Kate. You will get by."

"Well I can't cope. I'll go mad if I don't get some soon. I think it's time I went on a serious pick up."

"Why don't you just spend time with your girlfriends until someone special comes along?"

"I have no women friends," Kate retorts. "They bore me, I am far too competitive. I find men much more interesting."

Just then her father comes out with more snacks and the conversation changes.

Kate is an excellent hostess passing around the plates of food and even manages to hide her annoyance when Nina resists the chocolate cakes she offers her. This must be all part of her well-honed discipline Kate reflects, needing every ounce of her own willpower to resist one.

At ten when the light is beginning to fade, Nina makes to leave. Alone with Kate for a few moments she counsels, "My advice to you is make sure you give all that desire and passion to someone who deserves it. I always thought it was such a pity your father didn't get married again. You need a mother."

It's the last thing I need, Kate reflects darkly.

In the doorway, watching Nina walk away, Kate feels a stab of envy wondering what she gets up to when that chignon comes down.

. . .

One Friday, unable to bear the oppressive heat in the office, Kate decided to take a half day. Strolling through the town she came upon a hairdressers, newly opened.

Just what I need Kate thought, I'll get my hair done.

Opening the door she made her way into the new salon. It was very impressive, decorated in black and white with splashes of cerise pink. At the desk Kate enquired could she have a wash and blow dry. The girl began scrolling through the appointment sheet on the computer.

"I don't think so," she replied. "We're very busy."

Kate was at first so irritated that she didn't notice a man move in behind the desk.

"I'll see to this," he said in a decisive tone.

Kate found herself looking at one of the most attractive men she had ever seen.

He was tall and tanned, with black silky hair tied back in a ponytail and pale blue eyes. The overall effect was strikingly gorgeous.

"This way," he beckoned.

Kate followed him and obediently sat at the basin he gestured to. Mesmerized Kate leant back and sat still as he soaked her hair. Applying some shampoo his strong hands began to massage her head, moving down its crown, his thumbs using slow circular movements pressing in. Kate began to visualize the top of her head as her body, envisioned his hands sliding down, down until just there … and imagined what his fingers could do.

He spoke very little. He asked one or two questions, commented on the rich colour of her hair, its silky texture. His silence surprised her. Usually her beauty reduced men to babbling buffoons. Kate admired his restraint.

A stylist came over and opened a drawer beside him.

"Not now," he snapped.

Kate watched with admiration. The power of his rudeness excited her. She liked the way he treated people in an offhand way.

Kate was dying to know more about him.

"I haven't seen you before," she began, "are you from around here?"

"I've been away for years in Australia," he said. "I came home with my brother. I've a sister still out there."

He seemed so absorbed in his work that Kate gauged it best not to continue with any more questions. Instead she concentrated on his appearance in the mirror, noticed the black suit, crisp white shirt and gold cufflinks. Everything about him exuded style and class.

Too soon he said, "I'm done" and made his way back to the reception desk.

Pink with pleasure, Kate followed him her walk appearing more like a scurry. Handing her change he let his fingers brush lightly against her palm. Their eyes locked and in that instant they made a pact, an unspoken promise that they would see each other again.

"Ralph Vaughan," he said, his self-assurance cancelling any further need to elaborate.

"Kate Tiernan," she replied.

He smiled a secret smile as she backed away transfixed; only turning to open and close the door behind her.

Kate charged home.

"Dad, Dad"! she called when she rushed into the house. "Do you know the Vaughans?"

"No, I don't think I do," he replied.

"Think, Dad think," she demanded.

"Vaughans, Vaughans," he repeated. He liked to be able to place people. He was taking too long for Kate.

"Oh for God's sake you know the seed, breed and generation of everyone in this town and the only person I've ever asked you about you don't know. Typical."

"Oh yes it's coming to me now," her father said, deep in concentration. "There are Vaughans out by the river. Quiet people."

"Where on the river?" Kate demanded.

"South of the river, about three miles out from town."

"Have you ever met any of them?"

"No, as I said they are quiet people. They stick to themselves."

"Why do you ask?" he enquired.

"Oh never mind," Kate replied.

Preparing a bath Kate thought up a plan of action. She'd noticed a sign on the door of the salon stating that it shut at six. Well guess who will be outside at six Kate vowed smiling, watching the white fluffy bubbles rise as hot steam enveloped her.

Just before six o'clock that evening Kate positioned herself strategically outside a shop near his on the south end of the main street. She had wondered whether it would be better to approach him from behind and decided against it. It would be best if she came towards him, that way he'd get a full view of all her lusciousness. Within a few minutes Ralph came out and locked the door using a thick bunch of keys.

Instead of walking towards her he turned the other way and began walking in the opposite direction.

Oh no, Kate thought, she had stupidly calculated that because he came from south of the river that somehow he would be heading south.

Chasing after him like a fool wasn't in the plan she thought as she followed him. He was a very fast walker and Kate had to break into a slow run to catch up with him. She knew that sounding out of breath would only imply desperation on her part and was not the impression she was after. A few feet behind him she tried to steady her breath. When she was sure she was as composed as she possibly could be and swinging her handbag in a nonchalant manner she called out his name,

"Ralph."

He spun round. She caught up with him.

"Fancy meeting you here," she began, trying to sound as confident as she could.

"Yes fancy," he said. He looked at her with appreciation. They fell in step together.

Kate held her breath as she asked, "It's such a lovely evening do you fancy going for a drink?"

His eyes lit up in surprise.

"Unless of course," she counteracted, "you are in a rush home."

"No, I'm not," he said reassuringly.

Kate was so delighted she had to force herself not to gush, "Thank you."

"Great," she said, keeping her tone as even as possible.

"Say where," he motioned.

"There's a lovely new place on the Quay, will we try there?" she asked.

"Sure," he responded.

They walked the few minutes to the new café bar. They picked a quiet booth and sat down so close to each other that their legs squished together. She could feel the tautness of his thigh through her thin skirt.

He bought some drinks.

"Are you glad to be home again?" she asked, opening the conversation.

"Well I don't view it as my home anymore," was his enigmatic response.

"Why, did you leave someone special behind?" she asked, rather too quickly.

"No," he replied. "I miss Australia."

"Well the weather's been good here this summer," Kate replied, sounding older than her years. "We can't really complain." Silence descended and for one horrible moment she thought he looked bored. Kate chastised herself. Did she really have to mention the weather, knowing it was the bottom of the barrel topic in a conversation? "What do you miss?" she continued more hopeful.

"I miss the casualness."

"Oh I see."

"Tell me about Australia."

He spoke for a few moments of the outdoor life, the sports he missed and the friends he'd made.

"I aim to travel myself someday. I have plans," she said with enthusiasm.

He refused to follow on and ask what her plans were.

Kate expanded on her dream to someday tour America. "Have you ever been to America?"

"No," he replied, giving another non-committal answer.

They paused, both taking a sip from their drinks.

Kate found his vagueness intriguing, if a little trying. So you want to play mystery man? she thought, seeing it as all part of his game of seduction. Well I can play the mystery game too. The challenge now was to crack open the mystery and he would then be revealed to her and she would come to know him even better than he knew himself and this information would give her power over him. She would then use this knowledge either for him or against him, depending on how hopelessly in love he was with her.

On their fourth drink a particular soft piece of music came on and pulling her towards him he leaned in close against her face and spoke, his voice heavy with intent. "I have a little secret I want to tell you."

"I love secrets. You can tell me," she smiled slyly.

"I fancy you like mad."

Kate could feel herself becoming slightly overpowered by the intense spirit of masculinity that emanated from him.

"And what are you going to do about it?" she asked softly.

"I'm going to act on it."

"Act? On what?" she asked, feigning innocence.

"Your desire. I can smell desire off you. It's your perfume."

Kate wasn't sure she liked his saying that, but he was sophisticated so it must be a compliment she deduced.

"Come back to my place and stay," he said, releasing her. "It's up to you, but I like to know where I stand," he finished, keeping his voice cool.

Kate looked away. Never on the first date was another one of her mottos, but something in his tone warned her to consider her answer carefully as inherent in his proposition was the threat that she may not get this offer again. Looking into his eyes at his piercing gaze she felt he already knew her answer and all she had to do was repeat it and the sweet reality would unfold. "Yes," she said.

They walked quietly together the few minutes to his apartment. Kate held back. She wasn't exactly comfortable. She felt compromised.

Silently Kate argued with herself. It was all very well, Nina's restraining advice, but what was the point of wisdom and no action, morals and only the mundane? Besides, this was the offer, take it or leave it and she was taking it.

In the apartment he told her to sit down and went to make some coffee. Kate looked around, searching for some clues of him to get a sense of his story. She spotted some photos on shelves and went over to have a look at them. He reappeared with the coffee. "We'll have these in there," he gestured towards the bedroom. Inside he placed the cups down on the locker.

He moved towards her and kissed her. Kate untied his hair and watched fascinated as it swung loose like a sheet of black satin. Entwining her fingers through its silky threads and feeling the contrast to the roughness of his skin she pulled him closer and whispered,

"You are all man."

In an instant there was a flurry of zips being unzipped, hooks unhooked. His arms moved so quickly over her it was like being caressed by layers of hands, each layer eliciting a primal explosion of intensity. Her body, sprung so tight was like a coil releasing once, twice, three times. Each time fueling in Kate a familiar surge of triumph.

Afterwards, Kate reflected smugly that she'd come three times, which seemed about right to her. It was her usual standard. Kate was into numbers.

He must have been happy too because the next morning rousing her with kisses he said, "Three days. I want three days with you."

"I can't ....my father.... work," she said faltering. "What will I say?"

"Just say an old friend is in crises you have to visit her."

I'll say it Kate thought, but I know he won't believe it. He knows I've no old friends.

"I have to go home and get some things," Kate said.

"I'll meet you in an hour."

In her room Kate headed for that drawer. From her wardrobe she took out a new unused silk robe with lace ruffles at the neck which she'd bought for Tim. Packing, she wondered where her father was. She left him a quick note of explanation on the kitchen table. Making sure she'd thought of everything she was interrupted by an irritating beep beep in her handbag. "Delayed by an hour," the text read, "meet you at two in O'Shea's pub."

Kate couldn't believe it. Delayed, how could he possibly be delayed? She supposed this was what she would have to get used to and put it down to the trials of dating a business man. She was definitely not meeting him in O'Shea's where he might meet up with some friends and they'd never get out of there. She texted him back with the message to meet her at the end of her road at the same time.

Her father was still out when she left the house. Kate hid her overnight case under her light summer trench coat.

They drove inland for a few miles past the neat fields of farmland before turning into the grounds of a hotel. It looked neglected with large patches of white paint peeling from the outer walls. A large ballroom was attached which looked as if it hadn't been used since the seventies.

They both left the car and walked towards the dingy hotel. Kate stopped. "No," she said, knowing she sounded like a spoilt eight year old. "Not here. It's a dump. It's not conducive to romance."

"Kate," he said, trying to keep his patience. "All my money is tied up in the business." Seeing the determination set in her face he relented. "All right," he said. "We'll go for one night somewhere else and then back to my place."

Kate smiled and practically bounced with victory towards the car. "I know a great place," she said in her chummy voice. "It's not too far from here."

Ralph drove in silence; the only interaction between them was Kate's directions. His face darkened as they drove up the entrance to a grand country house.

In their room Kate threw herself on the bed. "Oh I love it here," she said with glee. "The pillows and duvets are the softest I've ever slept on."

"I'm hungry," he said, cutting her off as he placed his car keys on the table. "You can follow me down."

"Oh, wait for me. I'm ready," she said, jumping off the bed.

Kate found his carelessness of her intriguing; the fact that she had to work for his attention.

In the dining room the waiter fussed over them.

Kate could feel Ralph's irritation rising at the obvious expense he saw around him.

"I'm not that hungry," she said. "I'll only have the one course."
He visibly relaxed.

He was so quiet. Kate had to work hard trying to draw him out, covering his lapses into silence. This reticence was so new to her, she loved the challenge. After a couple of glasses of wine his mood lightened and he told her stories of Australia and his previous life there.

Kate told her own tried and tested litany of anecdotes and was puzzled that he did not find them as funny as she had expected. The slight suspicion that he may have no sense of humour began to dawn on her, but even before she allowed the opinion to formulate she quashed it, dismissing it to the far reaches of her mind.

"I'm tired," he said, pushing his plate away. "I'm going to bed."

Kate thanked the waiter and followed Ralph. Kate judged it best not to indulge in her usual lengthy preparations for sex. Hour long baths, she knew, would not be tolerated by him. She lay on the bed and let Ralph take the lead.

He liked clothes half on, half off. He arranged her so that her boobs burgeoned above her black basque, her tight skirt riding up her thighs, resting on her hips. Even though she appreciated his artistic side, she really did, she had to suppress a giggle when he strategically arranged the bedside lamp to highlight the smooth mound of her breasts. Then, satisfied that everything was arranged to his liking and with a look of deep concentration on his face he entered and began pummeling her and she pummeled him back giving him her all. Then a terrible thing happened. In fact, the awful thing was, nothing happened - her body wouldn't respond. Kate had always held a degree of contempt for women who couldn't manage the big O and yet here she was putting on the performance of her life. He didn't appear to notice the difference and afterwards lay sated, his head resting on her shoulder.

"I love you," she said meekly, cradling the sheet under her chin.

"I love you too," he said, matter of fact, pulling away from her. She lay listening to him, heard his breath deepen and knew he was asleep. Kate was glad of the space his sleep afforded her. She needed time to sort out her thoughts.

Kate was appalled by her lack of responsiveness. Was the power she normally had over men the real turn on, the impetus that fed her desire? With Ralph she felt wary and self-conscious. This love she had for him left her feeling one down. Her power had dissipated under the strong emotion she had for him.

An uncomfortable feeling of loneliness settled on her. Kate viewed the emotion with irritation, an unwelcome reminder of her own vulnerability, an unwanted glimpse of her own timidity.

The next day, Sunday, Ralph wanted to be off home as soon as he'd finished breakfast.

"Would you not like to go for a walk in the grounds? Kate asked.

"No," he said. "I'm not much for walking."

In the car Kate was silent. She had run out of things to say and was disappointed with the way the weekend had gone.

Ralph noticing her despondency and not wanting to alienate her too much spoke of the great plans he had for the day. "I'll get some movies and a bottle of wine and we'll watch them together," he said, careful to infuse his voice with as much warmth as he felt he needed to draw her back in.

"That sounds great," Kate said, cheering up.

The two movies he'd chosen were good fun and Kate enjoyed the afternoon. He cooked a delicious Thai dish and they ate it sitting on the couch watching the evening news.

At nine Ralph's brother and a group of his friends called in to see him.

"I thought we'd have a game of cards," his brother said.

"Count me in," Ralph told him.

"What about you?" the tall, lanky one asked Kate.

"I don't play cards," Kate said.

She sat by herself for a while and then decided to get herself ready for bed.

In the shower while washing her skin she thought of how she wanted the night to go.

She wanted to slow things down. Kate knew she liked it hard and unsentimental, but Ralph was a little too hard and unsentimental. She thought it would be nice to take their time to luxuriate in languid movements, to talk and tease and have some fun. She hoped he would respond to her new mood of tenderness.

The atmosphere had to be right. She took the lamp from the bedside locker and put it at the further end of the room and was happy with the hazy glow.

Dressed only in her new robe she waited for him in the room.

After what seemed like an hour she opened the door and called out, "Ralph."

There was the sound of sniggering from the men. "You're presence is requested," one of them said.

"I'm out," Ralph said and walked towards Kate.

In the bedroom he emptied his pockets the change spilling out on the table.

Closing the door they stood opposite each other with Kate's back to the door.

Holding the ruffles of her nightgown up towards her face seeking to soften her countenance she looked at him her eyes full of love.

"That's pretty," he said, his tone implying he wasn't impressed "Take it off."

Somewhat reluctantly she let it fall.

She faced him, a hesitant soft smile breaking on her lips.

"Kneel," he ordered.

A shadow of uncertainty flickered across her features and in the split second it took to kneel to the floor, Kate realised it was an act of submission and in the background she could hear the full flow sound of someone pissing in the bathroom.

The next morning they ate breakfast together and just as his mobile rang his brother asked him a question.

"Miss Perfect will get it for you," he said, turning to answer his call. Kate was so shocked that she swung round expecting to see someone else there. There was no one. She began to doubt that she had actually heard what he'd said. He couldn't have said that, she reasoned. I must have been mistaken. She stood waiting for him to finish his call. At 8.45 when she knew she just had to leave for work, she mouthed, "I've got to go."

"I'll call you," he said, in between his sentences. Kate let herself out and walked to work. He'll call me she thought delightedly. I'm sure he'll call.

Kate spent the week carrying the idea of him, hugging him to herself.

Kate daydreamed of all the lovely places in Wexford she'd bring him to. She saw herself in command bringing him here and there. She wondered how many of the beauty spots he remembered from his childhood. She wished she had some friends she could introduce him to. She would see him next weekend she was sure of that. The memory of him helped her get through her work in an unusually lighter mood. Even the customers didn't annoy her as she smiled at them, wishing them well.

Returning home that evening she decided to surprise her Dad and make the tea. "Are you sure?" he asked, looking dumbfounded. "Well I should be able to manage omelette and chips," Kate said and began preparing the meal, thinking a little practice of domesticity wouldn't do her any harm. I'll have to start doing wifey things she thought to herself.

Kate realised he wouldn't ring that Tuesday since she'd only seen him the previous day. On Wednesday evening she came home and enquired of her father, "Any calls?"

"No," he replied. She checked her mobile again. She dialed 171 and heard the automated recording, 'You have no messages' – the cruelest message of all.

By Thursday she thought if she heard that voice recording again she would smash it against the wall. By Friday when she returned home and saw her father on a call she roared at him, "Get off the phone."

Then at nine her mobile rang, the sweetest sound she had ever heard. Kate raced to answer. It was Paddy. She was about to bite the head off him for not being Ralph when she remembered she'd better be nice to him, he might come in handy.

"Hi Paddy, how's the new job?" He spoke of targets, customer service issues, management meetings, for once he even sounded interesting.

She could mention him in her conversations with Ralph, her good friend with the top job in Dublin.

At ten the house phone rang. It was Ralph.

"How was your week?" he asked. His voice sounded warm. "I'm sorry I didn't ring earlier," he said. "I was tied up." They talked for some minutes arranging their next meeting. He concluded the conversation with, "See you tomorrow at eight at O'Byrne's."

He loves me, Kate thought. I was right all along. I know he loves me. Her will was stronger than the facts.

The next evening Kate relished getting ready. She had admired her aunt Nina's sense of style so much that she had gone out and bought a similar outfit. She took out her new pencil skirt the one that cost a fortune for the right cut. Putting on her stiletto heels she felt in the mood to totter. I'll just totter into town and enslave this man she thought, placing her box handbag on her crooked arm.

She really wanted to take this relationship up a notch further. She'd make subtle enquiries, the future plans, that sort of thing. She wasn't silly enough to come straight out with it, but subtly, tentatively, she'd find out some clue as to his intentions towards her. She was so looking forward to a romantic meal together, just the two of them. She couldn't wait to beguile him.

This was it, she decided. He was definitely 'The One'. It was hard to keep her imagination in check. She saw herself in a nice house in the town, bringing her babies to show off in the salon and then some days, when she felt like it, helping out at reception, enjoying the diffidence and respect of her employees.

Walking towards town a kid cried out, "Kate you've an arse like J-Lo." J-Lo? Kate asked herself. I don't think so, more like Ava Gardiner. Fifties glamour was what Kate hoped she was replicating. She was tall with that classic Ava Gardiner shape. It wasn't particularly fashionable right now, but real men admired it.

At the bar, Kate went in and had a quick look around. There was no sign of Ralph. Outside she sat at one of the tables on the pavement and decided to wait for him there. She ordered a drink. After twenty minutes when she had doubly saluted neighbours on their return journey up the road, she decided to head back into the pub. Where was he? He was half an hour late. She decided to visit the ladies believing that when she returned he would be there just like magic. She slowly freshened up her make-up and returned to the bar with her most dazzling smile on her face. Frustratingly, he wasn't there. The feeling of letdown was so huge it was hard to stay positive. Where the hell was he? She walked outside again standing in the shadows so that no one would see her. She would give him the benefit of the doubt; it must have been some sort of silly mistake, a misunderstanding.

Across the road on a corner Ralph stood watching her. He hid from view at the side of the building smoking a cigarette. He'd seen her go into the pub earlier and smiled to himself at her obvious discomfort. He'd finish this last cigarette and then he'd go over.

She'd waited almost an hour for him. She's pretty keen he thought as he'd suspected.

Kate was so agitated looking up and down the road that she didn't notice him crossing until he was a few feet away from her. Relief flooded through her. "It's great to see you, where have you been?"

"I got delayed, that's all. Let's find a big table," he said. Kate sat down wondering why he wanted a big table when there was only the two of them. Her drink had just arrived when what seemed like a gang of people came into the near empty pub and headed towards them.

"Hi Ralph," they all said in unison. They sat down.

"Drinks?" he offered.

When he returned and sat opposite her, Kate waited to be introduced, it didn't happen. After about ten minutes she whispered to him, smiling through her teeth, "Introduce me."

"This is Kate," he said.

"Hi," they chorused.

"We work in Ralph's salon in Enniscorthy," Lisa, the friendly one, noticing Kate's incomprehension, explained.

"I didn't know you had another salon," Kate said, facing Ralph.

"I don't have to tell you everything," Ralph retorted, dismissing her.

The effect of the drink with no food was beginning to make Kate feel woozy. She was starving. "Let's order some food," she said to Ralph.

"I've already eaten."

"Can I have a menu please?" she asked one of the waitresses. The menu looked delicious. I'm not going to sit here and eat a big meal all to myself she thought. Not to look too conspicuous she decided to order a sandwich and coffee.

"On the coffee already," one of them said to hoots of laughter.

"I didn't have a dinner," Kate expounded, looking at the desultory sandwiches in front of her, less ploughman's, more high tea she thought. I certainly won't sustain an arse like J-Los on these she thought ruefully. They were eaten in seconds.

Her attention was drawn to the girl sitting on the other side of Ralph. She had a short raven haired bob and blood red lips, a look that Kate had often admired but because of her colouring couldn't achieve. She wondered did she really have to place her hand on his arm every time she whispered to him. The rest of the girls were dressed in casual clothes. Kate hoped she hadn't overdone the glamour.

The company was in high spirits and Kate did her best to join in. Once or twice she asked their private jokes to be decoded. As the night wore on, the pub became full to the rafters and with the noise of loud music and people talking the volume was at crescendo pitch. It was almost impossible to have a conversation with anyone. Kate found herself imprisoned, squashed between four people. Ralph, sitting opposite, seemed miles away.

The thick satin of her blouse was too heavy for such a sultry night, the heat inducing a sauna like effect. Kate felt herself break out in a sweat. When Andy on her left and Mia on her right asked her a question at the same time, the two questions seemed to meet and implode in the middle of her brain. Under the strain of frantically trying to assimilate yet not comprehending either one, Kate felt dizzy trying to grasp the first question and formulate an answer for the second. I have to get out of here, she thought. Excusing herself she quickly ran to the ladies.

On her return the conversation turned to Lisa and her legendary lateness.

"I'm not always late," she laughed. "Ralph, you said you'd be here at nine o'clock and I was here at nine, well just after it."

Kate sat in disbelief. This can't be true. He couldn't have told her nine, he told me eight. It was definitely eight because she made a little rhyme about it, "I've a date at eight," she'd hummed to herself

When Ralph got up to go the bar, Kate turned to Lisa.

"Was that some sort of joke between you and Ralph, I mean, about meeting here at nine?"

"Oh no, he said nine and that's what he told everyone else too."

Kate felt if she tackled him now she might explode. She didn't want to cause a scene. In the bathroom she ran the cold water tap and put her wrists under it. Her heart was pounding with the injustice of the situation.

She didn't trust herself to go over to the group. Spying from the door she spotted Lisa. "Tell Ralph I am not feeling well and ask him to meet me outside."

Kate stood outside pacing up and down the pathway arms folded. When she saw him she rounded on him. "Why did you tell me eight and the others nine?"

"I wanted to see how long you'd wait," he said.

"You did that on purpose?" she asked, in disbelief. He came towards her.

"Listen lady, when I said three days I meant three days only, you're on extra time."

Kate became tongue-tied with the amount of expletives rushing from her brain and was barely able to form a coherent sentence. "You're a machine," she spat.

He laughed. "A machine," he repeated, "coming from you that's apt. You are robotic in the sack."

Kate's arm swung round and with her hand she landed a forceful slap on the side of his face. She turned and half walked, half ran back up the street. Twisting her ankle, she was so full of rage she didn't feel any pain – fury propelled her home.

Back in the house she sat at the bottom of the stairs crying and roaring with rage. Lifting her handbag she began belting it against the carpet and with every thud she screamed, "No, no, no. This can't be happening, it just can't be happening!"

Her father rushed out to the hall. "Kate! Not another disaster."

Kate moved towards him. "And what would you know you old fool pining, pining after some dead dream. I'm sick looking at you day after day, night after night."

He began to move back horrified at the violence of her words.

"I'm sick of you looking at me with those accusatory eyes," but it was Kate's eyes that had him spellbound; the hate in them had turned them light green, for once he felt scared of her, scared of her venom. Backing away he felt the creased rug catch in his foot and then losing his balance, he fell backwards onto the floor. He lay immobilized in agony.

Kate stared in horror and ran towards the phone. "I'll get help, don't worry Dad, don't worry. It's an emergency, it's an emergency!" Kate cried down the handset. "It's Matthew Tiernan, 4 Commodore Row." She replaced the receiver.

Kate loomed over him. "The doctor is coming Dad, don't worry, he's coming to help you. You will be all right," she said crying. Kneeling beside him she grabbed the loose folds of shirt that fell against his chest and began pleading with him, her face close to his, tears streaming down her cheeks. "But what about me Dad? What is there for me? He said he loved me. How could he do this to me? What will I do Daddy, what will I do?" Through her tears her cries rose from her stomach in great guttural sobs.

The ambulance came and the men took over. Matthew was placed on a stretcher and carried out.

Kate sobbing followed him. Out of the corner of her eye she spotted Sheila Redmond in her nightgown marching down the road towards them.

"Don't go Dad, don't go, I don't want to be on my own." She started shaking her cries becoming hysterical.

"I'll go with him," Dr Cleary said. "Take care of her," he said to Sheila. "Kate's not much use to him at the moment." He gave her a look of abject pity and disappointment. Tears were streaming down her face. "Don't go Daddy, what will I do on my own?" Mucus ran down from her nose mixing with her tears. Mrs Redmond handed her a tissue with one hand and with the other firmly pushed her by the shoulder. "Get in off the street. You're making a spectacle of yourself." The two of them hurried up the garden path. A small posse of people followed them. Once indoors Sheila shut the door in front of them.

She faced Kate. "I've kept my tongue for years but my God I'll say it now. You are the most selfish strop of a woman I have ever met and yes Kate, you are a woman, even though he still runs after you like a child."

Kate watched Mrs Redmond's mouth opening and shutting not hearing the words. She was thinking how Mrs Redmond's bright red hair had faded over the years. Redmond's the redzers, she used to call them and turned her face so that she wouldn't see what she was thinking.

After Sheila had finished speaking Kate wiped her face clean with a tissue and said calmly, "I'm afraid to be on my own, can I stay with you tonight?"

"You can, and I'll then get Jackie to stay with you for a few days. The only blessing to come out of this is that the man will have a bit of a break from you," Sheila added, watching Kate climb the stairs.

Kate packed some night things and followed Sheila from the house.

In the Redmond's house four doors down, Sheila made her a sweet cup of tea and a sandwich. Kate ate them in silence at the kitchen table. When she had finished Sheila said, "You must be tired, I'll show you to your room, I've put you in Tara and Frances' room. They are staying at friends tonight."

Kate prepared for bed and pulled back the sheets on one of the single beds.

Lying down she admired the neatness of the room, the many books and games the ten year old twins had, all stacked in perfect order on shelving in the alcoves of the bedroom. Kate wondered how so many people could fit into such a small house.

The bed was so cosy she felt her eyes grow heavy and pulling the sheets towards her she breathed in their perfume and wondering what fabric softener they used, she fell into a comfortable sleep.

The next morning Kate woke fully alert. She could hear people downstairs and got dressed quickly.

"We would have let you sleep." Mr. Redmond said when she entered the kitchen.

"No, no, I'm fine. I feel wide awake."

Kate was distracted by the attractiveness of the spread in front of her. The table was laid with a yellow and blue floral tablecloth with delph and serviettes to match. They had even got some fresh flowers from the garden and placed them in a simple vase for her. The table was full of homemade breads and jams. "This is lovely," she said.

"We rang and they told us he is very comfortable at the moment."

Kate was so intent on looking at the table that she barely turned her head towards Sheila.

"Who?" she asked.

"Your father," Mrs Redmond said, her eyes narrowing in exasperation.

Noticing the edge in her voice, Kate replied. "Oh yes, that's wonderful news. I'll visit him this morning, first thing," she said, before helping herself to the bounties of the breakfast table.

. . .

For the first few weeks that followed her Dad's accident Kate had never lived at such a frenetic pace in her life. Between hospital visits she had to clean the house, cooking became quick convenience meals. The pounds piled on. She felt her waist grow squidgy around the middle. Always starving coming in from work and used to the dinner on the table, she stuffed herself with chocolate until the meal was ready. Her grooming routine went out the window. A quick shower every day and a slap of make-up was all she could manage. She tied her hair back for convenience. Her features became distorted with the additional weight.

In the days after the break up she thought of Ralph endlessly. She couldn't accept her fate. She wanted to grab life by the scruff of the neck and demand, "Give me what I want, a man, a home and kids." Why was it so much to ask? Other women had it. Why couldn't she? For the first time in her life she felt like a caged animal, helpless, and no matter how much she flailed against the bars trying to escape her circumstance, she knew it would make no difference. She felt powerless, unable to determine her own destiny. Inwardly she roared with exasperation wanting to scream in frustration.

As the weeks passed, her internal roars were beaten, through sheer exhaustion, first into a whimper, then to numbness.

As she trudged from work to hospital to home she existed in a vacuum of nothingness. Depleted, she repeated to herself, "I am nothing, I know nothing." She felt nullified, vacant. She knew the process of existence was trying to grind her down. All she could see was a gaping black hole ahead waiting to consume her.

One morning she woke late and looking through her clothes in a state of distraction she could find nothing clean to wear. I can't go on she thought. The house around her was in a shambles. She hadn't had time to clean it for the past week. That morning Kate decided to let circumstance have its way – for now. She'd take some time off, recoup and get her energy back and proceed to the next phase. The next phase was seeing off Mrs Whitty, her Dad's new friend. She'd need energy for that.

Kate had no bank of goodwill built up with her employers. She'd caused ructions there too many times. The most recent was when money went missing and she mentioned a name – well she didn't like her anyway. The slim sheaths of money were later found to have slipped down behind a desk. Kate didn't see why she had to apologise. Some people were too sensitive for their own good.

There was nothing for it but to ring in sick again. She needed two days to sort the house out then she would get up earlier, get into a better system, she could see herself managing everything then.

After Kate had rang work she went back to bed. She lay thinking. A hospital visit was out today, she had too much to catch up on. A fresh house meant a fresh mind. Kate got up with a new found surge of energy and pulled the sheets off the bed; she went into her father's room and did the same opening all the windows. She polished and hovered and then tackled the bathroom and didn't stop until it shone.

Downstairs she gathered every old newspaper, magazine and old bill and threw them out. She threw out all the dead flowers that lay stinking in a vase in the hall. In the kitchen she scoured and sprayed until the place smelt like a fresh lemon. The house seemed rejuvenated. By this time it was three o'clock and Kate was starving. There was nothing to eat. She took her car keys off the hook in the hall and drove out to one of the supermarkets on the edge of the town. She bought plants and flowers and in one section bought a new cream tablecloth for the kitchen. She thought it would go nice with the blue of the walls. In the delicatessen she bought some fresh rolls and salad and headed home. She put a plant on the hall table and one on the dresser in the kitchen. On the kitchen table she draped the new tablecloth and retrieving one of the vases draining on the draining board she placed her new cream and pink flowers. The house seemed to have come back to life.

Later that evening there was a knock on the door. Sheila Redmond came into the house hesitantly. "I've made this for you Kate. I thought maybe you could bring some in to your father."

Kate took the casserole dish.

"Thank you," she said. This woman doesn't like me Kate thought yet here she is making dinner for me. I suppose that's kindness.

Sheila looked around the room. "You are keeping the place grand Kate. If you're lonely I can send Jackie down to stay with you."

"No, I'm fine on my own. I've got used to it."

"Your father is improving I hear. I haven't been in to see him yet, but I will go. I wanted to give him a chance to get better. Mary Whitty has been in and she tells me he is coming on very well."

"Yes, she's been in a few times," Kate replied, her voice flat.

"People are saying how great you're managing and how good you are to him. We know you're not used to," …she continued hurriedly, "well … keeping house."

Kate began to respond to her compliments. Do people notice she began to wonder? How interesting. It would be nice to be thought of as nice for a change, so unusual.

"Well I do my best for him you know. He is everything to me."

"Oh I'm sure he is, with your mother gone and all, it's only natural he would be."

Mrs Redmond stood up. "Maybe you'd like to come to tea one of these evenings, before you go to the hospital I mean. Would Wednesday suit you?"

"That would suit me fine," Kate replied, adding, "Thank you Mrs Redmond."

"Ah now, none of that Mrs Redmond business, call me Sheila."

"Thanks again Sheila, I'll see you on Wednesday."

Walking back up the hallway after seeing Sheila out, Kate pondered. Well that's one for the books, I'm the new Florence Nightingale, my fame is going before me.

There were now more urgent matters to consider. Sheila had confirmed what Kate had suspected, her father was getting lots of visits from the widow Whitty. She was one of those merry widows, full of fun. Next he'd want to go away with her on weekend breaks, needing money, he'd remortgage. She'd put life back into him. Kate was having none of it. She could handle her father on her own. She liked it that way. She would squash this burgeoning friendship before it took hold.

The next day, Kate struggled into the ward laden down with bags for him.

Her father was sitting up in the bed laughing.

Mrs Whitty was sitting beside the bed regaling him with her stories.

"Ah Kate, come and meet Mrs Whitty."

Kate smiled sweetly at her. "How are you Mrs Whitty?"

"I'm fine Kate. I was just saying what a good colour your father has. He's definitely getting better. I see an improvement in him every day."

"Kate, where are you going with all the parcels?" her father asked. Turning to Mrs Whitty he said, "Kate spoils me so. I literally can't fit anything more in these lockers. The nurses say they are almost poisoned with chocolates; she brings so many boxes in. Mrs Whitty, I'm a happy man. When the chips are down Kate's the best."

Kate stared at the happy scene in front of her and felt cold. Her mouth was fixed in a static smile, her mind was racing. Her father and the widow continued talking and laughing amongst themselves. Kate stood with her hands in her pockets a few feet away. This situation was desperate. Something had to be done. It had to be broken; this bond just had to be broken. It would take time and time was what she had.

She thought of a plan. She'd have to wait until he was home to convalesce. She'd invite Mary Whitty around for tea, two or three times. She'd feign friendship, build trust then sew the seed of doubt. It wasn't too dangerous; she'd wait until he was under her control again when he wasn't capable of going anywhere.

With the decision made, Kate visibly relaxed and moved towards them. "When can I take you home Daddy? I must speak to your doctor. Did he give you any idea of when you will be allowed home?" she asked.

"He said towards the end of the week, near the weekend. I take that to mean Friday, although he could have meant Thursday, I'll have to wait and see."

"Come round to the house on Sunday, Mrs Whitty, we would be delighted to have you for tea. The company will do Dad good."

"Why that's very kind of you Kate, I'd be delighted to."

"Come round at 5.00 o'clock that will give us plenty of time to chat."

"That will be lovely, thanks Kate," Mrs Whitty said, beaming at her father.

He sat up in the bed smiling broadly, delighted with the proposition.

"Well, I'll head home now," Kate said, taking her bag from the end of the bed. "Do you need a lift?" she asked, turning to Mrs Whitty.

"No thanks Kate, young Gerard is coming to collect me in a few minutes."

. . .

The tea went well that Sunday and the subsequent one. Kate found an old recipe for Victorian sponge and made a salad with traditional ham and turkey. On her second visit she made scones and bought a Bramley apple tart and they had cold roast beef and beetroot salad, the three of them sitting close together in the cosy kitchen.

A few weeks later on Mrs Whitty's third visit, when they had finished eating, Kate nonchalantly leaned back towards the dresser and retrieved a white box from the drawer. She turned fully facing them and began counting her father's tablets. "Did you take your tablet today?" she asked with authority.

"Yes, I did," he replied. "I'm certain I did."

"Well there are ten here now and there are only supposed to be nine. There were ten in that box this time yesterday. You'd forget your head if I let you," she said, handing him one.

Later, when her father left the room, Kate stood with her back to Mary washing some cups in the basin. She turned her head slightly towards Mary as if too upset to look directly at her. "Mary I am very worried about my father. That's the second time he forgot to take his tablets. He seems to be losing his train of thought as well and last night I woke up to hear him rambling, having a conversation with my mother."

"Ah, I'm sure it was a dream he had," Mary said reassuringly.

"I don't think so. It's happening so often I'm afraid it could be something else, something much worse; the forgetfulness, it frightens me." She turned her head and slowly raised her eyes to look at Mary's expression.

For a moment Mary looked frightened too and when her father returned she looked at him in a new way as the one awful possibility crowded her mind.

Kate was pleased. Doubt now prefixed every question put to him by Mary and suspicion followed every answer. His sentences were dissected for slips of recall; an unnaturalness grew in their conversing and later when Mary left there was no mention of a further meeting.

The following evening, Kate stood territorially at the bedroom window looking down on the road. Mrs Whitty walked past with fear in her step, her eyes drawn watchfully towards the window. The coldness of Kate's stance emanated from the house. There was a shadow cast over it, a gloom that seemed to say stay away, stay away. When she was sure she had passed, Kate closed the curtains and resumed downstairs.

TIM

That Tuesday after finishing with Kate was one of the lowest nights he could remember. He sat in a chair in his living room for hours when she left, just thinking of her, unable to believe he had got her so wrong. He had misread all her clues. She had let them fall like threads and he, on picking them up, had woven a tapestry telling her story, a story that he himself wanted to believe, but which simply was not true

He thought the clue of her mother dying young meant she had suffered and because of that suffering was a deep feeling person. The truth being Kate was an extremely intelligent woman yet lacked emotional depth. She seemed happier seeing herself as a victim of life rather than taking constructive action. Tim thought when listening to her problems that she was seeking solutions from him and gladly provided them offering her any support he could whilst she resignedly soaked up his own energy like a sponge until he felt they were both spiraling downwards into a vortex with these issues spinning round and round them, all seemingly unsolvable.

"I'd like to strip you away, get to the core of you," he said to her one night. He thought there were layers to her that when patiently peeled back would eventually reveal some sort of gem. He was mistaken, there was nothing there. He had projected onto her what he wanted her to be, what he had needed her to be, not what she was and the reality was crushingly disappointing. In the end he felt lonely in her company and chose to reach for the newspaper in preference to her.

At 2.00 a.m. he went into his bedroom. Evidence of Kate's feminization of the room was everywhere. Small lampshades with beads, candles and dried flower arrangements were on every available surface. He was smothered in her. It was her smell that was driving him mad. Her perfume was in his nostrils, there was just no escape from it. He pulled opened the bedroom door and walked out onto the small balcony. He lit a cigarette and stood watching the darkened houses on the street below. Back inside he lit another cigarette and smoked that. The smell of tobacco was preferable to her smell, anything just to get rid of it. He lay on the bed fully clothed and pulled the covers around him. He dozed and woke intermittently all night and was falling into a deep sleep when the alarm clock rang.

"Hold all calls," were his first words to Lyn that morning when he arrived for work. He sat at his desk brooding, unable to concentrate. Lyn's tap on the door brought him into focus. Her face looked strained. "It's Mrs Rowe, she's called three times this morning. She says if you don't answer she's coming down to see you."

"Alright, put her through." Dread filled him as he lifted the phone. A tirade of complaints came down the receiver. "I haven't had any viewers to see my house in the last two months never mind offers".

Tim interrupted her. "I had two offers for you," he said.

"They weren't serious offers," she scoffed, "they were well below the asking price."

"That's the problem, you keep changing the asking price, shifting the goalposts."

"Look, will you get back to me as soon as you can?" Mrs Rowe entreated.

"Yes, when you make up your mind I'll get back to you," he snapped.

"Well I never. You really are the most arrogant man I've ever met in my life."

Tim slammed down the phone, "That's it, I'm out of here. I need a break."

On his mobile he rang his boss. "Dan I'm taking three weeks off. Can you step in for a while? I've some personal matters to deal with." Dan agreed that he would ask his nephew to step in and between them they would work something out.

Back in his house he turned on Sky sports and watched it for hours, revelling in the luxury of daytime T.V. It was a drizzly summer's day, a Wednesday, midweek, halfway, in transition or stuck, depending on the way you looked at it. A metaphor for himself he decided. Where was he? he pondered, looking out at the dismal back garden. An ending had taken place, although in reality he reflected it was only the beginning of the end.

Tim wanted to take back possession of his home. Upstairs the bed dressed by Kate in velvets and satins was an oasis of sumptuousness.

He left it as it was. He placed all her trinkets in a box and placed them under the stairs. Already he was beginning to feel better, to feel free of her. With the clutter gone he could begin to think straight again

'Arrogant!' the accusation stung him. He'd always known he was decisive, able to cut through an issue quickly with a tendency to see things too much in black and white, but arrogant? Was it arrogant to expect Kate to be what she wasn't, to feel that he knew what was best for her? He'd always played to his strengths which was his golden rule. His self-assurance, had he honed it too well?

But being with Kate was like being out of control. It was as if she had cast a spell over him as if all the forces of nature were propelling him towards her, compelling him to follow her every step as though in a predestined dance.

Gradually he had awoken from this stupor and wondered had he existed on a different plane with her. He now felt himself snap back into his reality where she seemed diminished, her goddess qualities gone. He wondered what had he seen in her?

In the beginning he had enjoyed her company. At first he thought her stories about people were funny until her wit became bitch, he eventually realised they were just endless bitching sessions. She seemed to appeal to his baser side.

All the same there were things about her he would miss. He loved her coming home from her shopping trips. The way her shopping bags were thrown across the couch, her excitement and there was always, always something in them for him.

Even now, every time he opened a press there was something in it from her; a set of coloured glasses, a coffee pot. A reminder.

He had loved the sense of occasion she created when doing a simple thing like deciding to eat in. She'd set the table with a decorative centerpiece, then order a take away – the one which came in the fanciest boxes appealed to her. She cleverly aimed for the minimum of effort for the maximum appeal.

Kate didn't like to waste too much time eating when Tim was around. So it was never what's for afters, always where to afterwards. That was one of the things he loved about her. She was always so available. Her sexuality was full-on. She wanted him and made no bones about it.

The next day after breakfast he decided to phone Clare and arrange to bring down the children. Although he was slightly apprehensive as the previous time in April, when Clare had rang and told him about Helen being home, he'd been abrupt, but he couldn't imagine her holding that against him. He hoped she wouldn't.

CLARE (APRIL)

I hate the way Tim cuts me off like that, Clare thought as she replaced the phone on the hook. It made her feel so lonely. She wished he understood how important he was to her, him being her only brother.

She would have loved to have spent more time talking to him. It would have been nice if he'd asked how she was for a change. If the conversation had gone well she might have even told him of this worry she had. She knew what his reaction would be. He would have sighed sharply, told her not to be ridiculous and nudged out of her worry mode; she would have said a grateful thanks and put the phone down. But he'd brought their chat to an abrupt end and Clare was still worried about David. He was just always working now and seemed preoccupied when he was at home.

To try and distract herself she looked out of her bedroom window, out onto the quiet cul de sac below. The large mock Georgian houses stood solidly, looking self-satisfied in their own importance, with an air of indifference to the temporary absence of their owners.

Taking some folded clothes off the bed, Clare thought no, she shouldn't doubt David and vowed to talk to him when he was relaxed at the weekend.

She placed the clothes on top of the chest of drawers. A tallboy it was called. Clare loved her pieces of furniture. It was like the furniture she used to see in those American movies when she was a child, solid and dark and furnished looking. She opened the drawers. The contents lay neatly folded. Everything was in order. Clare loved order. She felt her surroundings growing up were chaotic, so it was important she put order on things.

On the landing Clare opened the hot press. She'd had it custom made. There were shelves made for every item of clothing and linen. Her mother's hot press was always in a shambles. A jumble of bunches of odd socks, thread bare towels, old sheets. You could never find anything. Clare gave up asking where things were. She thought of her mother now and tears filled her eyes. It was so sad that she had missed all this. Clare would have loved to have shared her life with her. Rose would have doted on the kids, enjoyed

61

staying over in her beautiful, spacious home. Clare had everything good in life to offer her yet her mother was dead and couldn't enjoy any of her good fortune.

Clare remembered her mother coming up the stairs in their family home on Mountain View Road, her steps heavy, seeing Clare clear out the hot press. "You're such a good girl Clare, always tidying, you're the best girl in the world. I'm just going for a rest now," she'd say as she headed towards her bedroom. "Will you bring those books back to the library for me and get me some more? You know the books I like." Yes, Clare thought. I know, romances, always romances.

Puffed up from water retention, Rose drank tea by the bucket load. Every ten minutes the kettle was put on. She drank tea before she did anything and after she did anything. It was the drug she chose to keep her going.

Clare made her way down the grand curved stairs of her new home into the huge hallway below. The front rooms of the house were designed in the American style Clare admired, open plan with tall folding doors leading off the hallway allowing full view of two gracious reception rooms on either side. She had intended to decorate in a more casual style, but found herself drawn to ornate gilt framed pictures and formal furniture and was rather overwhelmed with the grandiose result. The back of the house she felt was more successful with more homely living quarters made up of a spacious kitchen, living room and sunroom.

Opening the front door she took the post from the postbox and walked slowly back up the hall. Leafing through the envelopes she wondered what was she hoping to find, a note from a friend, a 'Thinking of You card' some personal recognition to ease her loneliness? She placed two utility bills and a bank statement on the large circular table in the middle of the hallway, in the place where the father in the American apple-pie family movies always placed his briefcase before calling out, "Honey I'm home."

She thought of David again. She wished she could shake off this doubt. Things weren't the same, she could feel it. There were subtle changes in his interaction with her, an impatience which wasn't there before.

Tim came into her mind and how she would love to visit him, to reconnect and catch up. She thought if she had never felt she needed him before, she needed him now.

They were brought up together in what she now described as that dysfunctional excuse of a marriage of her parents. Although Clare thought what's unfolding in front of me now is not much better.

Clare couldn't remember the hall door in her family home ever being fully open. When people called she normally held the door ajar with her foot and spoke to her friends through the gap. On the really bad days Clare stood outside on the step with her hand on the doorknob, holding the door closed over in case anyone might hear the awful roars and shouts from her father.

They lived at the mercy of his moods. Theo was a vain, angry man. One night was particularly bad. He was normally home at six and that night he arrived home early unannounced. There was a general mad dash around the house trying to make everything perfect. He stormed into the kitchen, his presence oppressive and menacing, his anger simmering. Tim stood drying the plates and one fell, smashing on the floor when his father roared, "This place is a mess," when all that was out of place was the odd book, the normal detritus of everyday family life.

Almost every evening he left the house to go for what he fondly called his constitutional. It was his new favourite word. Beautifully dressed he would pass around the corner at the bottom of the road and smile broadly at Clare's friends who stood in groups.

"Lovely evening boys and girls," he would say, blissfully devoid of any insight into how he was perceived by others. Clare's best friends kept a straight face, acquaintances stifled giggles.

Twice a week her mother visited the local grocers. Mr. Dwyer, the owner, always served her.

"How are you Mrs Brady?" he'd ask her warmly.

"I'm fine, thank you Mr. Dwyer," her mother would reply enthusiastically. Clare watched embarrassed as her mother's face glowed with pleasure from his attention and she became girlish in her manner. It was only now she understood. Her mother, so used to the negative, was sensitive to even the most innocent of comments from a man. A beautiful woman reduced to gratitude for even these small, friendly pleasantries. She never remembered her father complimenting her mother or even remarking that she looked well.

Rose had met Theo at the local dance when she was nineteen. Theo had tawny wavy brown hair. He was tall and dark and had the dashing air of a colonel. Rose was smitten. He was so charming to her, witty and he seemed kind. When he asked her to marry him there seemed no reason why she shouldn't. Rose was the most beautiful girl in the neighbourhood with the same shaped face as Liz Taylor and a figure to match. They were married within six months. The following nine Clare arrived. They settled in one of the new suburban housing estates at the foot of the Dublin mountains.

Clare walked back into her own pristine kitchen, surveying the range of open shelves fully stocked with a vast array of glasses and delph on display so unlike her mother's kitchen.

It was a huge ordeal if anyone called in to her parents' house. There were never enough cups without chips or glasses for people. Once Rose called Clare into the kitchen and in a panic said, "Run up to the bathroom and get the glass that's there." Clare had the embarrassment of having to hide the glass from the visitors as she walked through the living room into the back kitchen.

David made no comment when she returned on almost every shopping occasion with more boxes of delph and glasses. The amply stocked shelves acted as physical insurance against ever running short again.

During those rare visits Rose got into a terrible flap. Visitors watched as the circus unfolded in front of them. Each one of the family fell into their part. Theo and Rose became happy husband and wife. Clare took over as dutiful daughter.

Tim very early on refused to take part. On the rare occasions that people called, he made his excuses and left.

Clare felt Tim operated more independently within the dysfunction. He managed to create distance between himself and his parents. This separating out from the family happened early on, from the time he went to college. He studied late in the library only returning home when he had to.

Things came to a head one summer evening when Tim was eighteen. Tension was rising in the house. Tim was happy, he had received news he'd been accepted on the auctioneering course he wanted. Their father was in the kitchen brooding. He was angry with the world. The subject of money for college fees had been raised. Downward mobility was his mantra.

"You'll work like everyone else I know," he snapped at Tim. "I'm not having any son of mine prancing around college grounds." And Clare always blamed herself for what happened next. It happened because of a simple remark she made. Tim had never looked so handsome she thought. He had worked outdoors all summer and had a tan. His dark hair gently curled on the collar of his new bright blue shirt.

"Tim you look beautiful," Clare exclaimed, genuinely happy for him. Tim stood near his father. A flicker of jealousy danced on Theo's face.

"Ponce," his father spat. Tim turned in shock and then his shock turned to anger. He charged against the slim body of his father and pinning him against the wall with one arm under his neck he threatened with every ounce of venom he could muster.

"You'll pay for college or I'll make sure this face of yours is marked for life."

He tightened his grip then roughly let him go.

Taking the chequebook from inside Theo's jacked pocket which hung on the back of the kitchen chair, Tim laid it on the table.

"Sign," he ordered.

His father shaken and beaten sat down and signed the cheque.

"And £500 for mam and £500 for Clare."

He continued writing until all three cheques lay on the table. Clare thought she never loved Tim as much as she did then.

Meeting David at fifteen was like a dream come true for Clare. He was so beautiful with blond curly hair and a soft face. She loved his sensitive nature. They were so in tune. He only had to look at her and he could read what she was thinking. She could talk to him for hours at a time. She told him about her parents, their awful marriage, it all came pouring out. At the local dances they used to sit together in their favourite place on a platform beside the DJ, her dark head resting against his blond head, his arm around her protecting her, protecting her secret.

Clare remembered the first time she went to meet his family. His three sisters and brother sat on the floor of their sitting room listening to CD's.

"Hi Clare," they chorused in unison when David introduced her. It was impossible not to warm instantly to their friendly faces. Their attitude to her was any friend of David's was a friend of theirs. She didn't have to win them over. She was accepted by them. Anna, the eldest, came over to her. "David told me you like U2, you can borrow my CD." Lorna went out to get some lemonade and brought back a plate of cakes she had made especially. Just then the living room door opened wide and David's mother came through.

"Clare," she said, taking her arm and shaking her hand. "It's lovely to meet you. David has told me so much about you." From that moment Clare and Mrs Bateson got on so well. She was such a lovely woman Clare thought, so warm and relaxed. Nothing fazed her. She had the art of genuine hospitality. Whether there were three visitors in the house or thirty she set everyone at their ease with her relaxed manner. Clare sensed she knew about her background. She must have known as they only lived around the corner from each other and because of this, Clare felt herself being gently enfolded within her care, safely enclosed in a warm blanket of concern.

She felt happy and proud to be associated with such a normal lovely family and watched carefully how Mrs Bateson ran her home. The table was laid properly for every meal, a sense of order infused the house and Clare vowed that was the way she would run her home when she eventually married David.

The same age, David and Clare passed through school together, he moving on to college and she to a florist's shop. A year after he got his first job as an engineer they married and moved twice before eventually settling in this, their dream home in the seaside suburb of Dalkey close to Dublin, a large five bedroomed house whose price tag had hit the property headlines when first advertised.

Up until the last few months Clare was happy and content. She knew she had a wonderful life and took it as her due. Clare felt it was God's way of making up to her for her miserable childhood. It was as if life had balanced out.

"You'll be very happy when you're older," a relation said to her with a knowing look. "It's the way life works; good will come to make up for the bad," and David, thought Clare, was the good.

Yes, David was good. She would talk to him on Friday about the excessive hours he was working. Friday night was Clare's favourite night. It was sacrosanct. She had two whole days to look forward to with David. Early in the morning she journeyed out to Dun Laoghaire and bought fresh fish. She set a beautiful table, chose a wine carefully and when David returned from work the fire was lighting, fresh flowers covered the house and the silverware twinkled in the candlelight. The children were washed and in their pyjamas ready for bed. This night was special. She had to force herself not to have his slippers ready.

Friday couldn't come quick enough. She would talk to David then. He was too tired during the week. She would talk to him then and everything would be alright. Everything would be alright after Friday.

On that Friday morning Clare woke with a great feeling of excitement and anticipation. The kids left early for school and Clare set out to Dun Laoghaire to buy fish for the evening meal.

On her return Clare was in her element. She began her preparations for her evening dinner with David. Clare was so happy. She loved her home. She tended to it daily, maintaining it, lovingly developing an attachment. Some of the other women had cleaners. She didn't. Clare loved doing ordinary, everyday things. It was what they had built up, their life together, the kids, the house. She loved it all. She couldn't understand why other women didn't like being at home all day. She was her own boss. She ran the family unit like a corporation - her way, only she didn't have any shareholders or subordinates to answer to. On her computer she had files on the kids' vaccinations, school holidays and extra curricula examinations.

Every day she looked forward to David coming home. He would tell her about his day and she would talk of topical things she'd heard on the radio, giving her opinions and asking for his.

This coming Saturday she had arranged a small dinner party with a couple, Mike and Liz, their new neighbours. It was a return invitation as Clare and David had the week before been asked to dinner at their house. Clare was looking forward to it. They had got on well and Clare hoped that Liz would become a friend.

She felt full of joy at the idea of welcoming and entertaining her new neighbours. She poured over her cookery books to find the best recipes for her ingredients. Clare loved cooking. She felt that, apart from the obvious, there were very few pleasures in life and decided that eating was definitely one of them. She decided early on every morsel that passed by the lips of her husband and children would be delicious food. At seven every day the juicer was turned on. At 10.00 a.m., after the children were gone to school, she made fresh bread. Holding her recipe book in her hand she checked that she had everything she needed in the cupboard for the evening meal.

Clare had all the groceries packed away and had finished arranging the flowers when she saw a flashing light on the answering machine.

It was a message from Mike, their new neighbour.

"Sorry we can't make tomorrow night, will be in touch, bye."

Why were they cancelling Clare wondered dejectedly? What had she done?

Had she said anything to offend them? She racked her brain going over in minute detail the conversations she'd had at their dinner party. Having meticulously scrutinized her input, she couldn't find any cause for having given offence.

This coming meal was very important to her. She had hoped they would be friends. She'd ask them over again, make sure no feathers were ruffled she reasoned trying to appease herself. Still she was anxious to know the real reason why.

She listened to the message again. Mike's voice gave no clues. It sounded neutral in tone, cheery almost. It never occurred to her that they might have a genuine excuse. It had to be something she'd done.

Clare viewed this cancellation with a sense of catastrophe; saw it as evidence of the inevitability of future opportunities closing down and with them all hope for new friendships. Clare mentally registered this occurrence as yet another example of her being out of sync, of forever travelling in parallel to people, never to connect with them.

She felt helpless yet with the undercurrent feeling of resentment at being dictated to, of being at the mercy of others' whims, a passive spectator in her own life, like someone unable to participate without their say so.

If she spoke to them now she knew she wouldn't have the courage to say how she really felt. She would smile and say, "I don't mind, not at all," and not speak of her sheer disappointment and annoyance at their late cancellation.

"The world won't fall apart if you say what you really feel now and then," Tim had said to her one day. Clare wasn't convinced.

Still she wondered why.

She felt the familiar tension rising. She couldn't wait to tell David. She needed him to mop up her anxiety.

Just then she heard a beep from her mobile.

She rushed to the silver phone hoping for a reassuring message from David.

The text read:

"Clare, I'm working late on project. See you later. Don't wait up."

Now even David was cancelling. It seemed a small thing, but she sensed something bigger behind it. She was especially rebuffed by the, "Don't wait up" part of the message.

All this communication, Clare considered, and yet no human interaction, no proper explanations to allay her fears. Clare felt flooded with uncertainties. Waves of worry came over her. Once one dissipated another rose up to replace it. Clare knew if she didn't stop worrying she might bring on the panic again and she didn't want that. She knew she could either tip further into the worry pit or get a grip.

She spoke firmly to herself. She would talk to David again express her concerns at his overworking. They were happy, weren't they? she asked, trying to reassure herself. Why wasn't she able to answer in the affirmative? The gnawing uncertainty wouldn't go away. She searched for a hook of conviction to hang her doubts on. She could find none. It was just that there was now David's newly found attractiveness to women to contend with. It had never been an issue before. He had always been very slight, but with all Clare's good cooking he had filled out. His soft face had matured with more interesting angles.

Clare remembered when David first became aware of his new appeal to women. His father had retired from Bateson Engineering and David was now assistant managing director, second in command. Women found this power very attractive. They were at the firms' Christmas party and one girl, Charlene, was talking to him – doing more than talking, she was chatting him up! The surprise on his face at all the attention was almost comical. While talking to her he kept looking over at Clare with an apologetic look yet he couldn't keep the delighted smile off his face. Looking between Charlene and Clare he was caught between two sets of emotions, delight at this new experience and guilt over the feeling that he shouldn't be. He glowed in the attention and when he sat down on his chair beside Clare again his chest literally expanded with newfound confidence and the realisation that he was now an object of desire. This was the first time Clare knew that the balance of power in their marriage had shifted and it was in his favour.

Who was this Charlene, the woman he had been talking to? It now seemed important to find out more about her.

"Where's Daddy?" Jack asked as the six o'clock news theme tune played out later that evening.

"He's working late," Clare said.

"Oh," he replied, absentmindedly twitching his nose with his finger.

"We'll play some board games," Clare said, retrieving some games from the press.

They all sat down on the floor by the fire for although it was early summer the evening was chilly. Clare let herself be absorbed by the games.

The children were good playing without too much bickering between them. At eight she put them to bed. It seemed a long night alone waiting for David. There was an atmosphere of expectation when he returned home.

From her chair by the fire Clare examined him closely looking for what she supposed may well be the telltale signs of an affair, elation perhaps or some inordinate sense of happiness. All she saw was a tired man in front of her. His face was grey with exhaustion.

"You look shattered," she said.

"I am."

"Do you want a drink?"

"No thanks, we stopped off for one on the way home."

70

"We?"

"Fergus and I."

"Oh? Is he the one you are working on the project with?

"Yes."

"I'd like to meet him."

"There's a work dinner in a few weeks' time. You will meet him then. It's to mark the second anniversary of the business."

Saturday passed quietly. David didn't bat an eyelid when she told him of their neighbours' cancellation. Normally she'd badger him into giving her a supposed reason for the cancellation, but now she didn't feel she had the same permission to harangue him, sensing she could no longer take for granted his high tolerance of her angst. That premise had changed between them and with it the assumption that she could rely on his continuous bolstering of her fragile sense of self. There was a need now she gauged, to grow more circumspect, to consider the level of his endurance before unleashing her fears on him. But how was the hard question. She felt defeated, incapable of the discipline needed to ease her own fears.

On Sunday David woke smiling and said, "I'll bring you up breakfast in bed. You stay there."

It was their Sunday morning routine. He was so good, Clare thought, feeling guilty at doubting him, at her betrayal of his loyalty. She felt weepy trying to sort out these conflicting emotions when she heard the phone ring downstairs.

After a few minutes David popped his head around the door. "There's a party in my mother's tonight. Uncle Des is on a flying visit; it's late notice she knows. She wants us to come." He went back downstairs.

Clare lay back in the bed. As if she didn't have enough to contend with, she now had a family reunion to get through. She wondered had she the energy required to negotiate all the different personalities, especially Greta. How would she face Greta feeling like this? Clare didn't like Greta, Andrew's wife. She was cold. Greta didn't trust Clare's niceness. She thought she was insincere. Greta had that bored jaded air in peoples' company as she looked to see who was worthy of the effort of her attention only coming to life when she thought someone was. Greta put people into boxes and

Clare was in the box labeled 'boring'. In her eyes if you had an interesting job, you were an interesting person. Once in conversation with her, which felt more like an assessment, Clare pushed Tim in front of them and introduced him hurriedly as, 'My brother, the auctioneer,' and then felt annoyed with herself for having fallen into the trap of justification. Later that evening, Greta came over to join Clare with an expression indicating that she had gone up in her estimation.

The last three family invitations had seemed more like a summons to Clare. There was no choice but to go. Now was her chance to practice some directness. "I don't feel like going," she said out loud to no one. How did that sound? It wasn't an option. She remembered the uncle was visiting.

There was another worry – what to bring. Normally Clare loved the rapturous approval she received from Mrs Bateson and her sisters when she revealed her trays of homemade desserts, and she especially enjoyed the inevitable comparison with Greta.

"Oh you can always rely on Clare," the inference being, unlike Greta. Clare normally welcomed this one favourable comparison, embracing the accompanying pierce of virtuousness, acknowledging their opinion as recognition of her goodness.

Now she was beginning to resent the fact that she was thought of as being so predictable. She felt angry at being coerced into something she didn't want to do.

She would bring nothing she decided – it would be her little rebellion.

Clare looked through her wardrobe of clothes. She wanted to look sharper, sharp for Greta. She wished she had a classic summer suit to wear. Clare didn't bother much with clothes feeling bamboozled with the variety of styles on offer. Even after three children she still had a good figure. She settled on one of last year's spring dresses in navy with white piping and was glad the shoes to match had a substantial heel. Clare fixed the belt on her waist and decided that it was as sharp as she was going to get.

That evening the children were dressed in their best clothes, sitting in a row on the living room couch, deeply absorbed in the television, all waiting to go visiting.

Christine Masterson

Clare and David were in the kitchen. David was looking for his keys, switching things off. Clare stood quietly beside the presses, one hand on the counter. Before they left the house it was important for her to feel he was on her side. She had a question for him. If he would just answer this one question with conviction then everything would be nice again. Clare loved everything to be nice.

"David," she said. "Is Fergus the only one you are working on the project with?" She smiled at him willing him to answer her with the conviction she needed.

He stopped, hesitating for a moment too long. He was unable to look at her. He half turned his face towards her, keeping his eyes cast down. Colour rose in his cheeks.

"Yes," he said, his tone weak.

"Are we going yet?" Tommy asked, rushing in to the kitchen and throwing his arms around David's leg.

"Yes, let's get going," David said, relieved with the interruption.

Dazed by David's evasiveness and flatness of reply, Clare mechanically summoned the children, foregoing for once the usual close inspection of hair, face and neck.

In their people carrier Clare sat high up in the front passenger seat. David was unusually animated. Clare half listened absorbed in her own thoughts trying to gather her wits. David's answer had heightened not lessened her worry. She wished Tommy hadn't interrupted them. A few more seconds and she would have been better able to read David; in the revealing moments following his answer and in the conviction, or otherwise, of his recovery as he struggled to regain his authority. The opportunity was lost. Clare felt alone.

Clare was vexed with David for another reason. David's evasiveness was bringing up uncomfortable feelings within her, feelings of doubt, resentment and envy. She didn't like being confronted by her darker side. Clare loved harmony, to feel magnanimous towards her fellow human beings. If he was co-operating then she wouldn't be forced to face this aspect of herself. It was unsettling, disturbing her peace of mind.

Clare hated having to deal with injustice and worried more about the bad feelings in her than the bad behaviour of the other person.

73

Clare looked at her empty lap, dessert less. She despised herself for the dishonesty of not saying that she didn't want to go, aware that her anger was seeping through into the petty gesture of not bringing a gift. Clare hoped she could put up with the discomfort.

The journey to the party brought them along the foot of the Dublin Mountains through the familiar suburban villages of Dundrum, Ballinteer, then into Rathfarnham. David swung the car into the long road of houses. Cars were parked a good few houses down from his parents so he picked the nearest parking spot and they walked towards the house. David rang the bell.

"Come on in join the party," called his mother good humouredly from the kitchen. "I have a bouncing castle for you children in the garden," she said, addressing them. "Your cousins are out there." The children raced out the back. David began talking to his mother and Clare walked towards the living room. On the way she had to pass the long dining table heavily laden with plates and plates of food. Aunty Marjorie stood, head bent, peering into the desserts, daintily licking cream off her fingers. "Which one is yours?" she asked absentmindedly, still absorbed in the cakes.

Clare ignored the question and left the room.

With relief she noticed there was no sign of Greta.

Clare could see Mr Bateson weaving through the guests making his way towards her. He was one of those people who felt he was an authority on everything. Luckily, for Clare he had a keen interest in flowers and Clare studied them as much as she could until she had almost an encyclopedic knowledge which she used to impress him.

"Well Clare any tips for the garden," he asked in his usual jocular way. Clare couldn't help laughing. Every season he asked her the same thing. She listed the same tips that she'd given him the same time last year. His friends called him away and Clare was sorry knowing that if she'd stayed talking to him she would have a safe enough partner in conversation for the night.

Watching him Clare reflected how at these family gatherings she was tired being the friendly, cheerful one. The one who made sure she was sociable, included everyone in the conversation, was amenable, personable. This damned niceness was driving her crazy. She felt it was a mask she couldn't go out without. Greta never made any effort and no one thought any less of her.

That night she decided to pull back, to go quiet. She picked a comfortable chair in the corner behind the folding doors and curved her legs beneath her. With a drink in her hand she placed her head on the back of the chair and started to watch the world around her. Uncertain of David, she wasn't sure if it really was her world anymore. Suddenly she felt tired of the lot of them, of these repetitive gatherings with the in-laws. It was impossible to miss one. Any excuse for not being able to attend was taken as a personal affront. This family seemed to move in a herd. Where one went, they all went. It was Sunday and already they were beginning to discuss seeing each other again on Wednesday.

How had she let this happen? They had always got on well, but gradually over the years she had let herself be taken over by them. It had suited Clare too as she always had someone to go out with, but her world had become very small. Seeing the same people all the time.

Keith, Anna's husband, came over to her. "You're very quiet tonight Clare, what's up? You're not your usual chatty self. Why aren't you joining in?"

"To tell you the truth Keith, I just couldn't be arsed."

He laughed. "What's in that glass, a little truth drug?"

"No, I am just seeing things clearly for a change."

"It does get too much though, doesn't it?"

"I think so too." she agreed.

Talking about the in-laws was a risky business. Clare didn't want to be misquoted. Looking at him she could sense he was thinking the same. They both smiled at each other and decided to leave it at that.

Clare relaxed back in her chair beginning to feel safe, safe from Greta. Unfortunately, there was no escape. Greta had hunted her out. She stood in front of Clare with a plate of food raised high to her chest. Clare hoped the cake she was eating would slow her normal bullet like pace of questions. Greta was in animated form. "And what have you been up to recently?" she asked, demanding an account from Clare.

Clare stumbled an answer, "Oh the kids, house, etc."

"Oh goody," Greta replied, patronizing her.

Just then it seemed like a mill of guests arrived and Greta's attention was drawn away.

What have I been up to? Clare repeated to herself. What sort of a dead end question is that? Busy minding my kids, that's what I have been up to. In comparison to Greta there was no comparison.

She vowed she'd never get caught like that again. She was sure Greta put the question in that way on purpose. The next time she'd embarrass Greta by switching the subject to politics or world affairs. Greta hadn't a clue. She was vacant on current affairs. Clare was an avid listener to the radio and knew everything that was going on in the world.

Testing her new found assertiveness, earlier than usual, Clare stood up to leave heading out the back to call the children away.

On the terrace Greta stood talking to a guest. "This is my sister-in-law Clare," she said. "Clare this is Dan O'Leary. He has the franchise on 'Bakes Cakes'. You kept very much to yourself tonight," Greta said accusingly. "Were you thinking up new flower arrangements?" she continued, smirking into her glass.

"Actually," Clare responded coolly, "I have been reflecting on the latest news of our trade surplus. Would you say that this upwards curve is set to continue?" Clare smiled sweetly. Greta looked stunned. "Well," she stuttered," I suppose.. .I think ..."

Dan O'Leary turned to Clare. Fortunately the two of them had similar views and they stood discussing the possible effects on the economy of the positive news.

Clare said a gracious goodnight to them both, barely managing to hide the enjoyment she'd got from getting one up on Greta. The feeling felt good.

Clare had begun to realise that Greta saw her as some sort of barometer, as an example of how not to turn out. She used Clare to bolster her own confidence. It was a revelation, a sort of final straw.

It was time to fight back, Clare decided. Doormat time had come to an end and David? She would deal with David. She wasn't living through this fog anymore. She would find out the truth and as much as she didn't want doubts and fears and bad feelings crowding her mind, they were there and she would just have to deal with them. And deal with them she would.

The following weeks after the party they lived their lives through their usual routine.

Clare let the matter of her concern for David rest for those few weeks. Quietly in the background she did some thinking. Clare viewed the forthcoming work dinner as more of an opportunity to hone her amateur detective skills than of a social outing. There was information she needed and this was where she hoped she'd find it. Clare couldn't take the risk of asking David whether Charlene would be there, but couldn't see a reason why she wouldn't. In fact, so afraid was she of raising his suspicions that she refused to make even the most tentative enquiries of the arrangements.

It wasn't until they were on their way in the taxi that Clare felt it was safe enough to ask where the meal was being held.

"Ricardos," David replied.

This choice of restaurant was a surprise to Clare. The Managing Director, Ian Parish, normally preferred restaurants with the air of a gentleman's club and Ricardo's was a modern restaurant all chrome, brown and fawn.

At the reception desk Clare studied the modern flower arrangement and admired its pared back simplicity. I must update Clare thought, reflecting on her trusted arrangements. These new pieces are very interesting.

They were led through into the far end of the restaurant. Ian Parish and his wife Maura were already seated at the table. Ian was the trusted friend and work colleague of David's father and had been chosen by Mr. Bateson to run the company on his retirement. David was seen as second in command, heir in waiting.

Fergus and his partner Gemma came along just as they were being seated.

Clare was happy. Maura and Ian held her in high regard and they listened to her opinions even laughing at some funny stories she told.

Someone asked where Charlene was. Evidently she was on leave. Clare really began to relax. The first course was delicious and the wine was sweet and mellow. Charlene. Clare reflected on her name. She must have been born when Dallas was at its height.

Just then, as if through suggestion, Charlene stood before them smiling.

"I'm sorry I'm late," she gushed. "I decided to come along at the last minute." All attention was focused towards her. Clare shivered. Charlene had brought the cool evening air in with her.
Unfortunately, for Charlene, most of the younger single people had decided not to go. Her presence seemed inappropriate. Instead of being uncomfortable with the fact she seemed to bask in it. She hasn't the grace to look embarrassed thought Clare. Clare's eyes searched the faces of the three men at the table to see who was most happy to see her. David looked particularly pleased with himself. Her breezy confidence didn't fool Clare. Was there an agenda here? Clare surveyed Charlene, observing the deep cut top, noticing how the push up bra seemed to be doing its job properly – making the most of a little. Clare reluctantly also noted the brazen set of her jaw. Clare wouldn't like to get into a row with her, the word mincemeat came to mind.

An extra place was set for her.

Charlene sat beside Fergus.

"Am I in for a treat?" she asked. "What's the food like."

"Very good," he said.

"Did Mr. Kinsella ring back today?"

"He did," Fergus replied.

"What's the latest on the offer?"

"Oh, he seems happy enough with our offer," Fergus replied.

The rest of the company watched spellbound at Charlene's instigation of what seemed a private conversation.

"Maybe you'll both share the details with us tomorrow," Ian said, leaning forward, exercising his diplomatic skills.

"Oh yes, we'll give you a full update," she said smiling.

Charlene stirred the discussion to a more neutral topic, her speech fast and sharp as though determined to prove a point, deftly rearranging her place settings, her movements exacting in their neatness. Clare sensed a whiff of desperation on her part and couldn't understand why. As Charlene continued speaking there was an acceleration of this desperation, fuelled by an undercurrent of a strange energy which threatened to burst through to the surface yet was held in control by Charlene's steely constraint.

Clare felt trounced, snuffed out by the strength of will emanating from Charlene. Clare's status suddenly reduced from valued guest to mere participant.

With relief Clare noticed a flicker of suspicion cross Maura's face. It isn't only me she thought, Maura can see it too.

It wasn't Charlene's looks that Clare was jealous of; it was her confidence, her authoritative command over the assembled company. She had the skill of shaping a situation her way as if gratitude for her presence should be theirs, her attendance their reward.

When Charlene had settled and everyone had returned to eating their meal, Clare looked closely at this woman, observing the lank hair, non-descript features and then with deflation her wonderful peachy skin. Clare had to force herself to resist from self-consciously touching her own face. She knew Charlene would notice. It would be like handing her a victory.

Assured of having established her presence, Charlene relaxed, her voice became warm and mellow, her honeybee tones, thought Clare, coating a waspish centre.

At the end of the evening the party broke up, they all stood to retrieve their coats.

"I'll get yours," Charlene volunteered, nodding towards David.

Clare noticed how David looked at her with a too tender look in his eyes. There was a level of familiarity between them that seemed inappropriate for work colleagues.

When Clare was on the sidelines of the crowd putting on her coat she quietly asked Fergus under her breath, "Is Charlene involved with the projects that David works on?"

"Oh yes they work together constantly. She is his right hand woman."

In the taxi on the way home Clare asked David, "Do you work with Charlene?"

David coughed and spluttered. "I hardly see her," he said.

The lie was considered nonchalantly. A new approach was called for Clare decided. For the coming weekend she needed to sort out some sort of a plan, a strategy even. Being calculating was new to Clare, but this was serious and serious called for change.

She thought up Plan A and Plan B. Both plans involved booking a babysitter without telling David. If David came home at the normal time on Friday they would go out for the evening, she would say it was a surprise. If he rang to say he was working late then Plan B would kick in.

Clare did all the usual things on that Friday, shopped for fish in the usual shop, brought her children to all their usual after school activities. At four a text message came from David saying he was working late again. Clare quietly prepared the evening meal earlier for herself and the children. At six the babysitter arrived. Clare was ready with her coat on; the children were already in their pyjamas.

Driving into town Clare wondered on the possibilities of what she might find. Was he seeing her? Would all her hunches add up to something concrete? If he was seeing her what were the mechanics of an affair? Where did they go? Had he a house rented somewhere? She couldn't imagine furtive fumblings in a car. David had so much money, he could afford a double life.

Outside the office block David's company shared on Harcourt Street, Clare sat in her car. If she was spotted by anyone she would say she was surprising David. Clare wasn't known for impulsive gestures of any kind. Her predictability was her best defence. At seven David's car turned out of the underground car park and turned onto the street. Clare let two cars pass before pulling out from the kerb onto the road and followed him.

They drove around Stephen's Green and out towards Ballsbridge. Past the canal David took a left turn down a residential street and pulled in. Clare drove past him and pulled in front of some parked cars. She saw in the back mirror that he had gone into the gates of one of the large Victorian houses. When she reached the house a discreet sign outside the basement said "Restaurant Vico." She walked down the steps of the basement and looking in the window where she saw, what she knew she would see, David embracing Charlene as they sat down snugly to enjoy their evening together.

Clare turned and walked back out onto the pathway. Heaviness descended on her stomach. She felt full to the brim. A burst of regurgitated air hit the back of her throat bringing with it the whiff of the fish she'd had for her evening dinner. The foulness of her breath made her gag and she crouched low, vomit purging from her mouth; a double indignity, discovering her husband's infidelity and now crouching, like some helpless drunk, with sick belching from her mouth. She cried out in shame wanting it to stop so badly. She feared her guts would spew out of her, her insides in revolt at the injustice that had befallen her. At least the panic didn't come back. Clare felt no sign of panic.

Back in the house Clare calmly paid the babysitter. "Would you mind asking your parents for a lift home?" she asked. "I don't feel too well," and gave Roisin an extra amount of money to make up for the inconvenience.

Clare trudged up the stairs to her room. She undressed, keeping to her usual routine. With the thinking part of her mind she felt it important not to raise suspicions to keep everything looking as normal as possible.

She placed her book on her locker to give the impression she had been calmly reading. She lay in the same position as normal and when David returned it looked as if nothing had happened.

"Good night?" Clare asked.

"I had a great night." He seemed eager to talk. Clare shut her eyes to the spiel of lies.

An Ed was mentioned. There it was the phantom friend. She had read about them in magazines, the alibi in an affair. Had he no imagination? Could he not think up a better name? It was only dawning on her now, he had none, he thought in straight lines. David fell asleep practically straight away. Clare lay still in the darkness, her gaze strained on a thin strip of light projected on the bedroom wall through a narrow gap in the curtains.

In the morning Clare woke later than usual. Lying there untangling herself from sleep, her body felt stiff and sore. Easing herself out of the bed her movements were slow and languid. David was getting dressed at his side of the room.

For some moments she sat on the edge of the bed, then with her left hand she pulled the sheets off the bed and they lay in a pile on the floor. Clare stood at the bottom of the bed and raising the white sheet high she let it fall dreamily back onto the mattress. The hypnotic rhythm of this action momentarily induced a trance like state and a memory returned to her. Sometimes when she was young and the pressure got too much she used a little trick to cope.

She let her mind become detached and like a moveable camera pan over the scene before her, silently observing and by being removed from the scene becoming anaesthetized from the pain. And in the safety of the space between her mind and physical self she could coldly evaluate what was before her and now she stood watching herself, watching him, wondering placidly who he was, had she ever known him. In her disjointedness she gauged that she did not know him and the realization brought no stress. It brought her time.

TIM

Driving towards Dublin Tim reflected on his last telephone conversation with his sister. He was embarrassed to have been asked, "Are you ill" so surprised was Clare to hear from him. "No," he'd laughed. "I want to invite the boys down for a holiday."
They'd then arranged for him to collect them on Sunday at lunch time. This plan suited Tim as he got the benefit of a Saturday night on his own and would arrive just in time for one of Clare's superb lunches.

He found it interesting to draw an analogy between Clare and food and blancmange, he decided, seemed to describe her best – wobbly – so unsure of herself.

What was it that had impelled him to contact his sister? he pondered. Was it this sense of loneliness he had begun to admit he was feeling since his break up with Kate - an awareness of his invincibility, giving way to a new vulnerability?

Still, he wouldn't confide in her about Kate. It was always best, he thought, to keep Clare at arms length. His aloofness, acting as a screen of protection, had served him well. Any gap and she'd come rushing through, pouring herself over him. Even worse, he suspected there was an avalanche of emotion there.

It always amazed him that even at his most dismissive she ignored his rudeness and kept reaching out to him and he, safe in the knowledge that she always would, felt no compulsion to bridge the space between them.

Right now he needed her warmth. He wouldn't even mind drowning in her niceness.

He would try and be sociable this time. Try extra hard to hide his annoyance at her probing about his personal life and yet, he knew, in their communication, there existed a distance as subtle as a layer of Perspex, he was unwilling to puncture due to indifference.

Coming within ten minutes drive of Clare's home he tried to remember as much as he could about her children. Jack, the eldest was ten, then Danny who was eight and Tommy, three years old. He remembered Tommy's christening so well, it was where he'd introduced Helen to Clare and they'd become firm friends. He viewed their friendship with suspicion. He didn't mind them getting on well, but getting on like a house on fire? That was another thing altogether. It unnerved him. He didn't like the idea of information being passed back.

For a moment he thought it strange that she'd never mentioned David. She'd met him when she was fifteen. There again, she was looking for a husband from the time she was fourteen, she was just that type and once she found him had stuck to him like glue. He was happy for them in an I'm-glad-it's-not-me sort of way. They had it all, three great kids, a huge house and pots of money. Driving in to the gates of their house was like driving into fairyland. Big sis had done well he thought and checked to see was the emotion he felt admiration or envy and was relieved it was the former.

The front door was ajar and he let himself in. The house seemed unusually quiet. Toys lay strewn across the hallway in a trail leading to the living room. Going past the kitchen he could see it was in a mess dishes stacked high in the sink. "Clare," he called.

"I'm in here," Clare answered from the dining room.

On the table were three suitcases with piles of clothes beside them. Clare was busily putting the clothes into the cases. She looked distracted and barely looked at him.

"Where are the children?" he asked.

As if in answer a ball hit the window. Clare rushed towards the window and pounding it with her fists she yelled at the children to stay away. Tim watched in amazement. Clare shouting at her children? That was new. He found it refreshing that she'd developed an edge. Closing the cases she looked at him.

"Tim, I've something to tell you."

Just then another knock came on the window. This time it was Tommy roaring crying.

"Oh this is hopeless," she cried exasperatedly. "It will have to wait."

Calling the children in she showed them how to wheel the suitcases down through the hall.

"Oh I'm sorry Tim, would you like a cup of tea before you go?"

Tim declined thinking it best to make tracks quickly.

Moving towards him to say goodbye, Tim sensed one of her lunges coming on and bristled at the thought of his personal space being invaded. He decided it best to surrender to it and get it over with quickly. Throwing her arms around him she seemed to cling for longer than usual and when she pressed her check against his he could feel it was damp. Sympathy stirred within him.

"Are you all right Clare?" he asked.

"Yes," she said, wiping away her tears. "I'm fine."

She ushered them quickly out of the house and as soon as they were outside shut the door quickly behind them. Usually she stood on the porch and waved until they were out of sight.

Something is wrong Tim thought as he drove out of the gates. All is not well in paradise.

"How are things with your mammy and daddy?"

"Fine," Jack said.

"They sleep in different rooms now," Danny piped up.

"No they don't," Jack said in denial.

"They do." Danny reiterated, not afraid to contradict his older brother.

Jack sat quietly staring out the window looking perplexed.

Kids, thought Tim, always the first to know.

That evening in the spare bedroom the kids were getting ready for bed. Clare had been so distracted packing that some of their clothes were missing. Danny was in the bed.

"I can't sleep without pyjamas bottoms. My bum is cold," he said.

"Here put on those shorts, they'll keep you warm," Tim said, throwing the shorts in his direction.

"I can't sleep without a pyjamas top," Tommy asserted.

"Wear one of your t-shirts."

"I can't they're for the day."

These kids are unbelievable, Tim thought. Have they never heard of improvisation? When he was a kid he got a new pair of pyjamas when they were way past his ankles. He remembered his skinny legs peeping out.

On the first morning Tim got up in plenty of time to have their breakfast ready. He'd bought three boxes of cereal and there were still two types they wanted and which he didn't have. One liked toast done on both sides with butter, one liked it without. Three slices had to be thrown out because it was toasted the wrong way. Tim bristled at the waste. Their fussiness was unbelievable. How did Clare cope with this? He thought he might ring Clare and find out their likes and dislikes. Then he thought the better of it. Something in him warned to leave Clare alone.

Realising he couldn't put up with their pickiness at every meal, after breakfast he said, "Listen lads, we'll write down a list of things you like. The only rule is that it has to be a mixture of healthy and I'll allow some unhealthy as well, just because you are on holidays."

Each child gave their favourite dishes, even Tommy. At the end of the session Tim decided that if he was to survive he'd bring them out to eat at least two or three times.

Jack was a stocky kid. He followed Tim everywhere and had the irritating habit of dangling loose change in his pocket like an old man Tim thought. He talked endlessly of money.

"Are you getting the paper today?" Jack asked, standing beside him.

"Why?" Tim asked.

"I want to look at the business pages."

If he mentions money again I'll scream. Who is talking to him about these things Tim wondered. It didn't seem like it would be David. He never came across as a hard-nosed business person.

"Who is giving you all this information?" Tim asked.

"My grandad Bateson is."

Grandad Bateson? I suppose that made sense reasoned Tim. He'd had a business once, although Tim didn't think he'd any interest in business at the moment.

"I have great plans for the week," he told them. "We can go to the beach and the fun fair today. Tomorrow, I thought we'd try some fishing. We'll go off out in a boat. What do you think of that?"

"Hurray!" the three kids jumped.

"There's a famine ship and a famous park I'd like you to see in New Ross."

"Can we go to the beach?" Danny asked.

"Of course," Tim replied. "It's great weather. Wexford is welcoming you. It's a great day just for you boys. Have you all got swimming togs?"

"I don't know," each one of them said in turn.

"Go and look for them now." They all came back to him with their togs and no towels.

"Have you towels with you?"

"No," they replied.

Tim looked in the airing cupboard and took out the three biggest towels he could find.

He put them into a big holdall bag with a book he wanted to finish and wondered what they would eat for lunch and how he would go about making a picnic. He simply had no idea how to make a picnic and decided that they would take the day as it came and buy some food when the kids were hungry.

They all trooped into the car. Suddenly Tim felt nervous. He had never been responsible for children for a whole day. "Have you all got your seat belts on?" he asked, "and make sure all the doors are locked."

Suitably ensconced, Tim headed towards the beach at Curracloe. He parked easily and they walked up the mound of sand onto the beach. The beach was near empty and they quickly found a nice sheltered spot and spread out their towels. We'll go for a quick swim and then I'll get back to my book thought Tim.

"Let's get ready for our swim," he said to the boys.

They changed quickly and the four of them ran shrieking down to the water. It was icy cold. Tommy stood frightened at the water's edge.

"Ha, ha, look at Tommy," Jack jeered, "he's afraid of the water."

"Leave him alone," Tim ordered.

He took Tommy by the hand and gently coaxed him into the water.

"Come with me Tommy, we'll paddle for a while before we go in deeper to the water."

Tommy wasn't that enamoured with the water and letting go of his hand he ran out of the water back onto the beach.

That's the end of my own swim, Tim thought. I won't be able to take my eyes off him. They spent some more time in the water and then returned to their temporary home on the beach. Tim flopped on to the towel. Now I might get some time to myself he thought as he reached for his novel. Three little bodies stood before him. "We're bored. There's nothing to do."

"Play chasing," Tim suggested.

"Chasing?" they scoffed as if they'd never heard of it. "Or have a race."

"We can't race, Tommy keeps falling over, his feet are wonky. We've no ball to play football," Jack moaned.

"I want to play volleyball," Danny chorused.

"I want a frisby," Tommy added chuckling.

"All right, all right. I can't listen to you all. We'll have to go back into town to get those things."

They all dressed again and packed up the car and into town they went.

In the main street they walked down the pedestrianised walkway four abreast. Tim held Tommy's hand. Tommy leaned back looking at the people going by. In what seemed like a split second he tripped and hit the concrete of the street hard, blood gushed from his leg. He let out an almighty scream and big tears rolled down his face. Tim picked him up and dashed towards the nearest chemist. He stood in the middle of the shop in a blind panic.

"Child, eh hurt, can you help me?" he asked the assistant. He hadn't a clue what to do with Tommy or how to pacify him.

"Sit down and let me have a look," the woman said calmly. "It's a deep enough cut," she said, examining his knee, "but I don't think he needs stitches."

She went behind the counter and brought out some TCP and cotton wool. "There, there," she said soothingly to Tommy, "this will fix it and you will be as right as rain in no time. Aren't you a great big fellow," she said in child speak trying to distract him while she put on a bandage on his knee.

Tommy sat, his tears abating, watching in wonder at the magnificence of the bandage being rolled onto his knee.

Tommy's sandals caught Tim's eye. They were too big. They were open toed, the white insole of the sandal seemed to stretch on forever. What was Clare thinking of? That was why he was always tripping up. He wasn't in the proper shoes.

Saying their goodbyes to the chemist and with a lollipop in each of the children's hand, they made their way up to the street to the shoe shop.

Tim didn't really know where to go and sat where the shoes looked the smallest.

A man came towards him. "Tommy here," Tim explained, patting the child's head, "he needs some shoes."

"No problem," the man said. "I'll just measure him first and see what we have in his size."

Tommy was measured and the man went into a back room returning with four boxes. "These are all in his size."

"I'm more interested in a good fit than design," Tim explained.

"These little navy ones are very secure. They come up high at the back and have laces."

Tommy tried them on and the decision was unanimously made that they were a perfect fit. Kids cost a fortune; Tim reflected, the guts of €100 gone in the blink of an eye.

Tim, as a concession, asked could they be left on him and the four of them trooped out onto the street again. They stood in a little circle, Tim thinking aloud about how best to spend the rest of the day. "I think it's too late to go back to the beach," he said. "We'll go again tomorrow. I think we'll have our lunch now and go to the park for a few hours."

At night when the kids were asleep, he couldn't get away from his rumination. Having the boys around reminded Tim of his own boyhood. He'd kept his childhood frozen in his memory and now that memory was beginning to thaw. He didn't want painful memories of lack and want unsettling him, disturbing the peace he'd created, yet they refused to be quashed. The more he tried to ignore and compress them the more powerful they became, gathering momentum, rising bigger every time. Sitting alone while the kids slept there was nothing to do but face them He poured himself a drink. He couldn't afford to have a few too many to block them all out, the children were relying on him.

Recollections of his family home came back sharp in detail like snapshots zooming in on his mind. The God Bless Our Home plaque hung on the wall beside the cooker, a single shepherdess ornament on the living room mantelpiece.

They were the cleanest kids on the road, soap and water making up for what the well washed and faded clothes couldn't do. He squeezed his closed eyelids trying to cancel the images but they wouldn't go away.

He remembered his slippered feet on the lino, his big toes protruding through holes punctured by the pressure of having grown too big for them, polishing the floor, a duster underneath each foot, his mother's grateful smile.

Her smile: its range fluctuated mainly between silly and hapless, the strain of living with Theo having forced her to regress into a childlike version of herself. As Tim grew older he longed to shake his mother to get her to wake up to what was happening, but it was like trying to relate with a vague presence, someone lost in their own world of denial. She always made excuses for Theo. There was too much pain in the truth that she had been rejected. Her mind developed its own way of coping.

He did remember when Theo was out and the house was peaceful, lying with his head on her lap, she stroking his hair, the baking smell of her apron. Rose smelt of safety – a contradiction, he never felt safe with her. He'd looked to her for solid emotional support, but she was intangible. Growing up he didn't take on the role of mammy's protector. Something in the deepest part of his being told him not to, that he might not survive the weight of it. Who was there to protect him? He'd learnt to rely on himself, to dig deep into his own resources.

Clare's relationship with Rose was different. She had more patience and was better able to operate within the dysfunction. Tim tuned out mentally, planning his eventual move away. In a sense he felt he'd abandoned her and now he was feeling guilt spreading out and over him, sapping him. What could he have done?

Sometimes they got the upper hand on Theo. One time Tim and Rose were sitting at the kitchen table listening to Clare romanticize about the magnificent dress she had just seen, saying how much she would love to buy it. Their father was in the living room watching television. They hatched a plot between them. Tim came up with the idea which he knew would appeal to his father's vanity.

"Tell him," Tim said, "the €35 is for a yearly raffle in the school and that the nuns will put up the first five names on the notice board."

They held their hands over their faces so that Theo wouldn't hear them laughing. Clare sat up and sat down twice. "I can't do it," she said.

"Go on," Tim said, encouraging her. "If you ask him out straight you know you won't get it. You're sunk then."

Rose held her apron up to her face giddy with fearful excitement, scared stiff at Clare's daring.

"Go on," Tim said again.

Clare walked towards her father and repeated word for word what Tim had told her.

"Notice board?" her father queried and then miraculously his wallet came out stuffed with notes as usual and lingering over each note, he lovingly counted three tens and a five. Handing them over he snapped it shut and hurriedly put the wallet in his back pocket.

When Clare returned to the kitchen she closed the door tight and they jumped up and down in a silent dance of triumph, their faces wreathed in smiles. Tim punched the air in victory.

Each week in her typing class in school, Clare diligently wrote out fictitious winners and in the evening handed the list to her father. "No luck again Dad," she'd say to his mutterings of, "Never again, that's the last time I'm giving to a raffle."

The more Tim thought about Clare the more he began to doubt the seriousness of her situation. It was probably some minor blip between her and David. She was always on the dramatic side. There again he didn't believe her when she'd told him their mother was dying.

"How can she die when she hasn't even grown up yet," he yelled at Clare.

In the hospital during the last few days of her life as Rose spoke to Tim she became more true. Her silliness was wiped away. She spoke frankly about her life as if she'd woken up and wasn't afraid anymore. What a pity, he thought, that she hadn't lived like that, then she would have been more present to them. It was lovely to see the real her.

"I hope you're blessed in love and that luck and timing go your way," Rose said to him. They were her last words. Her breathing became easier then. He held her hand and then just before lunch as the clatter of trollies began to trundle down the corridor she eased out of this life.

CLARE

With the children at Tim's, in the kitchen on the following Monday morning Clare said to David.

"I don't want you to go to work."

"Why?" he asked.

"Because I know."

"What do you know?" he asked scoffing, staring warily at her. "Is this you being ridiculous again?" He laughed a panicky little laugh.

"I know, I followed you."

His mouth puckered downwards drooping in panic. "It was only a quick meal out. I was starving."

"You are lying," Clare said quietly.

Clare distracted by a blob of butter on the tablecloth said almost to herself. "I don't even see what the attraction is. She is not that pretty. It somehow makes it worse."

"You don't know what it's like out there," he said, running his hands through his hair distractedly. "There are millions of pounds worth of contracts at stake. One mistake in a contract could be catastrophic for us. Since I've taken over from my father they are all waiting for me to fail. There are knives out to get me."

"But why, why her?"

"She is a clear thinker," he said helplessly.

He was avoiding the real issue for Clare.

"How much did you expose me emotionally? My family? What did you tell her?" His face creased in despair as the enormity of what he had done suddenly hit him. He started to cry. For a moment Clare thought she was going to hurl towards him and maul him with her fists. Instead with iron will she composed herself and decided to use the more deadly ammunition. She spoke. "It's obvious then isn't it?" she said quietly. "You've been promoted beyond your capabilities," and raising her voice in anger she shouted, "and what would your Daddy think of that?"

He sank down on the chair. "Clare I'm sorry, I'm truly sorry," he sobbed.

Clare's feet pounded on the stairs. In the bedroom she opened the part of the wardrobe especially built for suitcases and heaving the biggest one out began piling her clothes into it. She didn't know how long she was going to stay away, but for the moment a huge suitcase seemed to confirm that she was adamant. It would give him the biggest shock.

"Clare don't go. Please, please don't go."

At the hall door she turned and said, her voice threatening, "When the children return from Tim's - you make sure you mind my children. The experience should be new to you."

Clare was startled by the screech of the brakes on the gravel as the car jerked forward out of their driveway. She wanted company. Not from people, from inanimate things like street lights, traffic. She headed for the city centre, Dublin city. She wanted to get as far away from the sanitized suburbs as possible.

On the quays beside the Halfpenny Bridge, Clare booked into a hotel. It was an elegant four storied building wedged in a terrace.

Inside her room she locked the door and placed her bag on the floor. She undid the belt of her coat and placed it carefully on a chair by the wall. In her rush to leave the house she had taken her good coat. Suddenly feeling exhausted and slightly dizzy, Clare walked towards the bed and lay on it. She had barely taken in her surroundings. As she lay there she was aware of a freestanding wardrobe, a dressing table and a small sofa in the room. Closing her eyes she breathed in the atmosphere of her surroundings. The room felt welcoming and warm. The rosy hue of the wallpaper cast a comforting glow.

At first she viewed the tall buildings on either side of her as being claustrophobic, then she decided to judge the experience as one of being cocooned; the city was cradling her. She felt soothed and safe. The momentary squish of tyres on the wet streets the only reminder of the outdoors. She liked the idea of being anonymous, the fact that nobody knew she was there. It was a tremendous freedom. She sat in her room thinking of nothing. Her mind was in neutral; it was too painful to be anywhere else.

The truth was so ugly it had to remain hidden from view until she felt ready to deal with it and only then by approaching it warily, peeling it back partially, bit by bit, revealing only as little at a time as she could bear.

Staring at the ceiling, she spent some minutes pondering on the origins of the plasterwork of the cornices and the ceiling rose, wondering if they were the original period features. Studying the tiny plastering details of the roses and leaves, she decided that they were, the heaviness of the plaster being the clue. She imagined the workmen who had created these designs, their lives, bringing them to life in her mind, their memory acting as a presence, as company for her.

Through the blinds the muted street lighting chaperoned her. The city was providing everything she needed, anonymity, light, safety. It was supporting her, supporting her bolting.

The next morning Clare woke with a strong sense of her mother. In the familiarity of the city she could feel Rose all around her. She had this overwhelming need to be close to her. Clare's distress had evoked intense memories of Rose and the place where Rose had been happiest - in her own parents' home. Clare was being drawn there, drawn back to Rose's home.

The absurdity of going for a walk to a house where everyone she knew in it was dead did not resonate with Clare. She wanted the memory of them to enclose around her, to comfort her. It was also where she hoped to best evoke their qualities of compassion.

The simple phrase "God help them" came back to her now. She could hear her grandmother say it and had heard her say it over and over after any unfortunate news about a person. Compassion was a guarantee, a given. It was recognition, sympathy beyond pity to an understanding. Love flowed from her, seeing the humanity in each and every case. Clare now felt greedy for what had been so freely given to others, for them to bear witness to her story, to give credence to the injustice of her situation.

If she was to go out for a walk she needed clothes. She lifted her suitcase onto the bed and examined the contents. She had in her case two good pairs of shoes and three good dresses some underwear and toiletries. In her haste she had opened the part of the wardrobe where her good clothes hung and grabbed what first came to view. Good clothes seemed appropriate.

Leaving the hotel half an hour later, Clare walked along the quay. Conveniently, this was the same route that she and her mother often took on their regular visits to her grandparents. Retracing the route,

Clare walked passed Eustace Street with its cobbled alleyway full of pubs, past Capel Street Bridge, turning left into St. Michael's Hill.

Ascending the hill, Clare walked with the ghost memory of her mother beside her; the echo of her dainty steps from back then, full of purpose, going home. Between them her shopping bag with a tray of fresh cream cakes balanced on top. Rose seemed more alive in death than in life. Picture like postcards showing her various facial expressions filed towards Clare, procession like, the images sharper now, meticulous in their detail, their effect compounding Clare's loneliness.

Clare continued on her walk up the hill, walking back two decades. It was years since she'd walked this part of Dublin. Clare passed Christ Church on the left and turned into High Street on the right, out onto Francis Street then left to Meath Street up towards Pimblico by the back way, the towering presence of Guinness at the side. Within minutes she came to her grandparent's house in Reginald Street.

The artisan red brick houses looked summery with pots of red geraniums outside their front doors, the polished brasses shining through the bright morning light.

Since their death other people had been living there. Clare stood outside the house. A young woman was at the door of the neighbouring house pushing her key in the door.

"My mother used to live here," Clare said, needing to explain to someone.

"Why don't you knock on the door," she suggested, her voice friendly, "and see who's there?"

"No, I'll leave it thanks."

Walking away Clare wondered what had her grandparents thought of Theo. He was probably too clever for them. They were simple gentle people, ill-equipped to deal with his deviousness; their innocent trust in the good in others blinding them to him. They were joyous people who let the vagaries of life rest lightly on them. They believed that God is good. That simple belief was expressed several times a day. It was what sustained them.

And her mother, what advice would she have given her over David? None. This situation would have been beyond her. She remembered Rose when Clare was distressed sitting in the kitchen picking at the folds of material in her skirt distractedly whilst patting Clare's hand with the useless comforting words of, "There there, there there."

Clare crosses the road to St. Patrick's Park, the park where Rose played as a young child and where she had brought Tim and herself many times to play on the swings.

Strolling on the pathway, alongside the railings, Clare lapses into a daydream. She imagines her mother walking towards her now. Rose is younger and better dressed in the dream than in Clare's memory wearing a brown princess flared coat similar to her own. Her hair is lightly curled and shiny falling just above her shoulders. They hesitate and stop some feet away from each other, mother and daughter both the same age. Clare's expression is one of query, her mother's is relaxed, open, seeking understanding. There is peacefulness in each other's presence. A youth runs from the road onto the pathway in front of Clare. A driver beeps in annoyance. The pathway clears, Clare continues walking.

Still walking along the street Clare can hear her mother's clear voice repeat, "It was the wedding, the wedding; the wedding was the awful turning point." It is like as if she is trying to get across the significance of that event.

Details of a wedding invitation came into Clare's mind. She remembered the weeks before the O'Connor's wedding. Although Theo was not popular with the neighbours, he wasn't unpopular either, so it was with fantastic excitement that Rose received the invitation to a wedding of the neighbour directly across the road from them. The problem was how to get Theo to go. Theo would never accompany Rose anywhere. She couldn't get him to go places. Then the intricate dance of appeasing, cajoling, of trying to draw a positive answer from him began. If she pressed too hard he would withdraw completely. Rose had to use her limited skill to try and get the balance right, to ask yet not to appear to demand him to go. To feign nonchalance would only reveal to him her keen interest in going. She somehow had to try to show him the benefit of going. If she appeared to want too much to go then he definitely would not go.

Theo took the invitation from her and read it through with interest. "Will you go?" Rose asked.

"I might."

So delighted was she at his non refusal that she took this as a possible yes and hoping against hope over the next few weeks she planned as if they were going to the wedding.

She lay gentle reminders during those weeks. Placing his breakfast on the table she began, "When we go to the wedding."

His face seemed to open in recognition as he remembered the invitation. "Oh yes," he said.

Later that day she dared brooch the subject again. "The neighbours are all talking about it. It's out by Donabate, do you know the way?"

He was watching the television and seemed to nod. "Yes," he said. "I know the way."

Normally he'd choke her off for going on and on about this and she took his lack of verbal rebuttal as an acquiescence, that he was willing to go. Rose took his suit to the cleaners and ironed his best shirt again in readiness for the occasion.

It was a communal life on the avenue where Clare lived and children played outside between their neighbours' gardens, and out on the road. On the day of the wedding the bride appeared from the house opposite theirs and she walked like a moving fondant of pink silk and white netting with cascades of pink and white carnations draping from her arms.

Clare ran in to tell her mother that Sandra O'Connor was coming out of the house, to come quick and see her dress.

Approaching the front living room Clare stopped when she heard a conversation between her mother and father. Eavesdropping, she peered into the slightly opened door.

"And why won't you go?" Rose asked.

"Because I don't want to," he said and walked out of the room past Clare.

Rose sat with her back to the window on a hard wooden chair. She was half dressed in her best slip, the invitation in her hand. Her hair was tightly set before its final brush out. Her face was made up. Laughter and joyous shouts came from across the road. Her brown eyes were pools of tears crying silently and in that moment Rose knew she was beaten. Clare slunk away. There was no question of Rose going now.

From that moment on the more adult Clare became the more childlike her mother grew. Years of mental pressure from him had ground her down, she regressed, it was her way of coping. Clare remembered the day she rushed home from work and calling happily to her mother she asked, "Did you collect my dress?"
Her mother looked aghast. "What dress?" She shuffled towards her in her battered slippers.

"The dress you said you would pick up for me from the cleaners."

Her mother's face crumbled in distress. "Clare I'm sorry, I completely forgot."

"Mother you promised me," Clare roared at her. "I could have got it myself, but you promised me. How could you, how could you forget. I need that dress for tonight."

Her mother sat down at the kitchen table and placing her head in her hands she started to cry. "I'm sorry, I'm so sorry, I keep forgetting things. I am just so tired, I am so, so tired. It's all the time now. I never have any energy. This cloud is over me always."

"I'm taking you to the doctor," Clare said, taking her hand. "This is not normal. You can't go on like this."

Two days later Clare took the day off work and they went to the doctor. Rose spoke of her tiredness, the cramps in her stomach. Hospital appointments were made for tests and from one of those tests it was gleaned that she had cancer. Five months later she was gone. She died too young from stomach cancer, her stomach having been in knots for years.

"Life goes on," her father said, too many times as if he couldn't wait to get on with it. And get on with it he did. A few months later he met Fran a large Kerry woman who completely controlled and dominated him. "Isn't that right Theo," Fran would roar demanding compliance from him.

"Yes Fran, yes Fran," he would say when in her company. He seemed desperate for her approval. The interaction was so hurtful for Clare to watch. She wondered why the dynamics were so different between them and what had been between her parents. "Fear," Tim had explained one day. "It's out of fear he is like that with Fran. He knows he will be on his own forever if he isn't. She is his last hope and he will do anything to avoid being alone."

Clare remembered how Rose had lain in the hospital bed clutching her rosary beds. She turned her face towards Clare. "David," she spoke weakly, "such a lovely boy, such a lovely family." The expression in her eyes willing happiness for her daughter. Choose well was the unspoken message. How well had she chosen, Clare wondered? Her certainties had since been cancelled.

By now Clare was near Christ Church. She breathed in the familiarity of the city; she could feel it empowering her. Near Exchequer Street she stopped for a coffee and decided to sit out on the pavement. The children weren't due back from Tim's for another two days. Let David take time off work she decided. He'd never assumed responsibility for the kids for more than a few hours at a time over the years. Let him go through the embarrassment of explaining why he needed time off to his bosses at work, trouble at home, difficulty in my private life… let him, let him, let him.

Sitting there drinking her coffee she felt strong. She marveled at how strong she was. Clare had always seen herself as a wishy washy character, weak, whilst everyone around her seemed so strong. She waited. There was not one sign of panic. She waited again for some moments, listening to her body, half expecting the nervous hum in her tummy to emerge and rise again, but nothing came.

Clare's loss of her mother at seventeen was so acute that the physical world seemed in shock, bereft of her presence, the very earth grieving for its daughter. It's core needing to rearrange, to adjust to her loss. Clare was like a young tree with roots trying to establish themselves, arms like branches tentatively reaching upwards towards the sun, but those roots had been hacked, those branches tremulous, reaching unsure, frightened with her core sense of equilibrium damaged.

It was some weeks after her mother's death when the panic attacks started to happen. Clare felt herself becoming very nervous over what she couldn't pinpoint, just a general sense of unease and fear. She didn't feel safe. The world seemed such a hostile place. There was a constant sense of fear and dread that something terrible was about to happen.

The first panic attach came out of nowhere. Clare was walking on her way to David's. She passed by a group of girls she knew.

"Hi Clare," they said.

Clare felt unwell, their voices seemed to echo in her head, "Hi Clare, hi Clare," their words repeated in her brain. Oh God, I feel weird she thought. A sense of disconnection swept over her. She felt separate from reality. Panic began to rise through her. What's happening to me she wondered? Her rational thoughts were trying to break through. Calm down, they were telling her. Her heart was hammering in her chest. She was trying hard to fight the feeling of losing control.

She ran into David's house. Mrs Bateson answered the door. "Clare what's wrong with you, you look as if you have seen a ghost?" Clare started to cry. "I, I...," and in between the sobs Mrs Bateson got her to sit down. "What is it love?" she asked, holding her hand, "tell me."

"It's the feeling, it's the feeling that I think I'm going to die."

"It's the strain that you've been under that's all," Mrs Bateson reassured. "Your nerves have been affected. It's the shock you had. Sit there and I'll make you a sweet cup of tea." That day Clare's bond grew closer with her future mother-in-law. She became like a mother to her.

In the weeks after Rose's death, Mrs Bateson had become even more protective towards Clare. "Come around for your dinner this evening," she'd say. "Tell your father you are eating with us." David told Clare that his mother was trying to protect her from becoming a sort of unpaid housekeeper to her father. She didn't want him getting used to Clare being at his beck and call.

"Tell him to bring three bags of laundry to the launderette on a Thursdays, one whites, dark and coloureds and collect them on a Saturday. Tell him Mrs Bateson said."

One evening Mrs Bateson called in to see Clare on the pretext of wanting to see how her father was, but really she was sending a message to him. "Clare has her work Mr Brady, it's important she is not overburdened." Clare felt she was like an angel watching out for her.

When he felt the house was a reflection on him he suddenly took an interest, ordered a skip and threw everything out. Everything he replaced it with was cheap, but it brought an unusual comfort to the sad house.

If they broke up how would she manage without the Batesons. They were the only family she knew. If she lost David she knew she would eventually lose them. There would be sympathy at the start and then a falling off in contact. Especially Mrs Bateson, she had been like a mother to her. She knew everything about her, even about the panic.

Still revelling in her present strength, Clare walked back towards the hotel.

In the richly paneled reception area the receptionist asked her. "How long do you think you'll be staying?"

"I'm not sure," Clare replied falteringly.

"We need to know as soon as possible. We have bookings," she replied, her expression dull.

Clare climbed the stairs to her room more subdued from the reality check of dates, times, departures. Her mood fell into semi despair as she contemplated the reality of what lay before her. She wasn't even allowed this cocoon, her refuge was threatened. Now the hotel didn't even want her

In her room Clare sat hunched on the sofa thinking. Pin pricks of pain began to pierce through her numbness, bringing to her conscious mind words which articulated her suffering. Love and its existence had been the one certainty in her life. It was the well from where her essence sprung. How could she focus her life without love?

Her heart was now a cold dead place. There was a battle for her heart; a sinister stranger hovered over it, waiting for its possession. Clare pondered on whether to accommodate this frosty interloper. It would be so easy to allow it in and then shut down.

She wanted to present herself to the world as a neat package, three children, good husband, large house, a success. Now the hell of other people crept in, their judgements. She'd had enough of that when she was younger.

Her life, once ordered and contained, spilled out into a disordered mess. She wanted a dignified life and this was undignified.

Clare felt, through no fault of her own, she was forced to be on the defensive. Was it through no fault of her own? How much of it was her fault? Charlene was young, bright, independent and shaping a career. All Clare had ever wanted was to mind her family. To be a constant presence to her children was her dream having been brought up around so much vagueness. Now she felt vulnerable. Why did minding her family leave her so vulnerable?

She ran a bath. She felt herself slide into a depression and willed herself to stay on the edge of it, not to sink deeper in.

In the bath Clare thought about how she would tell Tim and decided understatement was best, she knew he would respond best to directness, no theatrics. She dried herself and dressed in an odd arrangement of clothes she sat on the bed and phoned him.

"Tim, I've a problem".

"What's wrong?" he asked.

"I've left David."

"Left David," he repeated, "but why?"

"I don't feel able to explain now. I just want to let you know that when you bring the kids back, I won't be there."

There was silence. "Where are you now?" he asked.

"I'm in Dublin in a hotel."

"Come down and stay with me. I am bringing them back later on this evening. Come down then."

"Look I'll leave it 'til the morning," Clare replied. "I should be there in the early afternoon."

"Are you sure?" Tim asked.

"Yes, I'll text you from Enniscorthy. Thanks Tim."

TIM AND CLARE

The next day as the Dublin to Wexford mid-afternoon train edged out of Connolly station, Clare placed her forehead against the coolness of the window pane and closed her eyes with relief. The physical sensation of movement, of moving away from her problems gave her a momentary sense of peace. Her reprieve was short lived. There was uneasiness in her excitement at the thought of seeing Tim. She worried about how they would get on, what would they talk about? Clare felt he expected more inane conversation from her and always perceived she lived up to his expectations. Their conversations never seemed to venture above the everyday. She didn't even feel she knew her brother. As the train began to gather pace, Clare tried to distract her worry by concentrating instead on the slicing metallic sound of steel on the rails beneath her.

Travelling past the suburbs, the train took the usual coastal route. The track was situated high on the embankment. On her left the sea lay wide and expansive. Through the blue of the sea the sun cast a pathway of silver widening towards the horizon that seemed to move with them as they sped onwards.

In Dalkey village they stopped at the railway junction and Clare watched as a suburban train passed. It was a shiny new train, so unlike the creaking, lumbering train Rose, Tim, and she used to take on their day excursions to that seaside village.

It was on those summer excursions with her mother that Clare grew to love Dalkey. The three of them had such fun on Dalkey beach on their Sunday afternoon trips out of the city. Clare smiled at the memories. Theo had a car and Rose couldn't drive. It was the same ritual every Sunday in the summer. Rose began by making a tentative enquiry, "Would you like to go to the beach Theo?" She'd get no reply. She'd wait another while and try again. "Theo, I'm thinking of going to the beach, would you like to come with me and the children?" Still no reply. It was like trying to get through to a wall. When she asked a third time she'd get a maybe and then on the fourth time she'd get a definite no. Rose got wise to his routine and even though she continued to ask him she prepared a picnic for only three as she knew he would never come.

They took the bus into the city centre and then a rambling train out to Dalkey. Rose, free of him, became lively and told them funny stories of when she was young. Her mother had a madcap side to her. One day on the beach she spilled some hot water from the flask and they only had a half cup of tea each.

"I can't stand a half cup of tea." she wailed. "I'd love another cup. Tim you stay with the bags I'm going to ask for some water in one of the houses."

"Mam, you can't ask for water from strangers," they protested.

"I can and I will," came her mother's retort. She picked up the empty flask and strode smartly in the direction of the road above the beach. Clare followed her.

"Which house are you going to go into?" Clare asked in amazement hurrying beside her. "Whichever one I get a good feeling from," her mother replied.

"This one looks nice," she said. Rose opened the gates and walked up towards the hall door. A woman of Rose's age answered the door.

"Would you mind if I asked you for some hot water?" she said, holding up the flask. "Not at all," the woman replied. "Come in."

They both stepped into the hallway and Clare felt like she was transported into another world. The house was magnificent. A carved oak staircase curved from the hallway to a balcony above. Silk apricot wallpaper lined the walls, rugs of coordinating hues adorned the floor. Clare was so enraptured she didn't hear the woman repeat, "Come in."

They followed her into a perfect square kitchen with open glass doors at the top of the room leading out onto the garden.

There were offers of tea and introductions. Sue explained that she worked in the house as the housekeeper. The Andersons, the owners, were out.

But it was the garden that had Clare transfixed.

"The garden is magnificent," Clare said, walking towards the doors, her view widening as she approached it. "I have never seen anything so beautiful."

"There's not much interest in gardening in our house," Rose said with genuine understatement.

"I let the lawn grow wild," Sue said, filling the kettle. "I want to encourage wildlife to flourish."

As Clare moved forward, a circular meadow of delicate cornflowers and bluebells bowing in the wind came into view. The meadow was surrounded by a pathway of pebbles edged with borders of lavender and lobelia. Tall cherry blossom trees sheltered the garden, their presence softening the effect of a high boundary wall.

Responding to Clare's enraptured gaze Sue said, "I'll give you some cuttings before you go, to get you started."

It was a friendship that began so innocently and yet gave direction to Clare's life as Sue kept her promise and during many visits gave her cuttings from every flower she had in the garden.

The train stopped at Greystones and fixing her clothes Clare roused herself to sit up straight when more passengers entered the carriage. The journey lasted another hour and then following the curve of the river Slaney the train slowed as it approached Wexford station which was situated on the mouth of the estuary.

She was seated in one of the first carriages and saw Tim almost immediately when the train stopped. Clare was surprised by the sharp feeling of joy she felt on seeing him. He looked relaxed yet from his stance Clare could see he was looking forward to seeing her.

Clare alighted from the train and walked towards him. He took her bag. She gave him a light hug. Immediately she began to apologise for her appearance. "I am thrown together; I don't know what I've got on me."

"You look fine," he said, leading through the gate out onto Redmond Square.

"I won't stay long," Clare said.

"Stay as long as you like," he told her.

"How were they up there in the house?" "How are my kids?"

"The kids are fine," Tim said. "David is walking around the house like someone haunted. He looks wretched. Mrs Bateson is staying over. She flitters around trying to make everything appear normal. The kids accepted the excuse that you had come to see me for a few days."

"I'm sure Jack knows," Clare said.

I think they all do thought Tim. "I only live a few minutes down the road, we could walk, but because of your luggage, I took the car."

They drove down the road beside the railway line going back in the same direction where Clare had come from, the sea a line of blue on their right.

Within two minutes Tim turned left into a mixed development of houses and apartments. "This one is mine," he said, parking outside one of the semi-detached houses.

He led Clare into a square hallway. The kitchen lay to the front of the house off a door to the right. The living room stretched the full width of the back of the house. A stairs was hidden in the left corner as you entered the room. Two brown leather couches one at the side of the room and one in front of the sliding door into the garden were the only pieces of furniture. The walls were painted white. A painting of a harbour scene was hung over the couch. The blue of the scene was the only other strip of colour in the room. The floors were covered in shiny cream marble tiles.

"I haven't got around to getting the things I need," he explained. "I have done some work on my bedroom. I'll show you that."

Clare followed Tim up the stairs to the square landing. "This is my room."

"It's lovely Tim."

"You can sleep here," he said, "and I'll sleep in the spare room."

Clare unpacked some of her things keeping most of them in the suitcase not expecting the visit to last more than a day or two.

Back in the kitchen she watched Tim carefully, but not too obviously, searching for signs of irritation at her presence. He seemed calm as he served up the meal, glad to be in her company.

Clare pulled out a chair and sat down at the table. "I feel as if I am a bit of an imposition. I know you must want your own space back after having the children for so long."

"It's no problem," he said reassuringly. "I've taken time off work."

During the meal they spoke about generalities. Tim talked to her of the children and the great time he had had with them. He told her where he had brought them. "I'm especially fond of Tommy," he said. They grew quiet and finished eating.

"Go inside," Tim said, "and relax. I'll bring you some more wine."

Clare sat on the sofa and couldn't prevent herself from mentally choosing cushions and throws which would enhance the room.

Tim came towards her and handed her a glass of wine. He sat down beside her.

Clare blurted, "David is seeing someone else."

"Who?"

"A woman called Charlene, an engineer in his job. Evidently brilliant at her work, a clear thinker he tells me. He relies on her heavily for his work and other things now, apparently," she added with sarcasm.

Tim listened taking in the information. He spoke carefully.

"David has always struck me as someone on the edge, not really coping."

"David? David's strong," Clare said, her loyalty asserting itself. "He's always been strong for his family."

"If anything, I'm the one who is weak."

"Maybe it's the other way round. Perhaps you don't know him at all."

Tim got up from the couch and went into the kitchen. Clare took this to mean end of discussion. She hated the way Tim spoke in statements like this. She'd have loved to talk this through to tease it out verbally, discuss all the different ramifications and implications of his statement, but she knew by the look on his face there was no point in asking him to repeat himself. He'd only give her so much. He'd expect her to work the rest out herself. She didn't want to spoil the atmosphere between them, but she vowed to confront him about it again the next day.

Tim returned. Clare continued redirecting the conversation.

"I can't understand women who have affairs. What about the sisterhood, the loyalty we should have for one another. We fought together for the vote, our rights and yet we target each other's lovers, compete with and dismantle each other over the opposite sex. They won't go into the pain of their lives, change what they can. They want a quick fix. They want to be rescued not knowing that no one can rescue you. We can only rescue ourselves."

"Maybe you're looking into it too deeply," Tim said. "Maybe she sees an affair as an appendage in her life."

"Like an accessory you mean? A pair of Jimmy Choo's?" Clare asked. "How can she rationalize it, justify it to herself."

"Or maybe," Tim explained, "through some convoluted/twisted logic she sees it as a sign of her strength."

"Or maybe," Clare's voice faltered, "she could be madly in love with him."

"Maybe," Tim repeated. "Trying to second guess this woman will lead you on the road to nowhere. It could be as simple as her being a lonely woman."

For some reason at the mention of the word lonely, Clare thought of her mother.

"You are miles away," Tim said.

"I was just thinking of Sundays at home when we were younger."

"I try not to think about that time if I can help it."

They sat quietly, each remembering the reality of what they'd lived through earlier in their lives.

Clare broke the silence. "It was awful."

"It was."

"He didn't love her."

"No he didn't."

"I never used to look back and now it's coming at me like a ton of bricks. I now have to cope with the sadness of my mother's marriage and also my own. I have so much working out to do."

They were still for a few moments, their thoughts occupied. The house was quiet in its restful Sunday repose.

Clare started to weep. Tim sat uncomfortable on the edge of his chair.

"Come here," he said, and holding her in his arms they gently rocked together.

"It will be alright Clare," he said, rubbing her arm, "David is a good man."

"I know," she said. "The pain is terrible."

"I know," he said.

They sat close Tim still holding her, absorbing her pain.

"I feel a bit better now Tim, thanks."

She began to pull away.

"Tim, you've changed, giving me hugs and everything," she said, trying to laugh wiping her eyes.

"It's your kids. They used to queue up every night for their hugs and now I've no one to give them to. I'm home alone most nights."

"You? You normally have two or three women queuing up."

"I fell in love Clare and it didn't work out."

"I'm sorry."

"I was attracted to the puzzle too, like mam, the working out, just as she tried to work him out for years, trying to solve the puzzle. It's like trying to understand a vacuum, to second guess thin air. These people can't be worked out because they don't even understand themselves. I was luckier than her, I got out quicker."

"She didn't crack up or dip into drink," Clare said, taking a sip of her own wine. "She coped in her gentle way."

"Gentle way?" Tim exclaimed. "By obliterating herself? That's not gentle. It's the most silent act of violence there is."

"You sound angry."

"The more I think about it the angrier I get."

"You seem to be able to cope with it though," Clare said.

"The end helps me. Do you know that in the hospital she asked me not to let him know when the end came?"

"I didn't know that," Clare revealed. "I thought he just didn't make it."

"No, she told me not to call him back to the hospital until it was over."

"You never spoke to me about that," said Clare.

"I never really spoke to you about anything," Tim replied.

They were silent each realizing that would change.

"She robbed him of his chance to tell his story to the neighbours, to show himself off in a great light," Tim continued. "He would have loved relaying all the little boring details of how many times the nurses came in, how many times they went out. His slowness in telling a story used to drive me crazy. She had the last word against someone who had taken away her voice," Tim finished.

"She won a victory in the end," Clare said with admiration.

"Yes," she died in peace.

Clare felt relieved her mother had been empowered. It made Clare feel stronger as if through her mother's empowerment she had been empowered as well.

The TV was turned on, but barely audible. There was no other light in the room. BBC News at Ten flashed on the screen.

"I've heard from him," Tim said, flicking the remote control. "He wants to see us. It seems opportune at the moment, a chance to tie up loose ends."

"Do you forgive him?"

"How do you forgive the greatest misery that ever lived?" Tim asked, placing the remote back on the sofa. "Do you?" he asked.

"It's hard. He has a chip on each shoulder."

"I suppose he's balanced that way," Tim agreed.

"Will I forgive David?" Clare asked.

"I don't know, but seeing the bigger picture with people all the time can blind you. There's part of them you like and part of them you don't. Trying to appease both sides of their nature can get you burned. It depends on how they treat you basically and how you feel after being in their company. You can't fight unreasonableness with reasonableness."

"What do you do?" asked Clare.

"You walk away," Tim replied.

"Do you think I should walk away from David?"

"I don't know. A lot depends on how sorry he is."

"I won't live my life the way so many other people do in a sort of limbo of wondering whether to leave or stay. It's like living within a constant question. It's a wait and see scenario. I don't want to live with that uncertainty, I want a resolution. He was all I ever wanted. If there isn't love, what is there?"

"There's yourself," he said.

Clare thought through this option and then spoke in a whisper, almost to herself.

"I don't know who I am, but who I am is not working."

"It's tedious loving someone who has no sense of themselves," Tim said, getting up from the couch.

Clare wanted to ask what do you mean, but Tim did it again and having made this statement he walked away. Clare reasoned at that moment it was safer not to ask him to explain. She wanted time to think, to test by trying on the tenet of the message to see if it fitted.

Sitting by herself she realised it did. Examples from her life matched his view; her tendency to dance around an opinion rather than frankly state what she really thought, her merging of herself with the wishes of others, a blending into neutral, into nothing. She once saw this evasiveness as diplomacy now seeing it for what it was, a lack of genuineness.

What she thought were positives, her devotion to David, did it spring from neediness? Needing him to make her whole implying she was only half a person? What she thought of as her gentleness was it passivity?

She could hear Tim in the kitchen, presses being opened, the sound of bowls being placed on the counter. He came towards her with bowls of snacks.

"You look tired," he said.

"I am," she replied. "I am disappointed with myself. What have I achieved? How can I support myself on my own?"

"You sound depressed."

"I am. I regret it. I regret it desperately. I should have made something of myself. Not relied on him."

"You went after your dream. Finding love was your raison d'etre for as long as I've known you."

"And look where it got me."

"It's not over yet. David is a good man."

"The only way I see it working is if I have one foot in the relationship and the other one outside it ready to run. It's an awful way to have to live. I will be watching him, always watching. Watching will be my life sentence. How can I get the trust back?"

"As I've said, a lot of this won't be up to you at all Clare. It will be up to David. Don't pile the pressure on yourself like this. It is so much up to him."

"We'll see. I can feel a hardening of my heart. I scarcely recognize myself."

"Talk to him. You need to talk to David."

"When I am ready, that's exactly how I feel right now; when I'm good and ready. Let him stew."

Tim took a handful of peanuts and sat back staring straight ahead thinking.

"And then there's Greta," Clare remonstrated, becoming animated with anger with the memory of her, "she does her own thing and no one thinks any worse of her. She never reciprocates any of the invitations I've given her."

"Do you ask her so that she'll return the invitation?" Tim asked.

"No, but it's just the way."

"Well it's obviously not her way."

"You're too bloody clinical for your own good." Clare said, raising her voice.

"And you stop trying to get people to squeeze into your expectations. Let them off." He paused. "I'm sorry," he said, trying to claw back some of the closeness between them. "Look here's something that might cheer you up. I have an invitation to a wedding. It's Lyn, the girl I work with, she's getting married to the dentist. You'll be doing me a favour if you come with me."

"I'd love to, just the two of us?" she asked.

"Yes, just you and me," he said.

"That would be lovely. When is it?"

"It's in three weeks."

"Great! I can come back down again."

The decision signaled a natural ending to their conversation.

"I think I'll go to bed now," Clare said. "I'll see you in the morning."

"Take your time getting up," Tim said. "Have a lie on. If the weather's fine, we'll go for a walk in the afternoon."

"That sounds great."

"We might go and visit Theo before you go home. What do you think?"

"That sounds like a nice idea," Clare agreed. "Goodnight." He gave her instructions from the bottom of the stairs on where light switches were, where extra blankets could be found if she was cold. She could hear him clearing up downstairs and fell into a restful sleep.

THE VISIT

Two days later they drove up to their childhood home, having decided they would visit their father before Tim dropped Clare home. Clare felt relaxed and calm from the care she'd received at Tim's. Slowing towards the gateway of their house, Tim stopped and made to get out of the car. "Can we sit here for a few minutes?" Clare asked, placing her hand on his arm. "I'd like to sit here for a while."

Clare looked out at the avenue where she grew up, at the rows of terraced houses. The area seemed old now, its youth and vitality spent. From the vivid technicolour memory of her childhood the scene before her had dimmed to washed out fadedness, as though colour had seeped from it over the years. It was like looking at a scene with a filter of gauze before her eyes. The gardens were pale, covered in a fine dust from the summer's dry spell.

"Are you ready?" Tim asked.

"No, not yet, he'll wait." Clare had grown up waiting.

Her thoughts returned to the quietness of the area on summer Sunday afternoons. She remembered sitting on a kerb on the road outside their house, her legs bent, the heels of her shoes pulled back tightly against the kerb, deep in concentration, diligently scraping the crevices between the kerb and road with her ice pop stick. All the driveways were empty of cars, fathers having driven off with their families for the day or on holidays. The few families who remained had transferred all living activities to the garden at the back of the houses. It was so quiet on the road as if the volume in the air had been turned down.

Clare used to wonder what everyone was doing. She wished the front of each house would fall down and reveal a dolls house view of her neigbours. What scenes would be revealed? she wondered. Were they all watching westerns like her father? Would the rumbustious Mr & Mrs Griffin be lying in bed, he on his back in his vest and underpants, she in her slip beside him both in a stupor of lazy rest, enjoying the illicitness of a Sunday nap?

They were long, hot boring days in August, especially in August when traditionally workers took their summer holidays. Rose hated the August bank holiday. No wonder she died on that weekend it was the time she chose to fade out.

"We'll go in now," Clare said, and they both got out of the car.

They stood outside the 1960's suburban house, the Dublin Mountains in the background.

Tim cast a cold auctioneering eye over the property. "It must be worth a fortune now," he said.

Clare remonstrated, "Take your auctioneering hat off Tim, for once."

They knocked on the door and were invited in by their father with Fran standing behind him in the narrow hallway. There was a flurry of welcomes and exclamations of how well they looked, how time went by so quickly. They were led into the living room which had been knocked through into the dining room since Clare had last been there with an arch separating the two rooms. It gave the room an unusual brightness from the light coming in from both ends. It was decorated in an updated version of brown and fawn with soft furnishings in pale pink, exuding an atmosphere of conservative security. They were in the company of two people who had everything they needed. Newer ornaments had been added, Tim noticed, not much different from the style of his mothers. Before long they had settled on the brown Dralon seats and silence descended.

"Tea," Fran said and left the room.

Questions were asked about Clare's children, their ages, their progress in school.

Her father spoke mainly to Clare, sure of a friendly response and occasionally gave an uncertain smile towards Tim.

Tim sat in a lone armchair listening.

Tea was brought in with a plate of freshly baked cakes.

"Fran's like you," her father said, nodding towards Clare, "loves the baking."

His face was eager, eager to make up, eager to win their approval. Clare knew by his expression that it wasn't their love he wished for, he knew that was out of the question, the possibility of their friendship he also knew was only a glimmer of hope and finally pity, he looked as if he would be grateful for their pity and compassion. Could they give him that? Should they?

At one point Theo looked directly at Fran with a knowing look and she left the room. "I have been wanting to talk to you both," he said.

"I want to let you know that I have made a will and this house is divided between the three of you. Let me explain. Fran has been living here for over fifteen years and I can't leave her with nothing. So when my time comes she said she will return home. There is nothing for her here in Dublin and I want her to have something to go home with. The other two thirds is between you."

"I hope this…" his voice faded. "I hope it's enough, I …" he began, "Well let's just say I know I had my shortcomings, many of them." Silence descended and if he wished for this statement to be denied he was disappointed. "I pray to your mother every day," he finished.

Ah that's it, Tim thought. That's your absolution, you say a few prayers.

What was the point? He looked old. Tim counted he was only over sixty, it was amazing how guilt aged people, he reflected. The bottom half of his face seemed to have collapsed in. The arrogance knocked out of him, gone.

"Why are you writing a will? Are you ill?" Clare asked.

"No, no nothing like that, I want to get my affairs in order. It's been on my mind a lot."

Fran came back in and had a cup of tea with them. She talked of the clubs she was in, updating them on news of the neighbours. She kept the conversation light and friendly.

When their tea was finished, Tim said, "We'll go now. I'm dropping Clare off home."

Their father followed them out into the hall with Fran after him. "Well goodbye now," he said as Tim opened the door. "Hopefully, I'll see you soon."

"Yes, yes we must do that," Clare said non-committally.

Driving out of the estate they took the road along the foot of the mountains towards the sea. Even with all the changes in life Tim thought, that view hadn't changed. The mountains stood dependable, indomitable through crisis after crisis.

"I feel bad not making an arrangement to see him," Clare said. "I just couldn't bring myself to, especially now with me and David and everything up in the air."

"You don't owe him anything."

"I know, but still. I'll think about it. If you ever got married would you ask him to your wedding?"

"I might." He said it lightly and Clare knew this was probably the nearest thing to a reconciliation they would get.

"I don't hate him. Hate takes up too much energy," Clare said.

"I pity him," Tim said.

"I do too," Clare agreed. "I'd hate to have his mind. It's sad it's all come so late, yet he seems so happy now with Fran."

"Is he?" Tim asked. "To me it seems a relationship of gratitude, who wants that?

Will David be there when you go home? Did you let him know you were coming?"

"No." Clare leant her head on the window. "I don't know what I'll find when I get home. I am dreading the confrontation with David. Do you remember how mam was suspicious of words," Clare said, turning towards him. "'Always be careful of words because you cannot take them back,' she would say. She believed that gossip spoken in secret was never secret, that once it was out in the ether it had a power of its own so that when the innocent party met up again with the offender, a change occurred because the awareness of what had been spoken caused people to react differently. She always kept her opinions to herself."

"And what happens when you don't talk?" Tim asked, and then answering the question himself he said, "You disappear as a person."

"Well I'm not disappearing," Clare asserted.

Clare was reluctant to say goodbye to Tim. She used the last few minutes in his company discussing all the issues that were on her mind, hopping from subject to subject, determined to cover all the things that were worrying her while she still had a chance before he drove away.

"I'm getting out from under the mountain of domesticity. I've decided I'm going to get a job," she said.

"Will you work full time?"

"No, I'll find some way around it. I'll find a balance."

Driving into their driveway Tim asked, "Will you be alright on your own? Do you want me to come in with you?"

"No thanks. I'm dreading this, but I will be alright."

Clare opened the door and got out. "Thanks for everything Tim," she said, bending down into the car.

"Good luck," Tim said, "and don't worry about Greta," he said smiling. "She's got the personality of a brick."

Clare laughed and shut the door and made her way towards the house.

Clare turned the key in the hall door and let herself in. The house had a strange empty feel. She could sense the atmosphere of quiet trauma. David came out of the kitchen towards her. He stood for a moment blinking trying to make out who she was. His face was unshaven. It was only four days since they'd last seen each other and yet it seemed as if a lifetime had gone by.

He walked towards her. "Clare I didn't know you were coming. It's great to see you." He went to put his arms around her and then stopped not really knowing what to do.

Clare walked past him. "Where are the children?"

"My mother took them out for the day. She thought I needed time on my own."

"Do you?" Clare asked, turning back towards him.

"You know I do." he said. Clare studied his face.

"Well, would you like a coffee?" he asked, turning away from her glare and moved towards the kitchen.

"Yes, I'll have one." she said. Clare walked past the kitchen door into the sunroom. The room was half-heartedly tidied with toys on the floor. Magazines lay strewn on the coffee table with what looked like an abandoned attempt to neaten them.

Clare sat on the couch. David followed through and sat opposite her. He took a drink of coffee and rested his arms on the arm rest. "Tim told me you were going down to him for a few days when he left back the kids, where did you go before that?"

"I spent two nights in town."

"Where?"

"In a hotel on the quay." Clare had replayed their reunion speech in her mind so often that she couldn't vocalize it. It was as if all she wanted to say was frozen in her head and she couldn't release it into reality.

Suddenly she felt exhausted. She closed her eyes. How to get across to him the rage, the hurt she felt, the magnitude of what he had inflicted on her and the children. She couldn't get it out. Where did she start?

David seeing her distress placed his cup on the table and came towards her. He sat beside her. "Clare I'm sorry, I'm really sorry, please forgive me. I'll make it up to you. For the rest of my life I will make it up to you."

"I don't know who you are," Clare said, her voice leaden, "and you don't know me."

"We'll date again," David said impulsively.

Clare gave him a withering look. "You are not taking this seriously," she said.

"I have never been so serious in my life. I want to change my whole life." he said. "I'm not happy. I have done a lot of thinking over the last few days and nights, I can't sleep. I lie there thinking, thinking; I am trawling through the minutiae of my life.

I've been thinking of my father a lot. I always held him in such high regard. I believed his story which I now realize is punctuated with myths. Myth one, thrown off the farm as a young lad, sending home nearly all his wages. Over the past few years I have heard his name spoken in reverential tones with the unmistakable whiff of fear attached to it. He has acquired masses of development land. How did he do that? He is worth millions. More than even my mother knows about. Why should I try and follow in the footsteps of a parody of a man? I had bought into 'My Dad the Hero' and I don't buy into that anymore. I don't believe the myth of his story.

In a nice way he held me in a vice like grip all my life, a steel hand in a velvet glove. His eldest son, I was the one who would take over his empire and yet somehow legitimise it. Put the stamp of education behind it and by doing so validate him. My back is breaking from the pressure. I can't cope, I don't want this life. I never have wanted it. I feel splintered trying to be what I'm not. I've decided I'm resigning as Project Manager. I'll work as an ordinary member of the team. I've had an idea for setting up a restoration division. If I could I'd leave altogether. I'd love to be a mechanic. I'd love to open a bicycle shop. I love motor bikes."

"You never had a bike."

"I'd love to sell them, to open my own shop. I want to work for myself. Be my own boss. From now on I want my life to reflect who I am, the truth. Truth is all there is in life. It's what makes it worthwhile."

"Your father won't be happy," Clare said.

"He'll just have to get over it. His dreams aren't mine. I will have to get through it."

"It will be impossible," Clare said.

"The only impossibility is life without you."

"How do you know I won't crucify you?" Clare asked.

"I'm crucified already."

Clare resisted the urge to put her arms around him.

"Clare I want to sell the house. It's worth a fortune. Start again. We could take a year off, do what we want. You love the city, we could move back there again."

"So much of this is only a distraction. The problem is you and me. Location won't change things. You are being evasive by bringing up the subject of your father, the house, you are using them as an excuse, you still haven't told me why. How could you do this to me, to us?"

"I have no excuse. There is none. All I can say is that she paid me a lot of attention and I was flattered. I became too dependent on her for work. She was so certain, so different from….." he stopped.

"So different from me you mean. This has changed me. There is steel there now. At the restaurant I got a sense of desperation from her, I couldn't understand it. What was that all about?"

"I had tried to stop seeing her, but she didn't want to. In a way I was flattered to see her there. I'm sorry."

"It may not work out between us," Clare said finally.

"But it might," David said, "please give me another chance to show you what you mean to me."

"You spoke about my family to her. You know that's unforgiveable. That subject is off limits outside these four walls."

"Why don't you speak about it? It's no harm to speak about it. You hated the way they kept their unhappiness a secret, why prolong the secret?" Clare thought about this for a few moments. Maybe it was time to move away from the pride, the pretence. The terror of disloyalty to her mother was still very high.

"I'm serious about this Clare, I'm going to ring my father now and tell him that I am resigning from my position."

David went into another room and came back a few minutes later.

"What happened?"

"He went crazy."

"Did you tell him about us?"

"My mother doesn't want him to know."

Clare was angry. "What is this thing peculiar to the Irish of not telling the mammy or the daddy, as if they are children and can't handle bad news? It doesn't make sense telling him you want to be demoted without giving him the background."

Clare stood over David. "Tell him," she said. He walked out the door.

Two hours later he came back.

"What happened?"

"He told me to get out that he can't stand the sight of me." As if to obey these instructions again David left the room.

Minutes later the phone rang. Clare stood by the door listening. Clare knew by his answer "I had to," that the question put by his mother was. Why?

David put the phone down and came back into the room. "My mother wants to speak to you."

Clare walked to the hall table and picked up the phone not knowing what she was going to hear. "It's Clare here," she said, trying to sound sure. She was determined not to be undermined.

"Clare, I want to let you know that I support you. I am here for you; I want you to know that. I do hope you can work things out. If I can be any help just let me know."

"Thanks Mrs Bateson. It means a lot."

"We had a great day, the children and I. I've given them their tea and I will bring them home now."

"No, I'll collect them. You've done enough Mrs Bateson, I'll collect them now. Thanks for all your help."

"Clare?"

"Yes?"

"Take care of yourself."

"I will, and thanks again."

Clare put the phone down.

She walked back along the hallway into the kitchen. The kitchen light was on. A moth flittered around it. It was that strange time of year the change of season when the day was shortening and it was too bright to turn on a light yet too dark without it. It was a closing in, the beginning of the shutting down of the year.

"You admire clear thinkers," Clare began, starting to set out her demands. "Well I am thinking clearly for once. I love your family, especially your mother, but their presence in our lives is claustrophobic. There has to be boundaries set."

"How?" David asked.

"Ask me before you agree to attend things."

"What do I do then, when I'm asked to go to something, do I say I'll ask Clare?"

"Don't say I'll ask Clare that makes me out to be judge and jury. Just say you'll see what's on and tell them you'll ring them back."

Over the next few weeks Clare couldn't stop herself from testing her new power. Anything she wanted she could have, he put up with it all.

David put into practice what he had agreed. Invitations came from his family and all were refused.

One evening another invitation came and was refused. He came into the living room looking particularly strained.

"What was the invitation?"

"It is a party for Uncle Ted again."

"I'd like to go to that," Clare said.

"Really?"

"We don't have to refuse everything David, we just have to get the balance right."

Clare feared there was a danger of him disintegrating, battling on three fronts, his family, work and herself.

That night she lay awake. Leaving her room she crossed the landing to the spare bedroom. Opening the door she saw David lying on his side awake. She walked towards the bed and pulled back the covers. Easing herself into the bed with her back towards him she breathed the luxury of his warmth. He put his arms around her and pulled her close to him.

"Forgive me," he said.

"I'm trying to," she said.

"All I ask is that you keep trying."
"I will."

THE WEDDING

The wedding was held in a hotel on the mouth of the River Slaney estuary. Lyn was one of a huge dynasty of Devereux children and grandchildren and the excitement of the wedding was palpable all over the town. Numerous shop fronts bore the name Devereux and even though it was a Saturday they were all closing down for the day. That morning every hairdresser was packed and all you could hear were snatches of conversations about "the wedding". On the main street people rushed down the thoroughfare carrying dry-cleaning or last minute purchases, racing back to their houses to prepare for the big day. Two policemen patrolled the street in anticipation of traffic chaos as the day wore on. Clare enjoyed the general feeling of excitement as she made her way down the street. She was glad to have had a reason to come into the town as she felt in some way she was part of the preparations.

In the chemist she paid for her purchases.

"Are you going to the wedding?" the sales assistant asked.

"I am. I'm looking forward to it."

"Have a lovely day."

Back in Tim's house Clare placed the outfit that she'd bought with Tim on the bed. She was so looking forward to seeing the whole look come together. She took her time with her make-up and then got dressed carefully. At last she put on her shoes and then the final accessory her earrings. She walked down the stairs and into the living room. Tim stood by the fireplace fixing his tie. He saw Clare in the mirror. "Clare you look fantastic," he said, turning towards her. "The dress is amazing on you."

"You look gorgeous too," she replied. "In your case, it's as usual."

"Come on, I want to be early. This wedding is both business and pleasure for me. I may bump into a few customers or potential ones. I have to be seen to be relaxed and convivial."

Heading away from the group of houses, they walked the few minutes towards the main street.

"This place is so empty," Clare remarked.

"They're all going to the wedding." Tim said. "There are hundreds of people going to this. The celebrations will be going on for days.

Lyn only told people five weeks ago that she was getting married even though they had been planning it for over a year. She wanted the surprise to add to the drama of the day which I think it has."

It was a beautiful warm autumn day. Clare felt her dress was perfect for the weather that she would be neither too hot nor too cold in it.

They took position on the top of the steps to the church and had a high vantage point overlooking the street. Guests began to assemble and chat on the steps, some strolled into the church. The mood was relaxed and carefree. Clare monitored the fashion. Some of the hats were amazing creations.

"Do you think I should have worn a hat?" she asked Tim.

"No," he replied. "Your hair is too nice to hide. In a way your hair is your hat."

"Why thank you brother. I shall take that as a compliment," she replied.

Clare decided to explore and have a look into the church. It was magnificent. It was more a small cathedral than a church. Small baskets of pink roses with pearls interwoven through them hung at the edge of every pew. The flower arrangements were pretty and neat just like Lyn herself, Clare thought.

Tim was one of the last people to be ushered into the church. He was able to catch a fleeting glimpse of Lyn as she emerged from the wedding car. Her dress billowed around her. She was a vision of tulle and lace. If this is a meringue he thought, then she was the prettiest meringue he'd ever seen. The wedding service was everything a wedding service should be; uplifting, full of song and hope.

The service was barely over when the newly engaged Dr. Cleary almost accosted him in his eagerness to ask about the best investment opportunities in Wexford at the present time. Tim had to use all his skills of diplomacy to calm him down and he hoped no one saw him pass his business card on to him.

Afterwards they all congregated on the steps. Tim met people he knew and introduced his sister to them.

Within a few minutes the crowd began to thin and in front of him at the bottom of the steps stood Kate beside her father who was sitting in his wheelchair. Tim hadn't expected to see her and from her dress he wasn't sure if she was one of the wedding party or not. He stood taking every detail of her in. He noticed the ill-fitting shape of her dress, the drab colour. Her hair was tied back and from here it looked ordinary brown. She had a peculiar look on her face, almost a half-smile as if she was witnessing all of her options closing down, but within her expression there was an air of steely resignation as if all was not quite lost.

Tim looked at her father beside her in his wheelchair and judging the scene he could see Kate was trapped. Get out, was what he wanted to roar at her before it's too late, get out and live your own life. At first she didn't acknowledge him, but Tim knew she could sense him there.

Kate stared back at him: I can feel pity coming through Tim. I know what those looks mean. He's urging me to get on with my own life as if there is still hope for me, but I don't want what he thinks I need. The wholesome life he has envisaged for me. If the good life doesn't come easily, then I don't care if it doesn't come at all. Effort is not on my radar. I'll get this house when he goes, that's the main thing. I'll be back on the marriage market as a woman of means. I'll be taken more seriously then.

If things were different and we were on speaking terms, I'd like to debate my life choice with you. I'd enjoy the sharp repartee between us. It's so logical you may even see the merit in it, although I don't think so, probably not. Underneath all that world weary sophistication, you're really just a good boy at heart.

The doctors say he's getting stronger every day. What do they know? The neighbours think I've worked wonders with him. I'm quite enjoying the praise. I'll play this role for as long as it takes. He can't go on forever. I'll wait.

. . .

After the ceremony, the guests were relayed by bus the short journey to the hotel on the outskirts of the town. In the gardens that wound down to the river, a number of tables with white table cloths blowing gently in the wind were laid out. A white circular canopy with garlands of flowers over its entrance was placed near the water with chairs placed inside. The weather was so warm guests merged on the lawn drinking tea or coffee or sipping bubbly champagne. Clare admired the colour coordination of the wedding party.

The little girls wore tulle dresses similar to the bride's and from a distance they looked like white powder puffs dancing with excitement on the lawn. Pastel colours were worn by the women, pale pinks, blues and greens and this gave the scene a light summer look.

For such a huge wedding Clare thought, there was a lovely homely feel to it. Everyone was friendly and even though Clare knew nobody she was made feel welcome. Clare strolled through the crowds of people.

She spotted Tim's boss sitting on a garden bench and sat down beside him.

"Do you like weddings?" she asked him.

"No, not really, it's all beyond me. The young people enjoy them though."

Inside the hotel the reception was taking place in the main ballroom which led directly out to a raised veranda with views of the river. Each table had flowers on it matching the theme in the church only on a grander scale with roses, gardenias and trailing ivy decorating the candelabras in the centre of each table.

At six the guests were summoned by a gong and everybody began to file into the ballroom. Tim and Clare sat beside each other at their place names and slowly the table began to fill up. Two middle aged couples walked over towards the table together. One of the couples sat beside Tim. To his right were two empty seats.

Just then a very attractive tall, willowy girl in her mid-twenties came over to the table and sat down. She was shortly joined by a young lad of about fifteen.

"Hi everyone." she said. "I'm Julie and this is my brother Jamie."

Julie, Tim repeated to himself. He thought her name had a happy ring to it.

One of the men sitting opposite Tim asked him, "How do you know the bride?"

"I work with her," Tim explained.

"We are all aunts and uncles of the bride," he said, gesturing to the other couple. "And Julie and Jamie are her cousins."

"All family," Tim smiled.

A bag pipe player entered the room and the bride and groom entered behind them. It's theatre, pure theatre Tim thought as he watched the couple being led in a parade to the top table.

Tim looked for Kate. He couldn't see her in his outer vision, but sensed she was there, seated somewhere on the periphery of the room.

As the meal progressed raucous laughter came from the table beside them. The table was full of young people in their early to mid-twenties. They all seemed to know each other really well. They had the same colouring, fair hair and blue eyes as Julie and Jamie.

"They are a really happy bunch," Tim said, nodding towards them. "Do you know them?" he asked, looking at Julie.

"I do, they are all my cousins, we grew up together and are great friends."

"You all look like each other," Tim said. "You could be brothers and sisters."

"Yes, people say that to us all the time."

After the meal people began to disperse from the room.

Clare excused herself and left the table.

"Are you and your wife living in Wexford long?" Julie asked Tim.

"My wife? Oh no, Clare is my sister."

"Your sister! Oh, I thought she was your wife."

"No, Clare is my sister."

"Oh," Julie said smiling and her smile, Tim thought, was warmer.

So that's why Lyn placed me here, beside the eligible bachelor, Julie thought to herself.

They chatted about where they worked. Tim liked her. There was a directness about her which he found refreshing. He didn't have to watch out for nuances. She had an open honest face and he liked the way when talking to her, her eyes stayed fixed on him as if she was really listening to him.

Tim found himself beginning to relax. "Would you like a drink?" he asked her and she told him straight away what she wanted. There was no coyness with her. Some women, Tim thought, work on suggestion only and it is exhausting trying to find out what they want. She was generous too and offered to buy him a drink soon after.

The band came on to the low stage and began to set up their instruments. Two of the hotel staff came towards them. "We have to move the tables back to make way for the dancing," they said, and began to pull chairs out from the table.

Tim stood up and was concerned that in the disturbance he would be separated from Julie. Thankfully, when the moving of tables had stopped their side of the table was still free, not squished against any other and they were seated at the edge of the dance floor with plenty of room and a great view of the dance floor.

The band began to play and people took to the dance floor.

Tim wanted to ask Julie to dance, but he couldn't face the humiliation in such a public place if she said no, feeling slightly emasculated from his time with Kate. He decided to watch how she dealt with other people first before he asked. Her uncle walked over and asked her to dance and she hopped up straight away joking with him. Another man asked her as well and she stayed with him for two dances. Tim was put out by this. Julie returned to the table.

"Do you know him?"

"He's an old boyfriend," she explained. The two of them were left sitting at the table. Tim decided to take the risk. He took a deep breath.

"Would you like to dance?"

"That would be lovely," she replied and they headed out on to the dance floor.

On the carpeted area, away from the dance floor, Kate stands leaning conspiratorially towards a group of women who are all listening intently to her tales of her father's demise. Gasps of sympathy are extended from the group. Words of praise and encouragement are offered to her in her role as carer. Her head is bowed as she absorbs their sentiments. Her demeanor is saintly in her mock devotion to him.

Matthew is on his own in his wheelchair in front of the entrance to the ballroom. Groups of teenage boys rush by him on their way in and out of the room. His face has a high colour from frustration. His tie is slightly undone and his shirt is crumbled over his stomach.

He looks around in bewilderment and asks out loud, "Why is everyone talking to me as if I am a three year old?" Some children at play, grab the chair and spin him round. He is rescued by an older man who says a few words to him and wheels him back to his place at the table.

As the night wears on, dance movements become even more fantastical. Normally quiet people become loud and by eleven even the shy have graced the dance floor.

At one o'clock the band stops playing and everyone stands for the national anthem. Afterwards some people start to make their way out of the room; others loiter in their chairs finishing their drinks. At their table Julie sits beside Tim as many of her aunts and uncles come up to say goodbye. Tim suddenly becomes anxious that she may go home with them and he may not see her again. He sits tense in his chair waiting for a quiet moment. A gap occurs in the stream of people heading towards them. Impulsively he asks, "Would you like to meet me at the Riverbank Hotel tomorrow night?" Julie smiles and says, "Yes, I would love to."

Tim smiles, a smile of relief.

. . .

The next day coming back from Tim's, Clare drove up the driveway of her home and was assailed by the smell of petrol. She was astonished to see a motorbike in the front garden outside the house. David was sitting on the bike, revving it up. The three children and the babysitter stood inside the house looking at them through the front window.

"What's this?" Clare exclaimed.

"I bought a bike."

"You've bought a bike?"

"I did indeed, dear wife. I think it's time we had some fun. Go inside and get your leathers on David joked."

Clare laughed and ran in to the house. She felt stirrings of hope in her heart, a new lightness in her being. Maybe it will work out. A dead feeling lifted and she became conscious of air and being able to breathe freely again.

Within minutes she reappeared in her black leather jacket and jeans.

"Hop on," David instructed.

Clare hopped on the back of the bike and waving towards the children they drove off towards the road. Leaning close to David Clare enjoyed the freedom of the undulating movement of the bike as they traveled along the coastal road.

As they travel a melody comes into Clare's mind, it's a song by Imelda May that Clare sings into the wind:

'Falling in love with you again
Yeah, I'm falling in love with you again
We've been together but it seems like forever
But I'm falling in love with you again'

MAUREEN VISITS DUBLIN

How am I going to get from one end of Grafton Street to the other without meeting someone she wondered? She felt she just couldn't face anyone. Walking hurriedly from the car park she planned her route methodically. She'd go by the backstreets parallel to Grafton Street. Then take a left off Georges Street, walk down through Trinity Street and into Andrew Street before opening into South William Street. She had just turned right when she heard her name being screeched behind her.

"Maureeeeen helloooo," a city of 1.2 million suddenly shrinking into 2.

Her shoulders flinched with the vibration of the piercing voice. Dread filled her. She knew exactly who it was before she even turned around. She faced the voice.

Daisy Talbot stood in front of her, breathless from trying to catch up.

"Ah Maureen," she said, "I'm glad I caught up with you. How are you?" she asked, and without pausing for an answer she went straight into the saga of her 25th wedding anniversary. "Can't believe it, I just can't believe we're twenty five years married. There's not many of us making it that far now you know," she said knowingly. "Of course my family have been plotting and planning what to do for us. You know my girls, they are so mad about us. So when I heard they were going to give us a party, I said, a party? Not another party, there's been a party nearly every year in our house over the last four years between 21st and then 18th birthdays. So I said, I said no. I don't want a party, I'd love a cruise. Well right, they said, we'll give you a cruise. So we're off on our cruise in two weeks time!" She paused.

"I'm delighted for you," Maureen muttered dully.

Her news imparted, Daisy turned to go. Walking backwards she remarked, "You're looking very drawn and peaky. Black isn't your colour," and then turning, she glanced back over her shoulder and with a sly smile added, "Harry's looking great these days. See you, bye."

"Bye," Maureen called back.

Automatically she started to blame Harry. Why did he ask me to meet him in town? I should never have agreed to it. I should have suggested a quieter place on the opposite side of the city. She was giving out to herself so much she didn't realise she had come upon the pub so quickly. Once inside her mood lightened. She loved these old Dublin pubs. The polished bar and tables, the gentle banter of the barmen to their customers, the witty remarks. It was so dim inside she hardly noticed Harry sitting quietly in the corner. He had a pint of Guinness in front of him.

"Well, what can I get you?" he asked when she came over to him.

"It's a bit early for me, but I might as well have a gin and tonic." They sat quietly with their drinks.

"Listen Harry there's been something on my mind. I do want to thank you for the way you looked after me all these years. I mean you were always very good to me with money and that. I don't think I ever said it to you."

"No, you didn't," he said. "Well I can't do it anymore. My lump sum is nearly gone and I am just about managing on my pension."

"Will you move in with Mai?"

"No," he replied tersely. "She told me straight she doesn't want to look after another man again. It seems youse are all the same these days."

Maureen could taste the sourness of the remark in her mouth and chose to ignore it.

"Look, I'll still do my best for you," he said, "but just don't go bringing fecking solicitors into this. We'll live as we are, go the way we're going. I don't want a divorce or anything. We'll sell the house and divide."

"That suits me," Maureen added. "Can we keep the cottage though, I love it down there. You can use it with Mai. It will be good for you. There are golf courses opening up all the time."

"Where will you go?" he asked.

"I'll move in with Pol for a while, then I'll get a small place."

"Don't go on at me about Mai," he said, preempting the discussion. "You forced me into it." He shifted uneasily in his seat. Maureen decided to let him stew in his guilt knowing full well how much of a hypocrite she was. Rescuing him, she conceded, "I made a friend myself, he was just passing through. Nothing came of it."

"Well Mai has had a hard time," he said. "Her husband left her with four small kids years back. We get along, she is good company."

Later that day on her way home to Pol's, Maureen felt the reality of the situation descend on her. Even though she knew she had wanted to be out of the marriage for years, she wasn't expecting to feel so sad about it. In her own way she was glad Harry didn't want solicitors involved. How did people do it? Sign those separation agreements? She didn't think she would have been able to come out from under the mantle of having a husband. She was glad that Harry still seemed willing to afford her that protection.

MAUREEN

The Dublin house was put up for sale and sold quickly. Whilst surveying the rooms on one of the last days before the sale, it was Shay Maureen felt sorry for. He'd lost his home.

"I'm sorry love," she said, sadly sorting through the paraphernalia of their lives.

"I'm going away mam," he said, grimacing expecting an emotional response from his mother. Maureen was too worn to provide one. "If it's any comfort to you I think it will be good for me," he continued. "I need a new start too."

"If that's what you want, as long as you are happy."

Ruth was her usual self, all moods and coolness. Normally Maureen could, through a process of elimination, work out what was wrong with her. This time she hadn't the energy to decipher her. As she grew older Maureen found she spent less time analysing people who weren't fairly clear to her. Anything difficult she let flow over her. Like her marriage. They were too different, the love had gone, that was the reason, no need for heart searching or soul searching.

"I suppose it's sad to see it go," Ruth said. Maureen was surprised to hear her speak in this way since she'd never really formed an attachment to the house, always wanting to move when she was younger. Jenny on the other hand had spent ages in her bedroom, mooching and crying over her old things as she packed them away.

Harry and she divided what they wanted between them. Maureen took the minimum. She wanted few reminders of the home which since her absence had become more like a tomb, the place where she had been dying for years.

In one way Maureen was lucky: Jenny was sentimental and left with her car loaded with stuff that Maureen had no interest in, but was somehow glad it was still in the family. Ruth chose carefully and only took a few pieces that interested her.

During those last few days of dealing with the physical separation, Maureen was conscious of a parallel energy working outside herself. It was the sense of a sundering apart, a falling away which was supported by a knowing deep within her that this was the right thing to do, that she was on the right path, in complete harmony with her spirit.

Maureen stayed with her sister until she bought her own apartment slap bang in the middle of Dublin city. It was something she'd always wanted to do, to experience life in the middle of her city. During the weeks she lived with her sister, Pol allowed Maureen to hang her favourite painting in her bedroom so it was the last thing she saw every night and the first thing she saw every morning. Thus, her last thoughts at night were of John and he also came into her mind first thing in the morning. Where was John in her life now? She'd heard a trick used by people who led different lives; in order to cope they compartmentalized their lives. Which compartment was he in? In the forgiven, but not forgotten compartment or in the dull ache one.

Maureen also used this time to ease herself into single life again. Walking through the streets of Dublin she was surprised at how vividly memories of her time with Harry returned to her. Their courtship was their happiest time together. The city was where they'd meet up three times a week, going to every play and film that was on. It seemed that around every corner of every street a different recollection came to her with such clarity and sharpness as to be almost painful. It was bizarre how the mind works Maureen thought since she'd walked these streets often as a married woman without this draw to the past.

One evening, watching Pol fix some shelving in her living room, Maureen commented on the three categories of man, "There's romantic man, intellectual man and domestic man and in marriage domestic man seems to be the most important."

"I think you need an element of all three to make it work," Pol said, hammering a nail decisively.

Maureen made contact with one or two friends who were shocked to the core with the news of her break up. Fortunately, they didn't request precise details.

"How do you explain a life?" she asked Pol one evening. "Don't, don't try to explain," was Pol's advice. "I'm not," Maureen agreed. She could easily have said on an emotional level, living with Harry is the same as living without him.

As December drew near and happily ensconced in her apartment, Maureen had more practical worries on her mind. All her capital was sunk into buying her home. It had all cost her much more than she had thought. Christmas was coming. There were presents to be bought, bits and pieces needed for the apartment. It had to be done, she concluded, she just had to get a job. The idea of painting seemed so far away, an elusive pipe dream. If she complained to Harry he'd only say sell the cottage and she didn't feel ready to do that. If the cottage went then her dream of painting for a living would go and she couldn't let that dream die. It was all she felt she had at the moment. It was keeping her going. Independence, financial and otherwise was what she most wanted.

She knew she faced a common dilemma. In order to live she had to work, but if she worked she wouldn't have time to paint. It was like being caught in some awful Catch 22. First things first, she decreed. She'd find a job and paint in the evenings or at weekends. Since other people did it, why couldn't she? Her children were grown; she had no one drawing on her energies.

The next day Maureen set out for town and heading into her favourite shop she decided to go all out in the style stakes. She bought a massively expensive grey suit and had her hair and makeup done. Her confidence restored she decided to pay a visit to one of the top employment agencies in the city. In the waiting area the receptionist handed her an application form and told her to fill it in. Within minutes she was called in to the interview room.

The interviewer looked at her form. "One year of art college and a short course in computer skills, is that the height of it?" she asked doubtfully.

"Well I have developed secretarial skills over the years working for my husband's business," Maureen enthused.

"Oh I see. What business is that?"

"Well eh, Event Management. He runs an Event Management company," she lied.

After a few more questions the young girl still looking askance at the form turned to Maureen, "You do look well," she said more hopefully, "and they are desperate for someone. It's just the phone, photocopying. Do you think you could manage that?"

"Yes I can," said Maureen, full of enthusiasm.

"Can you start tomorrow?"

"I'd be delighted to," she replied.

She gave Maureen the name of the company and the address.

At 8.50 a.m. the following morning Maureen sat in the foyer of a giant computer company. A girl of no more than 23 came down from the office above to greet her.

Maureen was relieved she seemed warm and friendly. Handing Maureen a pass card she explained, "You will need this to get in and out of the work stations."

"Work stations?" Maureen asked.

"Offices," she explained.

Maureen wondered why she just couldn't say offices.

"It's handiest if you clip it on to your lapel, you will need it so many times during the day."

They took a lift up to the third floor. On the landing two doors to the right and left marked the entrance of two large corridors. Sylvie took her card and swiped it through. With a click the door opened. Walking along the corridor Maureen could see people working at their desks through opened office doors. They came to a sort of clearing like an open plan office with room for three desks. "Maureen this is your desk," Sylvie said, pointing to the nearest one. She opened a drawer and took out a phone. "This phone is locked away every evening. You need to dial this password for it to operate." Walking over to another door she instructed, "This is where the files are locked away every evening. This password will open the door for you." Turning on the computer she said, "I'll give you your password to operate it in a moment." Maureen reached for a piece of paper and a pen and hurriedly wrote down the two passwords she had already been told.

"Oh, you're not supposed to write them down," Sylvie scolded. "You have to memorise them." "Oh I will," Maureen promised, "I'll memorise them tonight," she said, trying to hide the piece of paper behind her back.

"There is a massive backlog of filing for you to do. We'll ease you in gently today and start you on that." Maureen tackled the filing and was thrilled with herself for managing it so well.

At the end of day one Maureen felt exhausted but happy.

On day two Maureen was shown how to use the phone. She found it very difficult, people spoke so fast. She cut two people off by mistake and having successfully put two people through forgot their names. Berating herself all morning she found it hard to concentrate on the filing.

In the afternoon Sylvie came towards her. "There's a big boardroom meeting today for five directors. You will have to make them tea and coffee at three."

I'll manage that Maureen thought. I've been making tea and coffee all my life. Surely nothing can go wrong.

At 2.45 Maureen made her way to the small kitchen and began to set a tray with all the accoutrements required. On a plate she placed some biscuits and thought how plain it looked. She searched in all the presses for a doily to dress it up with. None was to be found. Filling a pot with tea and one with coffee, Maureen made her way delicately to the boardroom. A young man was walking past and she asked him to open the door for her. Walking across the deep carpet towards the boardroom table, Maureen couldn't believe how well it was all going. She carefully began to place the tray on the table, admiring how not one drop of tea was spilt, when disaster struck! The top right hand corner of the tray got caught on a file and when Maureen pushed it back onto the table, tea spilt over every cup leaving a puddle on each saucer. She stared at the mess ashen faced in disbelief.

"I'm sorry," she wailed.

"Leave it, just leave it," Mr. Dillon said crossly.

Maureen turned and ran from the boardroom and headed straight into the ladies in order to regain her composure. She felt close to tears. I'm hopeless, she thought. Why did that have to happen?

Aware of time passing Maureen tried to compose herself and headed back to her desk. She took the files off the desk and spent the rest of the afternoon filing in the cabinets with her back to everyone.

That evening in the semi darkness of her living room, Maureen tried to think of more practical ways to help herself in her work. She found a notebook and taking the piece of paper from her handbag with all the passwords, diligently transcribed them into it.

This notebook would be her bible from now on, every piece of information she learned she would write in this little book.

The next day, while working in the office, Maureen reflected on a new phenomenon. There was a general assumption made by management that clerical staff were mechanically minded and that office machinery, when broken down, was to be fixed by them. It was like a silent requirement of the job, a secret test of intelligence.

The photocopier in the company was positioned straight opposite their three desks in easy reach of all the other offices.

One day Alex Roche came to tell them that the photocopier had broken down. Knowing Maureen was new he looked over her head towards the two other women. Maureen relaxed assuming one of them would ring a mechanic and was surprised to see Sylvie walking towards the photocopier where she proceeded to open and shut paper trays until the familiar drone of the machine started again.

An unease settled on Maureen. She had learned how to do the basics, but as to what happened within the bowels of the machine she had no idea. To her the photocopier seemed to have a mind of its own. She hoped she was never asked to fix it.

Later that same day Maureen was asked to photocopy four pages of a document. Three pages of the document flushed beautifully from the side of the machine. While waiting on the fourth page Maureen heard the dreaded crunch of trapped paper. Maureen froze. She hadn't a clue what to do. Within three seconds she mentally registered her three options. She could own up, fix it or ignore it. Cancelling options one and two, Maureen hoped that by simply ignoring the problem it would go away.

Maureen prayed that whoever came to use it after her would be technically minded and able to fix it themselves. It was too embarrassing having to admit she couldn't fix it. She felt it was something she should be able to do. She sat back at her desk.

Bill Moore not known for his patience started to use the machine. He kept pressing the start button in frustration. "This photocopier is broken," he called out in their direction.

Maureen trying to hide groped for her handbag on the floor. Sylvie went to see what the problem was. This time it was serious, every mechanical piece of equipment that could manually be taken out of the machine was taken out. Maureen raised her eyes above the parapet of the desk to see Sylvie prodding a tweezers into a small part of the machine. A small group of people all with documents in their hands stood around participating in the drama of the delay. The whole office seemed to have ground to a halt. Maureen put her head back down when someone asked, "Who was the last person to use it?" A phone call was made to Des in another department and between him and Sylvie they got the machine going again.

Maureen sat back in her chair. The tension of the last few minutes had left her bathed in sweat. She went to retrieve a glass of water. Walking slowly past the machine she couldn't help looking in fearful awe at how such a seemingly innocent piece of equipment could cause such chaos. As if to avoid a jinx she made sure to walk a good few feet away from it.

Later that evening, Maureen sat with her bag on her lap ready to leave when Sylvie came towards her. "This is part of your document Maureen," she said. The fourth page, the evidence of Maureen's involvement, was placed in front of her. Maureen stared at the page. "I'm sorry Sylvie, I really am."

"Always call me if there is a problem with that machine," Sylvie replied firmly.

"Thanks," Maureen said, meaning thanks for not revealing me.

In a softer tone Sylvie continued. "Tomorrow our customer account details have to be printed off. There are thousands of them. It's best to start first thing in the morning. I'll talk to you about it then."

Maureen went home and spent another quiet evening by herself getting her clothes ready for work making sure she had everything she needed for the following day.

The next day in the office Maureen vowed to give this task her utmost concentration to make up for the disaster of yesterday. She wanted to be a good employee, to prove her worth. She felt the responsibility of being representative of all middle aged women everywhere returning to work, seeing herself as a showcase for the more positive attributes of the mature woman; her strong sense of fairness also underlying her resolve to reciprocate the opportunity of employment with effort.

Sylvie gave clear instructions explaining to Maureen that each invoice had a corresponding addressed envelope and it was important to keep the invoices in alphabetical order and remove from the printer when full and store in neat bundles on the trolley in the corridor ready for the post.

There are thousands of them. You can take all day to do it as long as you have it finished by 5 p.m. They have to be ready for the post the following morning.

Maureen worked intently all morning. Making sure the printer was constantly supplied with paper, the folding machine with envelopes, and removing the full boxes out to the trolley on the corridor where they were transported down to the post room.

With only ten minutes to go before lunch Maureen brought out a full box of invoices onto the trolley and was distracted by shrieks of laughter coming from Leeann's desk.

"Maureen look," one of the girls called. "Leeann has just got engaged, come and have a look at her ring."

Maureen was delighted for the girl and went over to congratulate her.

"We're all going out to lunch to celebrate. Will you come with us?" asked Megan.

Maureen excitedly went to retrieve her jacket from the print room when glancing through the door's glass opening she froze in horror. There in front of her eyes the printer was spewing out hundreds of invoices all falling into a chaotic mess on the floor.

The girls came towards Maureen.

Maureen turning to face them fell splat back against the door, her short neck disappearing with fright into her shoulders; her fingers splayed out in full stretch in defense of the entrance.

"Are you ready?" they asked.

"No, no, you go on," she said, trying unsuccessfully to hide her panicked appearance. "I've changed my mind, I'm staying in. I have my lunch with me."

"Are you sure?" they asked puzzled.

"Yes, yes," she said. "I'll talk to you later."

Maureen worked through her lunch hour and an extra two hours that evening until she had all the invoices in order and returned home to her apartment. Walking along the Dublin streets, her feet killing

142

her, Maureen looked with sympathy at the crowds of people waiting at bus stops and pitied their long commute. Fifteen minutes later she was home. Exhaustion pervaded her. She groped for the keys in her bag and slowly opened the door. In the hallway she dropped her bag and took off her shoes. Slouching past the kitchen she felt too tired even to eat and went straight into the bedroom. There she turned and collapsed into a heap on the bed still in her clothes. She tried to find a word in her mind to suitably describe the tiredness she felt. Banjaxed came to mind. It was an old Dublin word she remembered. It suits she thought. I am absolutely banjaxed.

She fell asleep and woke at eleven that night. In the kitchen she made herself a snack. I'll get used to it she thought trying to be hopeful. Other people can do it and when I get used to it I'll have more energy. She had a bath and headed straight back to bed again.

On the kitchen table the next morning she emptied and cleared her handbag of old receipts, papers, etc. to make sure she had enough room for all the items she needed for work. Without finishing the task she remembered she had left her mobile by the bed and went back to retrieve it.

Walking to work, she wondered would the tiredness ever leave her? Was it just something she had to get used to? She had plenty of time as she'd got up particularly early to be ready and relaxed for work and stopped for a coffee. She had got into the bad habit of drinking too much coffee and felt she needed one every hour just to keep going. Today will be better, she thought optimistically as she left the coffee shop. I will get through it today. She gave herself a rousing pep talk. She could do it, it was only a matter of being trained in, in time she would handle it.

Maureen decided the key was to act confident even if she didn't feel it. She decided to try to emulate the confidence of her co-workers, to feign their air of purpose and self-assuredness and then hopefully, these qualities would somehow transfer to her.

Maureen entered the building her footsteps quick and determined on the tiled floor.

In the lift she pressed the button with a deftness and certainty she did not feel. She worked carefully to settle her features into as blank an expression as possible in order to affect the demeanor of calm nonchalance she had witnessed from the other staff. With a jolt the door opened and as she stepped out onto the corridor, a new feeling of happiness and possibility lifted her mood. Enjoying the momentum of the moment, Maureen walked quickly to her desk slinging her bag on the table in as breezy a manner as she could muster and headed towards the door of the filing room. She stopped short. A password was needed. At her desk she began to forage in her bag for her notebook, it wasn't to be found.

Just at that moment Mr Dillon came towards her holding a folder in his hands his expression indicating he had a lot on his mind. "I want you to do a few things for me," he said.

Maureen searched in desperation for Sylvie and saw only a lonely workspace in the corner, Sylvie's empty chair pushed neatly under the desk.

"Sylvie is sick," he said and began issuing a set of instructions.

Maureen relied on Sylvie as a buffer between herself and management and now without that layer of comfort she had to take the responsibility herself. A mixture of shock at her exposure to his expectations and the terror of there being no way out left her immobilized on the spot.

Maureen, concentrating so intently on his instructions, was unable to hear them, her nerves rendering her temporarily deaf. She felt dwarfed by his physical presence and the power of his authority. He finished speaking and walked away.

Maureen rushed to her bag again and in desperation upturned the contents on the desk. She searched for the little blue notebook, willing it into existence. It wasn't there. She checked her pockets again to no avail. The realization that all the instruments of her work lay dormant around her; all needing passwords to bring them to life, her computer, her phone, the filing cabinets, the enormity of her impotence came crashing down on her.

Maureen gathering up her belongings literally fled from the office and running down three flights of stairs bolted out of the building into the bright sunshine. If anyone had timed her departure it would have been noted that it took exactly three minutes to exit the building and the world of GE Computers Ltd.

. . .

Two days later, Maureen stood in the kitchen eating her toast and glanced idly out of her window. In the small courtyard she saw Jenny get out of her car with her three small children in tow. Maureen balked. She was having none of it. The last time they'd visited, which was only the previous week, Jenny said she had to drop into town to see a friend who was desperate for help and would it be possible for her to mind the children just for an hour, please? she'd begged her mother. Maureen had said all right and Jenny had been out half the day with the kids running wild after the first hour. She wasn't getting caught like that again. She ran into the bedroom and quickly changed into her suit. Maureen greeted them at the door.

"Hi, lovely to see you all, but I'm just going out."

"Out?" Jenny asked, "but it's Saturday and I heard you've given up work. Where are you going in a suit?"

"Oh I have an important meeting with my accountant. Look I'd love to have time to see you all. I'll come over to you during the week for dinner." Bare cheek Maureen had begun to realize was the only tool that worked with her daughters. "I've something interesting to tell you," she said.

At the end of her first week of freedom from work, Maureen turned on the radio. It was a clear day in Dublin and she picked up the frequency of BBC Radio 4. She sat drinking tea, admiring the dulcet tones of the radio presenter who was in conversation with a distinguished invited guest asking her questions on her background.

"And your mother?"

"My mother worked as a live-in companion to Lord Canterbury in Argyle."

"A companion," Maureen spoke, saying the word out loud. Do people still do that she wondered. It seemed perfect.

A plan began to formulate in her mind. She would work as a companion and rent out her apartment. That way the rent would pay her mortgage and she could live on whatever salary she earned. The idea was just too good to be true. Wouldn't it be wonderful she thought if she could paint there as well, that wherever she went they would have space and allow her to paint.

She felt full of excitement, her despondency dissipating. Maureen had the capacity, once the initial depression lifted, not to dwell on her limitations, but to spring back into action full of new hope and vigor.

Finishing her tea she popped the cup in the dishwasher and made her way down to the newsagents on the complex she was living in. She bought three newspapers, hoping that the fact it was a Friday would mean more advertisements had been posted than any other day. In her kitchen she laid the paper out on the table and stood peering over the situations vacant column. She read through every column and every column again to make sure she had missed none. Folding the paper away she moved onto the next paper. Eyeing the detail carefully of the Situation Vacant column in 'The Irish Times' she couldn't believe that there was no hint of a position. With a huge sense of disappointment she closed the paper and began looking at the back page noticing the small ads for holiday breaks. Just then at the bottom left hand corner one ad caught her attention. It read:

Retired Theatre Director
seeks house companion for
light household duties & chauffeuring.
May suit someone slightly eccentric.
Please call 01 324512

Maureen dialed the number immediately. A woman answered.

"I am ringing to enquire about the position advertised in the paper today."

"Oh yes," the woman replied. "Mr. Hetherington is taking interviews tomorrow. Would you be able to attend at 3 p.m.?"

"I would," Maureen replied. "Is there anything I need to bring?"

"No, just bring yourself, that's all that's required. You will need the address it's 35 Lennox Avenue, Dublin."

"Thank you," Maureen said and replaced the phone.

The next day at 2.55 p.m. Maureen stood outside 35 Lennox Avenue. It was one of those Edwardian red brick solid family homes that she had often admired in Dublin, double fronted with a glossy red painted front door. Feeling nervous and not quite sure what she was letting herself in for, Maureen walked hesitantly to the door. Pressing the doorbell, the door opened almost instantly and a smiling woman greeted her.

"Hello, you must be Maureen," she said brightly.

"Yes," Maureen replied.

"Charles is expecting you, come this way." Maureen was led into a library at the back of the house to the right of the hallway. Maureen's first impression was that the desk was placed at an odd angle and jutted too far into the centre of the room. Behind the desk sat Charles and on seeing Maureen he stood up and extended his hand.

"Good to meet you Maureen," he said in his English accent. "Do sit down. You may wonder," he began, once they settled, "why I didn't ask you to bring along references, etc., it is because after fifty years working in the theatre, I pride myself on being able to judge people's character and I have never been wrong once," he said, bending his upper body towards Maureen as he finished the sentence. Continuing he said, "I wanted to put in my advertisement that this position would suit someone slightly mad, but I was advised to put slightly eccentric instead. Are you?" he asked pointedly.

"Am I mad?" Maureen said, blinking in bewilderment.

"No, no, no," he said. "Are you eccentric?"

"Oh yes, yes," Maureen replied, feeling relieved, "getting more and more every day."

"Good," he said. "There's so few of us left. Now about myself." He leant back in his chair and proceeded to roll out his achievements. "Ex Theatre Director. Winner of two Tony Awards, one Olivier, successful completion of three world tours and oh yes one disaster. Ah, don't mention the disaster. I have five children scattered all over the world and a wife scattered all over the garden."

Maureen paled. She had visions of limbs strewn over the lawn. "Your wife," she reiterated slowly, "is in the garden?"

"Ashes," he replied, compressing his lips. "Her ashes are scattered in the garden. It was her last wish."

"Oh I see." Suddenly Maureen felt the room very warm.

"Are you all right dear? You have rather a poor pallor."

"I hope so," Maureen said, not fully convinced. Holding her fingers against her forehead she began to explain hurriedly. "It's just that I've had a lot of changes in my life recently and I'm not really myself."

"Ah don't worry dear; I've made a career out of working with people who weren't really themselves."

He leant forward preparing to impart a confidence.

"Actors – very strange people. Imagine wanting to be someone else, act a part. I've never really understood it." He started to shake, mirth bubbling up inside him at the idea of it. "I just can't imagine wanting to be someone else," he said laughing. "I do like myself so. Although I've always pretended I thought they were wonderful, so I must be one as well."

"I suppose we all act a little to get through," Maureen said.

"I supposed we do."

He looked at her with a fatherly expression, his face serious.

"These changes you've mentioned, I do hope nothing terrible happened to you dear."

"No, just life that's all. Life happened to me."

"How interesting," he said. Peering at her intently he continued, "I think you are a woman of hidden depths Maureen. I think we'll get along just fine. Now if you don't mind," he said, banging the arms of his chair with his hands and standing up. "It's almost three o'clock and I'm a man of routine. Come over at two tomorrow and we'll talk in more detail. I find one hour is all I'm good for now at anything."

In the hall, opening the front door, he said pleasantly, "Good day dear."

"Good day to you too," Maureen replied.

The next day Maureen arrived promptly at 2.00 p.m. and was met at the door by Charles. He ushered her into the drawing room indicating that this meeting was less formal than the previous.

"Now," he said, "I have given some thought to your duties and if you don't mind I shall proceed with the small list of tasks I would like you to do. The main thing is I would like you to be here in the early evening. I do hate coming home to a dark house. Also, would you mind lighting a fire for me? I know it's archaic, but it cheers me so. Chauffeuring is another task I may call on you to do. These dreaded drink driving laws. Taxis are fine, but there are other times say when attending parties in the country or in the outer suburbs when I will need a lift. You can accompany me if you wish. You will have some fun, wonderful parties, absolutely glorious. Oh yes and keep the brandy stocked. I like a tipple at 3.00 o'clock before my afternoon nap.

I have been thinking of your salary. I propose the going rate plus some extra. I am a generous man."

They discussed this between them and the issue of time off. Then promising to work on a mutual basis of flexibility they shook hands on the deal. Maureen mentioned that she had an interest in painting and would like at some stage to proceed with her work.

"Don't worry dear," he conceded. "It's such a large house I'm sure we'll find space for you somehow. Come with me," he said. "I'll show you to your room."

Maureen followed him out through the hall and up the stairs on to the landing.

"I thought this room might suit you. It is the prettiest one in the house."

Maureen stepped into a bright bedroom decorated in lemon florals. It was situated at the back of the house with a south westerly aspect and had a bay window. He was right. It was pretty Maureen thought, but too nice to paint in. She wouldn't push this matter anymore for now. She needed the job and thought it best to bring it up later.

"Well are you agreeable to the terms I've offered?" Charles asked.

"I am," Maureen replied.

"When can you commence your employment?" he continued.

"In a week's time, if that's acceptable to you."

"Yes of course, we'll say next Monday, 10th December. Agreed?" he asked.

"Agreed," Maureen replied.

He started to lead her back down the stairs. "Oh, by the way, Mrs Cathcart is my housekeeper, she works here every morning from seven until nine and some afternoons. She will have a key ready for you next Monday."

His house was positioned between the Canals and Maureen decided to walk home, pondering on the likeability of this man she was going to work for. She loved the twinkle in his eye, his warmth. Even though she had only recently met him, she felt he

149

was one of those people with whom you know you will get on with, feel safe with. She sensed she could trust him, that he was a good person. Their energies clicked. The idea of going to parties with him seemed an unbelievable perk and she felt he may have only said that to humour her.

In her apartment Maureen went straight into her bedroom and began packing. Once a decision was made Maureen had no trouble seeing it through. Within a few hours most of her clothes were packed with only the minimum left in the wardrobe for the coming week. She notified letting agencies and told them of her plans. Later when Pol looked around the almost empty flat she said, "Unfurnished. I think I can safely say it will be let unfurnished."

Locking the door on the final day Maureen felt happy and relieved that the burden of home ownership had been lifted from her, even if she wasn't sure exactly how long it would last.

. . .

There was a level of awkwardness in Maureen's first few days with Charles Hetherington, an uncertainty of her role. It was, she knew, a role that would only evolve over time. She found it difficult to know when to disturb him and when not to, when to remove herself from his presence or when to be present. There was a mismatch in their expectations.

Often he'd sulk when he felt she wasn't reading his nuances, anticipating his needs. One day after clearing up a minor misunderstanding Maureen said to him, "Why don't you just ask for what you want?"

Unfortunately, once he started to ask he couldn't stop. It was fetch this and fetch that. On the second day of running up and down the stairs for him and in and out to his car he asked innocently, "Where's my cap? Fetch it for me will you."

Maureen exploded. "This is worse than having a husband," she roared. "You're taking advantage. Fetch it yourself."

She left the room and slammed the door with all the force she could muster. The house reverberated with shock, a hushed suspense descended on it and within this apprehension the unanswered question hung in the air - what happens next?

Both withdrew, Maureen to her bedroom, Charles to his study, each defending their position.

In her room Maureen sat reading, but was unable to concentrate and put the book down. She worried that he would miss his tea. Taking the book up again she thought, let him get it himself. As the night wore on she listened for sounds as to his whereabouts.

At ten she heard him come up the stairs. She couldn't bear to go to sleep without seeing how he was. She crept over to the door and opened it slightly. He stopped outside his door turning his head slightly to his left sensing she was there. With his shoulders hunched, his body shrunk smaller, an air of wounded misery pervaded it. He shuffled in to his room and closed the door quietly.

The next morning Maureen woke to a knock on the door. He stood in his nightclothes and slippers holding a breakfast tray in his hands. His eyes looked puffy from lack of sleep, his face had a dejected hang dog look. "Please don't fight with me dear, it makes me too sad," he said. Handing the tray to Maureen he turned and walked back down the stairs.

Later that morning, Maureen went into his study and found him sitting bolt upright in his chair. "I think I'll have an early nap," he said. "I didn't sleep a wink last night." Taking a rug Maureen carefully placed it on his knees and tucked it in around him.

She went to move towards the door. "I'm sorry Maureen," he said. She had never heard him use her name before. The fact that he used it now made his apology seem all the more poignant. "I'm sorry too," she said quietly.

Leaving the room she glanced towards him and saw that he was already fast asleep.

As the days turned into weeks Maureen found that she wasn't quite on tenterhooks as she had been and the synergy between them became more natural.

His promise to her to accompany him to parties did become a reality. The first party was to a friend of his, a musician. There was no formal invitation, no invite on the mantelpiece. Charles simply surprised her with the invite.

"Where is it?" she asked.

"It's up in the Dublin Mountains. I promise I won't stay out too long," he said with a half-smile.

They drove out towards the Dublin countryside. It was nine in the evening and traffic was light. After a number of missed signs and one or two wrong turns Charles shouted, "Ah, here we are, this is it."

They drove up to what seemed like a converted coach house.

"It's a charming house Maureen," he said, "come and see."

Inside the hall door they entered straight into a rustic style dining room. The focal point was a huge dining table laden with food – all organic she was told later and copious amounts of drink.

Through the dining room there was a more modern extension which served as a large living room with numerous glass windows. People sat on three couches which formed a U shape in the room.

Maureen was in her element. She was surrounded by famous faces, people she'd only seen on the television or read about in the paper and here they were in front of her.

The musical talent that was available was unbelievable and if anyone was asked to do their party piece they sang or played an instrument to such a professional standard it was the equivalent of being at a concert.

The other guests seemed to be fascinated by her.

"Do you act?" one of them asked her.

"Oh, only in real life," Maureen said earnestly.

They laughed amused to find a comic amongst them.

The party went on well into the early hours. At 4.00 a.m. Maureen sat trying to catch Charles' attention to indicate that she wanted to go home. It didn't work.

When most of the guests had dispersed Maureen asked, "Do you think we could leave now Charles?"

Heading home in the pitch black morning he said, "I think, in the future, it would be a good idea if you brought some night things to stay over. It's often hard to say which way the night will go. See it as a taste of what's to come." Maureen was to come to know Charles's indefatigable energy.

Over the weeks Maureen witnessed a near constant flow of visitors to Charles – mainly women.

Constance sat in the drawing room, arm outstretched, holding the handle of an umbrella, its point piercing the carpet like a dagger, her threat to the world. Go back one hundred years and Maureen could see parallels between Oscar Wilde's Lady Bracknell in 'The Importance of Being Earnest' and the severe woman sitting in front of her.

Maureen had the feeling of being presented to a Victorian aunt, of being an unwitting participant in the scene of a play. Slowly she came forward. "What have we here?" Constance asked, staring at Maureen her expression full of distain.

"Maureen is my new house companion Constance," Charles explained. "She started last month."

The two women eyed each other coldly. Constance seemed to want further explanation. Maureen stayed silent.

Charles sensing no hope of conversation between these two women tried to mend the breech. "What a lovely day," he said unconvincingly, looking out at a grey sky.

"I must be going, I have so much to do," Maureen said, hurrying towards the door.

"Don't let me detain you," Constance said acidly.

In the kitchen Maureen began to wash dishes on the dashboard. Imagine addressing someone as a what, she fumed. That woman for all her airs, has no manners. I had better get in there quick before he asks me to prepare refreshments.

Marching down towards the drawing room she knocked daintily on the door. "Charles one moment please," she said, beckoning him with her hand. Charles came out of the room. Maureen shut the door behind him and indicating to move further down the hall she began, "I will not be available to make that woman tea," she said firmly, leaving him in no doubt not to press the point.

Charles looked perplexed. He did not like to see Maureen unhappy. Relenting he confessed, "Alice couldn't abide her either," he whispered. "I will explain later. I have a full decanter of brandy, I'll offer her that."

Later when Constance had departed he explained, "I know she's rude, but she spoils me so and to be honest I quite enjoy it. Makes a marvelous banoffi," he said with relish. "You see, she thinks she is my special friend, but I'm too old for special friends. I play along though, does wonders for my ego." Leaning closer to Maureen he continued, "Hope never did anyone any harm Maureen and her little visits give her hope. What's wrong with that? She's held a torch for me for years and in one drunken moment even told me that she loved me. What am I to do?" he chuckled childishly to himself as he wandered out of the room.

One wet Sunday afternoon Charles sat reading his newspaper in the drawing room. Maureen tidied papers in the lounge, the intersecting double doors opened between them. On hearing a car pull into the driveway Charles turned abruptly in his chair and seeing a blue Fiat Panda stop abruptly outside the window, he exclaimed in horror, "Oh dear, how distressing, it's fey Faye on one of her bi-annual visits and I am totally unprepared. It only seems like yesterday since I saw her last." He got up from his chair in a terrible flap and all his newspapers came crashing onto the floor. He went to the door to greet her.

A tall, thin, gangly young woman in her early twenties entered the room. She had fine wispy hair and seemed gauche and nervous. They stood opposite each other.

"How is your mother?" he asked.

"Very well thank you," she replied.

"And your father?"

"Very well thank you," she replied again.

"Have you been to any auditions lately?"

"I have," she said.

"Well?"

"Nothing, I'm afraid," she replied with an embarrassed sniggering sound.

Charles finding it difficult to hide his exasperation, told her to sit down and came through the double door towards Maureen. He started to root through some papers. "I need a script. Ah," he said holding the script up. "This will do." He leaned towards Maureen and began whispering in her ear, "Faye is empty, but put words into her and she comes alive." Handing the script to Faye he instructed her to start from the top.

"Love's heralds should be thoughts,
  Which ten times faster glide than the sun's beams,"

And with these words of Shakespeare, she sprang from the couch her voice booming, her persona coming to life at its most theatrical.

154

Charles' face bathed in relief, the words like music drifting over him inducing a dream-like state, turned towards the double doors and with a wink he mouthed to Maureen, "All is well, all is well," before gently closing them towards him.

One day when Maureen was in the library trying to negotiate between the bookshelves and the desk she asked him, "Why is this desk at such an odd place in the room?"

"Vortex," Charles replied with a blunt tone. "There is a vortex under its previous position and I thought it prudent to change."

"Vortex?" Maureen enquired.

"Yes, it occurs when the horizontal and vertical energy lines from the earth intersect, that's when a vortex occurs.

"Oh I see."

"I feel a thousand times better since I've changed it. Before I used to find myself dozing off very early in the evening. Now, once I've had my nap, I can stay up long into the night."

During the party season leading up to Christmas, Maureen came to know again Charles' extraordinary energy.

The trouble was he was so popular it was hard to get him to go home. In the early hours any time he made a move towards the door, people kept pulling his sleeve asking him not to go, to tell them more anecdotes and as the evening wore on and they got more inebriated, they would pull his tie and insist he stay. He was so polite he regaled them all for hours with his stories of his time in the theatre and the famous people he'd met and of his earlier days in rep in England. He had an audience erupting in hoots and hoots of laughter.

Maureen sat slumped in a chair close by. The novelty was already beginning to wear thin. It was amazing how nearly all the same faces that had been at the party the previous night were at this one. Two parties in a row, she couldn't keep up the pace. He had such stamina for a man his age.

"Oh there's Faye," she said, trying to get his attention.

"Oh dear," he replied, "and not a script in sight," and did his best to avoid her.

The hostess came up to her. "If you like, Maureen, you can stay the night in the guest bedroom, from experience I don't think Charles has any intention of leaving just yet."

Maureen made her way to the bedroom and even the comfort of the surroundings did not assuage her annoyance at having to stay over.

Maureen lay in the bed trying to sleep in unfamiliar surroundings. Just then the bedroom door opened and a figure came through weeping quietly. Maureen switched on the bedside lamp. It was Faye. "Oh I'm so sorry for disturbing you," she said.

"It's all right," Maureen lied. "Whatever is the matter with you?"

"I've been rebuked," Faye replied.

"Rebuked?" Maureen queried indignantly. "By whom?" she asked, her voice shrill, the fact of being in the company of this prim young woman raising her standard of English by her rather old fashioned expressions from another age.

"By a young man and practically every young man I try to converse with," she started to sob. Maureen stared at the stiff hunched shoulders of the weeping woman. Maureen, in her annoyance, felt pity towards this girl. Her awkwardness was such a contrast to the self-confidence of her own daughters. Maureen could feel the old compulsion to fix things starting to rear its head. For some moments she fought against it, but this young woman really did seem so unhappy and what harm would a little advice do? She somehow had to be pulled from the 1930s to the present day.

"Could you not have brought a friend?" Maureen asked.

"I don't have many friends and the one or two I do have are married and live away."

"I'm sure they would have appreciated a night out; something surely could have been arranged."

"No, I'm afraid."

Friends Maureen thought, friends had to be found for this young girl.

The next morning, returning home with Charles, Maureen asked, "Where might a young girl meet nice, gentle people?"

As if reading her mind Charles raising his chin in defiance, his tone full of warning said, "Don't interfere Maureen, don't interfere, it may come back to haunt you."

Maureen thought it was worth the risk.

Whilst Maureen reflected on the importance of friends for Faye she assessed the current lack of friends in her own life for which she felt no great loss. Most of them did not know her address and Maureen liked it that way. She viewed this time with Charles as time out, a space she could use to transform her life into something new and worthwhile and then when the time was right reinstate herself back into her own social circle, or maybe not. The last few years she had found her nature changing to one of more introspection and personal space was now of paramount importance to her.

Maureen pondered on the contradiction.

After Christmas there was a particularly cold spell, and even with the central heating on full, the house still seemed cold. One evening Maureen and Charles were in the drawing room, Charles standing in front of the fire with a glass of brandy in his hand.

"Thank you for lighting the fire for me. I feel the cold dear. That's why I wear a cap. An actress told me once that hats suit me." Maureen lifted her head expectantly.

"Don't look at me like that dear, I never strayed. I always knew Alice could cope very well without me." He continued deep in concentration describing the character of Alice. "She was the most independent woman I have ever met. She had the most innate sense of herself. I found her stillness fascinating. Don't get me wrong she was a very passionate woman, tremendously so. Alice had her admirers too. She was an actress and drama teacher. Youth appealed to her and when the children were reared she devoted her life to the youth of Dublin."

"The way you said your wife was in the garden, I thought it was a derogatory comment. I assumed you weren't happy."

"Don't assume. We were perfectly happy."

As if on cue Maureen's eyes were drawn to a picture of Alice on the bookshelf.   She had such a wonderful strong face with the classic features of high cheek bones. A face created to convey the great speeches of literature through the roles of Helen of Troy, Medea, Joan of Arc; to hold an audience spellbound, transporting them through the power of her performance.

Maureen stared at the picture of this amazing woman married to one of the most dynamic men of his generation and yet she somehow managed to keep herself involved in and yet apart from his world, a very delicate balancing act.

In the pictures she could sense the woman's strength and it was completely alluring. "Such composure," Maureen said.

"Yes there were enough theatrics in the theatre," he said. "Coming home to Alice was like coming home to a soothing balm."

. . .

As spring approached Maureen felt a sense of calm, as if her equilibrium was returning. She felt drawn to the library. It was her favourite room. It was painted dark green, with mahogany furniture, the atmosphere exuding peace and warmth. She liked to spend time reading through Alice's selection of books, absorbing the knowledge within them. The titles of the books, 'Healing emotions', books on inner peace and self-love seemed to be sending messages to her. The tenet of all the books was the importance of self-love that no other relationship will survive unless love of the self is intact.

If she ever thought of John again it was in the context of never again. She would never love like that again. Sometimes though, when watching couples at events she wondered would she ever find love or was that part of her life closed forever. Deep in her heart Maureen knew that it wasn't closed, that she was still able to love. And if she did get the chance to love again, she wondered, how would she love? These questions Maureen pondered as she stood one day fingering Alice's books on the shelves.

Charles broke the silence. "What are you doing?"

Maureen turned reluctant to explain. "I'm working out how to love again and Alice is helping me," she said.

"I see," Charles said. He pushed his weight up on to his toes in order to assimilate this information trying to reach some conclusion then rocked back on to his heels, without having drawn any. Lowering his eyes he said, "My dear, you know Alice has been dead for the past five years, how is she helping you?"

"Through her books."

"Ah, an extraordinary woman."

"Do you think I'm strange?" Maureen asked.

"No, I don't think you're strange," he replied, the rhythmic tapping of his fingers on the desk betraying his sincerity."

Although this talk was beyond him, he decided to play along with it, seeing Maureen as an example of a particular eccentricity that interested him.

"You see," Maureen said, her tone matter of fact. "I've looked to men to know the secret of life and I realize that I know more about life myself. The ideal is that I become as whole a person as I can be on my own, not to look to someone else to make me whole. Then when I am more complete and my relationship with myself more intact, I stand a better chance of making it with another."

"Is that so?"

"It is."

"Maureen, I find you fascinating."

"It is fascinating. The secret of life is fascinating and it's all to do with ourselves, loving ourselves."

"Do you Maureen?" he asked with urgent concern bending down to peer under her fringe.

"Do you love yourself?"

"I think at this stage I can honestly say, I do."

"Bravo!" he said. "Let's drink to that."

. . .

Charles often went out on his own. One evening after returning home from the opening night of a play where Charles, rather than the play, had been very well-received he asked, "I feel wide awake Maureen; will you share a drink with me?" Maureen wasn't feeling particularly sleepy so she agreed.

In the drawing room she stoked the fire and threw some logs on it and in no time the room was cosy with their glow.

"You enjoyed yourself tonight," Maureen said, noting he was in particular jocular form.

"Wonderful." he said. "I had a wonderful night. I was so pleased to see people that I haven't seen in an age. I do love to reminisce."

Over three brandies for him and three vodkas for her, Charles brought to life his childhood in England. "My parents ran a travelling troupe of actors. All during my childhood we toured England. I never liked acting. In my childhood I found it just about bearable, but coming into my teens I began to view it as a form of torture. I love literature, but I am an unsuitable vehicle to express it. I wanted to stop acting but my parents refused to even let me entertain the idea."

"How did you manage to change their minds?"

"Sabotage," he said, in that direct way of his when certain of his actions. "Three times," he said, dusting flint off his sleeve, "I accidentally missed my timing at the most critical part of the play. I was surprised it took three times," he said, almost to himself, dusting more flint off his collar. "I would have thought two would have done. I loved organizing. I have great organizational skills. Eventually," he continued, "my parents reluctantly agreed to let me organize venues. It was when I procured the talents of the famous actress Clody Buttle that they eventually allowed me to choose and direct plays. It's how I honed my skills as a director."

"What about your schooling?" Maureen asked.

"Mrs Moffat," he said, "woman of all trades. She was a member of the travelling troupe. She was my governess, and she also stood in as a player, a rather fine actress actually, she played many parts. She could fix and mend props with the best of men. All the actresses in the travelling troupe doted on me. I had about ten mothers looking after me."

Charles spoke of his time in rep, his tours around dreary English towns, giving her hilarious accounts of dour landladies and the colourful characters he'd met. Maureen sat in stitches. He mimicked every accent all over England. He talked of early loves he had as a young man in particular with two women called Faith and Joy.

"You know in their particular cases their Christian names were entirely appropriate. In other cases I find peoples' names are a misnomer." Continuing he said, "I once knew a Hope who had none, a Prudence who was impudence personified and a Patience who tried me beyond endurance."

"And what is Constance consistent with?" Maureen asked dryly. "Her pursuance of you?"

"Now, now Maureen tetchiness doesn't become you."

Maureen gave a satisfied smile, not sorry for her sarcasm.

"Now that you ask, I think it's her tenacity I admire. Constance is consistent with her tenacity. I admire her for it in a way, I must say

I do. She's loyal too, a loyal friend to have. I can see you don't agree," he said. "You don't like her do you?"

"No, I must say I don't. It's her vibes."

"Nothing much gets by you." Charles said.

"No, unfortunately, it does not."

"Why do you say unfortunately?"

"Because, I do not need that much information. I sometimes think I'm too tuned in."

"You should see your sensitivity as a gift. It's what enables you to paint; it's linked to your creativity."

During the next few weeks Maureen was wondering how to broach the subject of painting. Luckily, circumstances were working in her favour. One day, for whatever reason, they kept finding themselves in the same space together. They got stuck between a doorway and had to take turns passing each other on the corridor. The final straw came when Maureen nearly bumped into him with a tray of tea.

"Dear, dear," he said, exasperated. "I think it's time I sorted out a studio for you. Come with me dear."

Outside at the back of the house there was a disused shed the whole width of the garden. "I think it should suit you if we got rid of the junk, dickied it up with a fresh coat of paint. I'll put in a heater; I don't want you to freeze to death. We'll start on Saturday," he said. "I do like the energy of a Saturday it has an odd jobs feel about it – a lets get things done sort of day."

Saturday arrived. Charles came out of the house with the most obscenely oversized white overalls.

"First," he said, "I need to test the building for geopathic stress."

"What is geopathic stress?" Maureen queried.

"The earth has a geomagnetic energy field which if disturbed becomes harmful to our health. It will help you decide the best place to put your easel." With a rod placed in each hand and with hugely exaggerated footsteps he crisscrossed the room twice. The rods did not move. "No geopathic stress my dear, I am glad to say. You can put your easel anywhere."

They got a skip and cleared away the junk. They then set about painting the walls white.

Afterwards, Charles stood with a brush in his hand staring at the wall. "That wall looks too perfect to me," he said, almost to himself. "My word, the strangest impulse has come over me and try as I might I just can't fight it," he said.

He stood poised halfway between thinking about doing something and actually doing something. Then Charles dipped his paint brush in bright blue paint and with a ping flicked the brush against the wall, "Whee!"

Maureen grabbed her brush and dipping it into a red tin of paint; she flicked it on the wall. They both turned to each other and with their faces full of divilment and exuberance, they dipped their brushes into every tin they could lay their hands on. Then Charles did it first. He picked up a full tin of yellow paint and with a huge yelp threw it on the wall. Maureen picked up the blue and flung it tears of laughter running down their faces.

"Well really," a deep voice boomed behind them. "What are you two doing?"

They both jumped in fright.

"Constance!" they screeched, their mouths dropping open in terror and if it had been one of those sci-fi movies their hair would have stood on end.

Constance, with her regal stance, stood peering down on them like a disapproving schoolmarm. Decades fell away from them and they stood like two schoolchildren waiting to be admonished by their headmistress.

"Really, you two are such a pair of nit wits," she said and stormed off.

Released from her spell they snapped back into the reality that they weren't children anymore and laughed and laughed, relief washing over them.

"Oh my Lord, what have I done," Charles said.

"It's too late," Maureen cried dramatically. "She's gone now. You've lost her forever."

"It's not Constance I dread loosing, it's the fear that I may have to face into eternity without ever tasting her banoffi again." They both erupted in laughter.

"Oh Maureen," he cried, trying to regain his composure. "What have you done to me?"

"Sure you've done it to yourself," Maureen said, collecting herself.

"You're as mad as a hatter. I knew it the moment I met you. I could see it in your eyes."

"Really"? He started to rub his face, pressing it with his fingertips, feigning to open his eyes in an exaggerated way. "Where Maureen," he asked. "Where in my eyes?"

"It's just there," she said. "It's an element of you as you would say yourself."

. . .

Maureen continued painting. There was dissatisfaction with her work. She felt she was in a rut and doubted whether they would ever sell.

On Sunday afternoons she liked to stroll around Merrion Square studying the displays of paintings exhibited against the outer railings of the small public park.

Maureen judged some of them to be of a similar standard to her own and wondered about the possibility of selling her work there.

"You have to apply in writing for a license and then go on a waiting list," the nice man from Dublin City Council explained when Maureen asked for details on street selling. Maureen, standing in the hatch in the public office said, "I'll apply now."

For two Sundays she had stood in the rain on Merrion Square trying to sell her paintings with not one sold, trying to look happy when her neighbours' had sales.

She had retrieved all her work from the boot of Pol's car, her practical nature coming to the fore, and had a fairly substantial body of work to show.

Sometimes she got chatting to potential buyers who stopped to view her work. Some comments were not complimentary.

"I find your paintings overwhelming," one man wearing a cream coloured suit with a blue cravat said to her. "I think they would work better if toned down."

I didn't ask for your opinion, Maureen thought glaring at him.

"Finesse," he said, "is a word you may find useful."

"Are you saying I've no finesse," Maureen said, moving towards him unable to hide the hostility in her voice.

"In my opinion, no," he said, and walked away.

163

Maureen slumped dejectedly onto her tiny portable stool the remark had struck her in a personal way. Overwhelming? How many more "overs" were going to be used to describe me, she wondered? "Over emotional", "over excitable", she'd heard them all before down through the years and yet here was another one.

Her paintings were too much she thought. Just like herself. The attack on her work was a simultaneous attack on her. She was crushed. Bounce back from that, she challenged herself sagely knowing this time there was no bounce in her left. Folding her work away she wished she could fold herself away as easily.

It took every ounce of courage Maureen possessed for her to turn up again the following Sunday. Two women stopped to view her work.

"Lovely colours," one of them said, "but I don't think they'd go too well with my duck egg blue walls." They laughed and walked away.

Maureen stared after them. Maybe they had a point. Not everyone was a serious connoisseur of paintings, with white or cream walls to show them off to their best advantage. If duck egg blue was what the masses were putting on their walls, maybe she should paint for the masses. They could be her market.

The next day she got up early and headed into all the interior design shops. The same combinations of colours were similar in all the shops. Duck egg blue with either brown of fawn. Fuchsia pink with green, rusts and golds were always popular. That afternoon in her studio Maureen began working on prints that would complement the accompanying paints and wallpapers. By nightfall she had some lovely mixtures put together and felt they enhanced the original colours.

Two weeks later Maureen had four pictures ready, but was still unsure about them.

She needed some advice. She spoke to Charles.

"What do you think of my paintings?"

"Oh my dear they look lovely to me, but I am illiterate when it comes to critiques on paintings. I have an artist friend who will help you. His name is Michael Wallis. I will arrange for you to meet him. Oh, I almost forgot, we'll see him at the weekend. He's attending the party that we've been invited to – a rather swank occasion. It's in the Irish home of Hollywood film actor Sam Hughes. There's no need for you to drive me, we'll get a taxi, so you can have a drink and relax."

THE PARTY

That Saturday in the taxi, on the journey to the party, Charles explained the background to their visit. "Sam Hughes has built a massive house overlooking the sea. It's quite the talk of the town. Tonight is the official housewarming. I'm looking forward to it. It's a very modern building I believe."

The house was built on a narrow strip of land between the coast road and the sea, at a lower level to the road above it. From the higher vantage point of the roadside, Maureen's first impression of the house was that of a bunker. Apart from the doorway, the only openings were narrow slit like windows high up on the walls of the concrete building.

Maureen followed Charles down steps towards the house. A small group of people waited outside the hall door and on joining them, the door opened and they followed them through. Inside the reception room was a huge open plan space, the ceiling double height, cathedral like in its effect. There was collective agreement amongst the small clusters of people on the beauty of the building. This approval was vocalized with words like wonderful, magnificent, which when spoken, hung in the air.

Charles stood in the centre of the open plan room, "Interesting" was all he said.

Charles spotted a man he knew coming towards him. "Ah Michael, how are you? Would you mind explaining to me," he began, "oh by the way," he stopped, interrupting himself. "May I introduce you to Maureen, who is the artist lady I was speaking to you about. Maureen this is Michael." Michael offered her his hand and smiled warmly.

"Now, as I was saying," Charles continued, "how is someone persuaded to build one of these modern mausoleums, what is the blurb used to convince. I cannot see the beauty myself."

"Well I think it is the execution of detail, the clean lines which attract people to buildings like these."

"I see," Charles said. "They are just so cold. Where's the personality?"

"Well, it is because of their lack of personality that people admire these homes. They act as a blank canvass for them. They find it relaxing. The lack of demands it makes on ones senses."

Charles drifted away from them.

"Do you like working for Charles?" Michael asked.

"I must say I do. We have a lot of fun together."

"He's one of the best friends I have ever had," Michael said.

"Really?" Maureen asked, before sipping her wine.

"He's been extraordinarily good to me throughout my career," Michael continued. "Dublin's art world is very small and you need every contact you can make. Charles has been so generous to me introducing me to people which enabled me to make as many contacts as I could along the way. Apart from my mother, I would say he has been the most important influence on my career and my success."

A dark haired petite woman approached them. "Michael darling," she gushed, "how are you." She kissed him on both cheeks and kept standing close to him. After a few pleasantries Michael still smiling said pointedly in her direction, "I'm speaking to Maureen."

"Why, yes of course," she said, only then acknowledging Maureen's presence. He stepped back and turned again towards Maureen.

Maureen was thrilled with Michael for showing a preference for her and admired how deftly he had dismissed the woman. It was like coming first in a competition she thought, the prize being his attention. She gazed warmly at him. They stood side by side.

Surges of people streamed through the hall door. Waiters appeared with drinks and canapés. There was no sign of the host. For some time they stood lost in the bustle around them. The room became extremely full. The ceilings were so high that sound travelled upwards and as the party warmed up and musicians started to play it became extremely noisy. It became harder to hold on to some personal space.

Maureen felt strangely claustrophobic standing in the huge cavernous space, the only outlets downstairs being two nondescript doors on either side of the room. From the windows high above, shafts of light streamed down onto the beech wooden floor. Maureen looked up to breathe; it seemed to be where the air was.

People walked freely all over the house. It was generally on show.

"Let's explore," Michael said, pointing towards a long corridor off the main room.

"Yes lets," Maureen agreed relieved.

They walked past different groups of people until they came to one of the doors opening on to the entrance of the corridor.

Charles stood in a corner of the room on his own.

"Charles is very quiet tonight, he is not in the best of form," Michael remarked.

"Don't mind him," Maureen said, "I think he's slightly put out that the house is star of the show." They laughed.

Walking down the long corridor this part of the house seemed particularly quiet as people hadn't discovered it yet. They both opened and closed doors. Some rooms were unremarkable and then on the left hand side of the house, on the side of the sea, they opened a door into the most glorious room they had ever seen. It was a large room, more expansive in width than in depth. Three of the walls were painted white. The fourth wall was a vast expanse of glass facing out onto the sea. Completely bare the only pieces of furniture in the room were two Corbusier chairs placed side by side facing the glass walling.

Outside a patio of about four feet in depth surrounded the house. A low barrier of glass at the edge of the patio was the only protection from the sheer drop to the sea.

There were no plants on the patio, no decoration of any kind. Lighting was the sole tool of decoration used. Beams of blue and turquoise light shone on the patio floor and one powerful light high on the outside window was directed towards the sea enhancing the view even further. The effect was enchanting.

Michael and Maureen stood for some moments entranced.

"This must be his private quarters," Maureen said. "Do you think he would mind if we sat here for a while? He might think we are intruding."

"I don't believe he would," Michael replied.

Placing their wine glasses on the wooden floor, they reclined back into the undulating shape of the chairs, the solid frame of tubular steel supporting them.

Through the glass the sea seemed only feet away and they had the sensation of being elevated and suspended out over the water. They stared ahead in wonderment.

"This is the most magical setting I have ever witnessed in my life," Maureen declared.

"This must be where he comes for his inspiration," Michael said quietly. "It's ingenious, in order to create he aligns himself with creation placing himself in its very centre."

"It must be why he keeps the room empty," Maureen said. "No distraction. Leaving his mind as uncluttered as possible to absorb the new ideas."

"It must be," Michael agreed.

They sat quietly, each absorbed in their own thoughts.

Michael broke the silence. "Charles told me that you are looking for some advice on your paintings."

"Yes I am."

"If it suits you, I could call over to you tomorrow and give you an opinion on them."

"Yes, thank you, that definitely suits me," Maureen said.

Just then the door opened and Charles came through.

"Ah there you are. I have been looking all over for you. Would you mind if we left now Maureen? I have a dreadful headache and it seems to be getting worse as the night goes on."

Maureen glanced at Michael and was pleased to see a shadow of disappointment cross his face.

Charles turning towards the door said, "Goodnight Michael. Maureen, I'll wait for you in the hallway."

They both stood up. "I hate having to leave so early, she said, "but I will see you tomorrow."

"Yes, I'm looking forward to it."

"It was nice to meet you," Maureen said, as they headed towards the door.

"Yes, lovely to meet you too," Michael replied. "It's good to meet someone real."

With that sentiment ringing in her ears Maureen almost floated out of the room and down the hallway towards Charles.

"Did you enjoy yourself my dear?" Charles asked as the taxi pulled away.

"Yes, I must say I did," she replied.

"Michael's a nice man," Charles said yawning.

"Yes, he is a very nice man," Maureen said, instinctively raising her hand to hide her smile.

The next day Maureen got up early and went down to the shed in the garden. Charles had reprimanded her for calling it a shed and had insisted she substitute the word studio instead. So, to herself she called it a shed and studio when in front of him.

Standing in the shed Maureen worked out her plan. She would show Michael some of her original work with the loud vibrant colours and then when she had explained the commercial idea to him, she would reveal the softer pastel collection of paintings. She hung the bright paintings on the wall and leaned some of them against the lower wall.

There was one new painting she'd been working on recently in between her commercial work. It wasn't finished, but Maureen was very happy with it. It was the view from the window of her bedroom in the cottage in Wexford. Maureen knew every detail of that view. This painting was different. It seemed more definite, more structured. In a way the painting signalled the end of her grieving for John. She was happy she was strong enough to revisit the place. It signalled closure.

Maureen began to feel nervous. What seemed such a good idea the night before didn't seem such a good one now. It was embarrassing having to show her work to someone so knowledgeable. She wasn't used to this scrutiny and could feel herself becoming defensive against any criticism that may come her way. She knew her defensiveness would make her seem edgy. She didn't want to appear rude.

Maureen heard the crunching of gravel outside and knew someone was coming. She stood in the doorway.

Michael appeared before her, smiling. "So this is where it all happens," he said.

"Yes it is, come in," Maureen gestured towards him.

They stood looking at each other. All of a sudden Maureen felt very gangly, with her hands flapping by her side.

"Would you like a cup of tea or coffee?" she asked.

"No, I've just had one," he said.

His attention was drawn away from her to the paintings and Maureen began to relax.

He studied them for some time. Holding one canvas in his hands he said, "You paint with great flourish and relish. I can see you love colour."

"I do. I love to infuse the ordinary with brilliance," she explained.

"Yes, they have a very unique quality."

"The trouble is they aren't selling," Maureen said. "Would you be able to explain to me the reason why?"

"I personally like the wildly painted splashes of colour, but for some tastes they may appear too random, too undisciplined. A little restraint I think, if introduced, could give your work a lighter touch. Sometimes it is worthwhile to contract; you don't always have to expand. It's a quality you could develop."

He stopped, thinking he'd said enough.

Maureen could see his discomfort. "Well, I have some more paintings to show you where I have used lighter colours." She led him towards the back of the studio. "They are based around a commercial idea I have had for some time."

"Good for you," he said.

"Oh," Maureen said, surprised and pleased at his approval. Then correcting herself she mused, I mustn't look to him for validation. I must find it within.

"I thought you might sneer at the concept of commercial art, at my plan."

He was silent.

"You know the snobbery attached to commercial art."

He stared expressionless.

"Come on, you must know."

"I don't think that exists as much as it did before. Do what you want to do that's my advice to you."

"Well I have some examples at hand. What do you think of them?"

"They are delightful. You draw well Maureen."

"Do you really think so?"

"I wouldn't say it if I didn't."

"My plan is to sell them in interior design shops to go with their furnishings. Do you think they will sell?"

"Well there is only one way to find out."

"Yes there is."

Maureen wanted more information about her older work. "Can you think of any other reason why my paintings won't sell," she asked delicately, trying to fashion a soft place for him to land the truth in.

But Michael was distracted by her newest painting. "Can I have a look at this one," he asked, lifting the new canvas in his hands. "This is very good, very interesting indeed. This is lovely," he stopped, admiring the work. "It is as if you have already put into practice what I have been saying to you, the lightness, the discipline; it has happened naturally. Your style seems to be evolving on its own. I love the cubistic shapes representing the hills, the patchwork of block colour signifying the fields. All the elements work well together. The entire piece dominated by the simple black cross of the window frame."

"Yes, it is a cross, although I wasn't conscious of that when I started to paint it. I wasn't aware of the symbolism of the cross with the bright colours behind it. It was only later that I could see the metaphor could apply to my own life. I do believe that after suffering there is brightness, that light comes after dark, always. If we believe and give it time."

"Yes," said Michael. "It is very interesting. I found that to be true in my own experience of life also," he said.

She liked the way he didn't flinch when she mentioned God. Like herself, he viewed Him as someone real in his life, like a friend.

"You choose to break up the block of jewel colour with small flecks of glint in the hillside," he continued.

"Yes, I think that's how we are. They represent paradoxes within us, which we have to work out and live with; the flaws at the core of our being."

"They bring more tension to the work. Are you more drawn to expressionism or cubism?" he asked.

"I don't know, is the only answer I can give," Maureen said speaking rapidly at her dread of having to critique her own work. "I don't like to over analyze my work, to do so would make me too self-conscious. I just want to paint. I find categorization tedious.

Why can't I just be unlabelled?" she asked, her voice rising in animation.

"You can. You are allowed have an individualistic approach. I think Modern Art can cope with your independence."

Maureen was thrown by his calmness. She was afraid he was tiring of her.

"Well, thank you for your help," she said. "I don't want to take up too much of your time. I'm sure you are busy."

"There is an exhibition in the National Gallery. I am going to it now. Would you like to come with me?"

"Oh, I'd love to," Maureen said. "Just let me get my bag." She ran back to the house and with her bag on her shoulder she met up with Michael at the front of the house.

They decided to walk into town.

"Charles is lucky having so much space near the city," Michael said.

"Where do you live?" Maureen asked.

"In town, I sell my paintings in a shop and live over it."

"That's fascinating," Maureen said.

"I moved back to the suburbs before my mother died. She was ill for some years."

"When did your mother die?"

"Two years ago."

"I'm sorry," Maureen sympathized.

At the entrance to the National Gallery, Michael knew exactly where to go. It struck Maureen that he probably knew every square inch of the building, having visited it so many times. Strolling through the rooms of the exhibition, Michael stood before each painting explaining light and proportion to her. They viewed the paintings for some time and then decided to go for coffee. They found a table by the window.

"You have a definite talent Maureen."

"You are very talented yourself," Maureen replied.

"I've been lucky. Many people are talented, but don't receive the recognition they deserve. I'm fortunate, my work has been recognised." He paused. "Have you studied art?" he asked.

"For one year only," Maureen said. "That's all I've done."

"Your work is good. I can help you to improve. I don't believe in overworked, pieces. I think it's important to let your own spirit through and you, Maureen, do just that."

"Well, there's plenty of me in my work," Maureen said sanguinely, stirring her tea. "I am not really sure if that is a good thing."

Michael noticing her despondency said, "Don't doubt your work Maureen. My advice is to let it go, release yourself from the pressure, let it go and see what happens."

Maureen liked his qualities of rock solidness, the unshakeable faith that emanated from him. "You are very confident," she said.

"I wasn't always like that," Michael replied.

Maureen was intrigued, but he was not forthcoming with any more details. Maureen let it rest. "What do you paint?" she asked.

"Well," he began, "I started off painting still life in the traditional style based solely on the value of aesthetics then, as time went on and my work evolved, it became more contemporary. In the last few years I have become influenced by the work of the artist Bill Viola. Now the intention of my art is not for improvement or aesthetic, but for the purpose of transformation."

"That's very interesting," Maureen said. "How do you hope to transform?"

"Through emotion," he replied.

These words were like some sort of miracle to Maureen - a man who valued emotion.

"Whereas Bill Viola works through the medium of video art in some of his work and uses actors to express emotions he wishes to portray," Michael continued, "I use actors and photography to capture emotions and paint from them."

"Is there an exhibition where I can see your work? I'd love to see them."

"You must come to my studio. Would you like to?"

"I'd love to," Maureen replied, not masking her delight at his invitation.

They moved from the restaurant to browse in the bookshop, the museum, a self-contained world of its own. Michael bought a book whilst Maureen looked through the catalogue of prints. Then strolling, they made their way outside of the building to Nassau Street.

Maureen turned to begin to say goodbye, fully aware that the minutiae of detail of their parting was crucial to whether she would see him again. "I had a lovely day Michael, thank you," she said, fingering a catalogue in her hands.

"I enjoyed it too," he replied. "Would you like to meet me some evening in town for a drink?" he asked. "Next Tuesday perhaps?"

"Yes, I'd like that very much," Maureen replied.

"How about," he paused trying to pick a landmark, "the Shelbourne Hotel at nine. Would that suit you?"

"Yes, that suits fine."

"Well goodbye then," he said smiling.

"Goodbye," Maureen replied.

Maureen turned to walk back to Charles' house. Tuesday, that was only two days away. She was so pleased with the short wait to their date, with the definite arrangement. She liked the way he was able to make up his mind, his certainty, the way he took control of the situation. She couldn't bear the uncertainty of waiting on a phone call. She felt too old for the cat and mouse game of dating.

The Shelbourne Hotel was quiet that late spring evening when they met. A small group of musicians in a corner of the lounge played low easy listening music. They listened to the music at ease in each other's company. Michael smiled as Maureen, lost in the rhythm of the music, tapped her feet absentmindedly in a world of her own.

Maureen was thinking how relaxed she felt in his company, as if she'd known him before. Sitting by his side she felt a bond forming. She knew he could feel it too.

Coming out of the hotel, walking towards the centre of town there was an atmosphere of peacefulness on the Dublin streets. Early evening was a strange time in the city, a time of waiting. Lines of taxis queued along the roadside for the anticipated night revellers to release themselves out onto the streets.

"I love to walk," Michael said, passing the taxis.

"I never used to," Maureen admitted, until I spent some months in Wexford. On a lovely evening like this though, I'd love a walk by the sea."

"We can walk down by the river if you like," Michael suggested, down towards the docks."

They walked enjoying the stillness; there wasn't a breeze in the evening air.

As they turned right from D'Olier Street onto the quays, the clouds out towards the horizon were dark and dramatic in the cobalt sky, folding in on each other, into tones of fluid blues, creating a magnificent foreground for their walk.

"It's lovely down here," Maureen said.

"I spent a memorable night here once."

"Oh," Maureen said, intrigued.

"It was a long time ago."

"Tell me," Maureen coaxed.

"It came back to me when I began pondering on what you said about my having confidence."

"Really?" Maureen asked, pleased that he had pondered on her comment.

"I learnt a valuable lesson very young. I was successful very quickly. After my second year at Art College they decided to put on an exhibition of student's work. I won student of the year. It was held on a Thursday night, I remember that because my mother was relieved she didn't have to ask for time off work, from her second job. She worked in a restaurant two evenings a week. All week we worked hard finishing and displaying our work to its best advantage.

There was great excitement around my exhibition stand. I had a number of people approach me wanting to buy my work. Towards the end of the night when I was standing by myself, one of the student's fathers came over to me. Back then some of the parents were even more ambitious than the students. I looked towards him expecting a smile of congratulations instead his grey eyes were full of contempt, his mouth curled in a half smile full of sarcasm and through his teeth he said, 'Beginners luck old chap, just beginners luck.' But it was the look of contempt intensifying to hatred as he turned away that unnerved me. My face was pale with shock at the negativity of the remark; his lone voice began resonating into a chorus of disapproval, piercing through to the non-expectation, the self-limitation that lay beneath my own tenuous sense of self. In that moment, I was split open. Belief drained from me.

My mother walked towards me ready to go home, the black fabric of her gabardine coat shiny from wear. She looked poor. She had witnessed what was said."

'Is it too good to be true Michael,' she asked in her soft Dublin accent. 'Is it all too good to be true?'

"She was full of fear too, looking to me for reassurance. I was hanging on by my fingernails to any feelings of self-belief I had. I had none to give her. I didn't want to be with my mother as she was a witness to what had taken place which somehow made it more real. I couldn't deal with her questions, with her doubt.

I put her safely on the bus home and told her I would be home later, that I had some thinking to do.

'You can think at home Michael,' she said, her practicality overriding her concern.

'Just tonight,' I said. 'Leave me on my own for tonight. Don't worry if I don't get home.' I walked towards the docks. The landscape of the docks was completely different then," he said, passing one of the fake Victorian lamp posts on the quays. "I remember empty warehouses framing the Liffey, tall ghostly grain stores with glassless windows punctured like black holes through the fabric of the stone.

I headed towards a late night pub and ordered a drink. It was a real spit and spittle sort of pub, hazy with smoke and the soft glow of lamp light. The décor was basic in the extreme, wooden floors, simple wooden chairs, furnished mainly with the company of men, mostly dock workers. That October night brown fog curled in off the sea winding itself along the river.

One man began to sing sad, wistful songs, songs of home and place, his plaintive voice expressing my loneliness and yearnings.

I sat on a bench against the wall, separated from the group. There was no expectation to talk. I was free to think, to wage war on my own thoughts. I was struggling to rekindle that which was extinguishing, my very essence, my creativity. Although intangible, I could palpably feel it leaving me. I was left in a damning, harsh place devoid of hope, faith or future, left staring into the abyss of nothingness.

After some time a strange acceptance fell on me. In a peculiar way I felt cleansed, cleansed of my talent, my ambition, my hopes and yet it was terrifying too. With my creativity gone, I had no tool to pull myself out of myself, nothing to enhance me. My work was my companion and now I was alone."

He stopped. They walked some more, Maureen linking his arm, gave it a little squeeze for encouragement.

He continued, "I drank and dozed on and off all night. In the morning, I awoke to the smell of fried breakfast. A plate of cooked bacon and egg was put in front of me. 'Fill up on that,' a man said, 'and get that pot of tea down you. There's a couch inside if you want a proper kip,' he said. I declined.

Walking back along the quay, back towards the college, the city centre was beginning to waken, a tiny flow of traffic moving on the streets.

In the Art College, I headed to my art room which was a double room on the second floor of the building, trying to be as quiet as possible as some loose pieces of wood on the old uneven parquet floor rattled beneath my steps. The bright morning sun from the east streamed through the high sash windows.

My easel was in the familiar place by the window. Someone had arranged the beginnings of a still life on a table in the top left hand corner of the room. I took up my brush and tried to paint. Nothing came. My hand, holding the brush, was midway between myself and the canvas, still nothing would come. Unbeknownst to me, Professor Cole stood at the door watching.

'Michael!'

I swung around my face stricken with grief, with despair.

'It's gone,' I said.

'And the one negative opinion cancels out the hundred positive?' he said, walking towards me.

'Yes. I've let it. His opinion is nearest the truth in my head.'

He faced me. 'Trust in God. God is the fount source of creativity.'

And heading towards the door he said, 'Don't let the bastards get the better of you.'

After he left, I stared at the still life, at the sweet coyness of the arrangement. My brushes seemed inadequate, my easel too restrictive, the palette of bright colours inappropriate. I found some large canvasses and cleared a space for them placing them against the window and began preparing palettes of black, charcoal grey and brown. The professor's words came back to me giving me courage. I began to feel supported by something good outside of myself as if some sort of benevolent force was encouraging me. My arms moved in expansive arcs over the canvas, the broad brushstrokes forming vast swaths of shade. Through the swirling mists of brooding colour, images began to form, a suggestion of a silhouette of a woman, the majesty of a horse's head; the bold gestures on the canvas liberating me from the restraining concept of aesthetic value."

Michael paused. "These are my most treasured paintings," he said. "They signaled a new direction for me, a loosening of the old forms, a releasing of a new confidence in my work, a power that hadn't been there before. Through these paintings my work became emboldened, more sure, more confident. His comment liberated me, liberated my style although his intention was to hinder, he actually helped me. Good came out of bad. That's why I understand what you mean when you say that light always comes after dark."

They crossed over the Samuel Beckett Bridge. Midway, Maureen stopped for a moment staring at the river towards the sea and as she stood the moon emerged behind breakaway filaments of cloud, casting a widening corridor of light down the river.

They continued walking back towards town along the quay for some time in silence, listening to the gentle lap of the river. They stopped at O'Connell Bridge.

"Can I see you again Maureen?"

"Yes, I would like that," Maureen said.

"Come to my home on Friday," he suggested. "I will show you my paintings there."

Michael's home was in Green Street, off Capel Street. The building stood out amongst the terraced row of shops on the street, having been refurbished. He led her into a side door beside the main shop entrance. They entered a narrow hallway.

"I live on the first two floors," he explained, as Maureen followed him up the stairs.

"My studio is on the third floor," he said, raising his arm upwards. "In an attic conversion." Patting the banisters he expanded further, "I had the stairway widened to allow access for the larger canvasses." Michael led her into a bright living space. The living room was to the front of the building and the kitchen was to the back. The furniture was modern except for a huge velvet couch under the window. Colour was provided by beautiful tapestries on the wall.

"These tapestries are lovely," Maureen said. "Where do they come from?"

"I got those in Argentina on one of my visits. I love that country."

"How did you manage to travel when your mother was so ill?"

"The rest of my family took over caring for her for some months at a time and I was able to travel. Argentina is a unique place, very European yet with a fantastic Latin American feel to it. I loved the artists' quarters in Buenos Aires. I toured the pampas as well."

Maureen noticed a mannequin in the corner with a shawl draped casually around its shoulders. "Is that where you bought that shawl?" Maureen asked.

"Yes it is. I always came back feeling rejuvenated, with my creativity restored. I also love the tango," he said, almost shyly.

"Oh, maybe you'll teach me one day," Maureen gushed, and then was mortified by the implication in her outburst of a presupposed future meeting.

He smiled cheerfully, ignoring her discomfort. "I'd be delighted to," he said.

Maureen was intrigued, thrilled by his liking of dance seeing it as a romantic side of his nature.

"Have you many brothers and sisters?" she asked.

"I have three brothers, all married. I am the youngest by a good ten years."

Since the subject of marriage was raised, Maureen was sorely tempted to ask him why he never married; her curiosity stronger than her fear of appearing rude. There was a gap in the conversation. Maureen filled it. "So you never married?" she asked.

"No, I was engaged once. Since then I never came close. I've had a few relationships, nothing came of them."

"I was married," Maureen said, not giving him the chance to ask, "for a long time."

"How are you now?"

"Oh everything is sorted amicably." Maureen knew it wasn't what he meant, that it wasn't the practicalities he was interested in, but she didn't feel ready to explain.

"It just didn't work out," she said.

"I understand," he said, "but painful all the same."

"Yes, very painful," she said, letting her guard down.

"But that's then and this is now," she said in an upbeat tone.

"Yes, and this is now," he repeated slowly. He paused wanting to speak, "Maureen I like your company very much, would you like to see me again?"

"I would very much," she replied, "I enjoy your company too."

"Come and I'll show you my studio." They climbed two sets of stairs.

"Northern light," Michael said, on entering the attic, pointing to two huge Velux windows in the roof, "it's what you need for painting." Some paintings hung on the gable wall of the room. Maureen recognized them from Michael's description. She moved towards them. Michael watched her. "These are the paintings I told you about. I've collectively named them "The Epiphany" even if it was a forced one. That's why I've given them such a strategic place in the room."

"They are lovely," Maureen said. Maureen viewed some other sketches tacked to the walls. "How do you work?" she asked. "What's the process?"

"From the photographs I take, I make sketches," Michael explained. "These are my most recent paintings, the ones depicting emotion."

"I like them," Maureen said, studying his work.

A group of five faces lined together in a row on the wall with expressions ranging from supreme joy to extreme dejection and despair. Michael spoke eloquently, almost lovingly, about his work. He is a person who is alive, interested, involved in the world Maureen thought. She felt herself being carried along by his enthusiasm, recognizing that this is what she had missed, this awareness, this vibrancy and the companionship of similar interests.

"Let's take a break from the intensity of my work," he said, putting his arm around her shoulder and directing her towards the stairs. They returned to the living room. Michael prepared a drink.

He pondered on Maureen. There was a brittleness about her even within her friendly nature. In her reticence he saw humour as a way of relaxing her, lowering her defenses.

He put on a CD of a tango. Maureen started to sway to the music.

"I think it's time I taught you the tango," he said.

"No, I can't," she said, embarrassed.

"Come on," he said, "it's a bit of fun."

Maureen followed his instructions enthusiastically getting so carried away that she grabbed Michael and twirled him around.

"Goodness you are a force of nature," he said, stepping back from where he landed.

"I'm sorry," she said. "I can't help it. It's how I react to music; I can feel it move through me."

"Wait for just one moment," he said and went out of the room and up the stairs. He returned with a beautiful handcrafted Argentinean shawl in tones of lilacs and purples with shots of pale pink throughout. "I had no one in mind when I bought this," he said. "I decided that I would keep it for someone special. It's for you," he said, and then he unfolded the shawl and placed it assuredly on her shoulders.

Maureen was speechless with delight. "Why thank you, what a lovely gesture. I shall treasure it always."

"It suits you. Now shall we begin again?" he asked. "And this time take it a little slower".

After they had exhausted his CD collection he asked, "Can I see you tomorrow?"

"I have to go to my granddaughter's birthday party." Maureen explained. "Sunday perhaps?"

"Yes Sunday," he replied. "Come to my place for dinner. I will cook for you."

On the following Sunday Michael was excited at the thought of seeing Maureen again. He prepared his favourite summer meal for her, chicken salad, slowly and methodically.

Maureen was enveloped by the homely smell of roast chicken and stuffing when she entered his flat.

He took her coat from behind and observed her stance. Maureen was subdued. This mood was new, she seemed out of sorts, preoccupied. He deemed it wiser to let his expectation of her slip into neutral and just see what happened.

They sat opposite each other at his small square kitchen table. Maureen was quiet.

"How did it go with your daughters?" he asked. "Did you have a good time?"

Maureen made a face trying to contain the exasperation she felt.

"Spoilt, both of them are spoilt."

"The kids?"

"No," Maureen laughed, "My daughters, chiefly my daughters, although Ruth is a bit more discreet about it."

Not wanting to appear disloyal to her daughters Maureen thought to herself, they are all bling and what they've bought, but to him she quietly said, "We don't see eye to eye on certain things."

"Oh I see," was all he said.

Maureen was relieved. He didn't try to quieten her with senseless platitudes. She didn't have the patience for token reassurances.

In time what Maureen came to love about him was his ability to appreciate her directness, his acceptance of what she saw as her awful side - her ambivalence towards her daughters. He never judged her, just calmly absorbed what she had to say. It was so freeing, his lack of judgment. Harry judged her all the time.

When they finished eating they took their coffee into the living room. Maureen began to feel unwell. Her family had exhausted her, things were moving too fast with Michael. She felt crowded and needed space. As much as she loved being with him there was a strain in the newness of their friendship. Normally she'd try and put on a breezy act to quell her misgivings. It seemed dishonest somehow. She wanted to go home. She was aware of the risk she was taking by pulling back from stoking the friendship. For a few moments she pondered on the wisdom of her leaving. A series of possible dire consequences crossed her mind. It made no difference; she wasn't good company, she had to go.

"Would you mind if I leave early Michael? I'm not feeling great."

"Not at all," he replied.

"Thanks for the wonderful meal," she said, getting up from the couch. "I enjoyed it very much."

"Can I drive you home?" he asked.

"No, I'll walk thanks; the air will do me good." Gathering her things, Maureen was relieved that the atmosphere had not changed. His manner was still warm and he was concerned for her welfare. There was no ill feeling emanating from him.

"Goodnight Maureen," he said pleasantly.

"Goodnight," she said.

On leaving the house, Maureen was glad he still seemed happy, she didn't want to have to take responsibility for his feelings.

Back in the house, Maureen was relieved that Charles was out. Turning on the light in the kitchen, the only sound for company was the hum of the fridge.

At the sink, Maureen poured herself a glass of water and looked out at the garden at the bright reflection of the kitchen through the blackness of the window. Her pale pinched reflection stared back at her.

Examining her mood she tried to pinpoint what exactly was wrong with her. Was it the fear of being subsumed by someone again? The fear of losing her independence in the midst of all the care Michael offered her. Maureen knew she had to gain some perspective. She liked Michael, she liked him a lot. She knew he cared for her. She decided that she would relax and see how things would go.

The next morning on hearing the familiar plop of post on the floor Maureen went to retrieve some letters. One letter was addressed to her. It was from the interior design shop. They had sold all of her prints and wanted ten more of each and were delighted to enclose a cheque for €400. Maureen was ecstatic. All her worries and feelings of unwellness vanished and she felt full of energy and zest.

The first person she wanted to tell was Michael, but it was too early to ring him. She went back to her room. With the good news she felt grounded again, back on track.

Shortly after 10.00 a.m., Maureen rang Michael and told him of her success.

"Michael I want to bring you out to celebrate. Will you come out for a meal with me?"

Michael was delighted with her invitation and without hesitation said, "Yes."

The following night Maureen arrived at her favourite restaurant. She was in high spirits. Two groups of people were already eating and their laughter and good humour pervaded the atmosphere. Candles and discrete lighting created the general ambience of sparkle, the restaurant itself reflecting the glittering mood of the diners.

The good humour was infectious and the waiter was in great form as he led Maureen to the small booth she had earlier managed to procure with an exaggerated flourish.

Maureen had just settled in her seat when Michael walked towards her. From the moment he greeted her Maureen knew the evening was special. There was buoyancy in the air.

"What wonderful news," was the first thing he said to her.

"Yes it is," Maureen said, clasping her hands together.

Michael was so delighted for Maureen and Maureen was so delighted for herself that they sat beaming at each other.

"And I have even more good news," Maureen said. "I have been asked to supply two more interior shops with prints. There seems to be huge demand for original pieces at reasonable prices."

"Well done to you," Michael said.

Unfolding her napkin Maureen said, "You know I am interested in sketching some prints with a Japanese influence, I admire the delicacy of Asian art."

"I've been to Japan," Michael said, "I have some wonderful postcards. They may inspire you".

Maureen realised whilst sitting opposite him that there were years in his life she knew nothing about. Over that dinner they really talked to each other, filling in the gaps of their lives. So eager were they to converse, they viewed the waiter's request for their order almost as an interruption, as precious minutes lost in their interest in getting to know one another.

As she ate, Maureen realised he was the happiest man she'd ever met. Not in a smug satisfied way but he had a deep sense of contentment about himself as if he'd dealt with all his issues and was at peace. He was the least angry man she knew, even tempered and kind.

As he spoke, Maureen reflected on his personality. There was a complete solidness about him; the sense of his truth which emanated from him was almost sacred. The attractiveness of his personality transcended in a physical way, it imbued his whole being. During the meal he was so attentive to her, interested in the small detail of her life, remembering what she had previously said. He was so present when he was with her. Maureen found herself being seduced by these qualities of his character.

"Don't you have goals you want to achieve?" she asked.

"To learn about life is my goal," he said. "If I need something specific I take on more work. Don't get me wrong. I think money is a great facilitator. It can buy you choice and comfort. I work to live not live to work." Maureen admired the rhythm of his life. It was a balance she hoped one day to achieve.

When their desserts arrived Michael gestured to the empty space beside him and said, "Come over here beside me." Maureen placed her dessert and wine on his side of the table and slid in beside him. They sat in close together and between sips of wine and snitches of laughter they snatched tiny kisses unable to resist touching each other with little squeezes and hugs.

They sat talking until the place had emptied and the waiters began to clear their table. Leaving the restaurant, Maureen began to worry a little about how the evening would end. Outside on the pavement Michael turned to face her and said, "Come back to my place." It was said in such a direct way that Maureen knew it was an invitation to stay over. It was still too soon for Maureen. She hesitated. Michael saw the hesitation in her face. "Whatever suits you," he said, his face kind. Maureen began to make excuses. "I'll come back for a quick coffee. I won't stay too long." He was not put out by her hesitation. "That's fine," he said. "I'll order you a taxi whenever you want to go."

Leaving his house later that evening Maureen was still undecided as to whether she was doing the right thing. She had mixed feelings about it and almost regretted her decision. She was in one way reluctant to go home and felt lonely in the taxi as if she'd clumsily bludgeoned the natural progression of their relationship.

. . .

In the early summer Charles began to talk of travel. He made several references to his children and his wish to visit them. Change was in the air. Maureen sensed that the phase of her life with Charles was coming to an end. Within her sadness she felt resigned to the situation, aware it had to happen, knowing her hiatus with Charles couldn't go on forever.

These changes brought up issues about her future. New living arrangements had to be made. Within the uncertainty, a vacuum was created. Michael attempted to fill it. He saw it as an opportune time to declare his intentions towards Maureen.

At first nothing was said directly by Michael, but indirect questions were asked about her future. Maureen could sense his need for a pinning down of her plans. The fear rose again.

One Sunday, soon after, Michael invited Maureen for lunch in his home. Whilst finishing their coffee Michal began, "I believe Charles is talking of travelling."

"Yes," Maureen replied.

"Have you given some thought as to what you will do?" he asked.

"I have given it some thought," she said, not wanting to expand any further.

Suddenly he sat up his back straight and pushing his cup and saucer towards her he said, "Why don't you move in here with me?" His face shone with excitement and he could hardly believe what he had come straight out with.

Maureen was flabbergasted, she stared back at him.

"Well, what do you think?" he asked again. "I have enough space for the two of us, we could paint together, we'd have a lovely life here." He raised his arms in a suggestion of inclusivity offering her all he had around him.

Maureen sat back in her chair. She felt the pressure of having to make some form of commitment. Maureen wanted to kick back against the pressure. She knew it was unreasonable to feel trapped. She tried to reason with herself.

"Michael, I like my own space. I want to go back to my own apartment."

He watched her in silence.

She felt what she was saying was an inadequate explanation of her fears. In her annoyance and frustration with herself she stood up from the table and in a moment of pure pique she turned away from him and exclaimed, "I'm not someone you can use for your art, someone you can file under 'Maureen Moments' and then preen over in your dotage."

"What are you talking about? How can you say that?" he asked, almost distracted.

He walked towards her taking her hand. "Maureen I love you, you are the most amazing woman I have ever met."

"No, no, no, you mustn't put me on a pedestal."

"Why ever not?"

"Because the books say that if you put someone on a pedestal you will only end up disappointed with their ordinariness."

"What books?"

"The books I've read about life."

"You can't live your life through books."

"Well, I haven't made too good a job of it on my own have I?"

"Why do you think you have to be so strong? he asked. You are not the titanic. All love involves a certain vulnerability. It is the nature of love in some ways."

Maureen wasn't convinced, she wanted to explain herself further. She walked towards the window and sat down on the couch and without looking at him began to speak her voice low.

"Michael, over the last few months I have viewed myself as a series of switches. The switch of hope and belief is switched on and it will always be on because I do believe that I will find love. All the other switches are turned off, like the switch for longing and desire because it's easier to live that way, but since I've met you they are starting to switch back on and the raw vulnerability this exposes is excruciating. It's like being split open."

"Don't you think I feel that too?" he asked.

Maureen was startled by his remark. "I never thought of it from your point of view," she paused, "and if I let my heart valves open," she continued, "how will I close them again if it doesn't work out?"

"But it will, it will," he said. "Look all I know is that I love you and want to protect you."

Maureen looked into the face of a man whose very soul was being exposed through the raw depth of his feeling. Like a furnace of love Maureen wanted to shield her eyes, to run away from it, to close this man down and only open him up again when she had time to think whether this was what she really wanted. But then the moment would be lost and his exposure was heartbreakingly genuine. What could she say to him, the truth, a voice inside her said, tell the truth.

"I…I am so afraid to risk loving you …."

"Take the risk," he said, his eyes almost pleading, offering himself to her in all his bare emotional vulnerability.

"Maureen I want to give you something," he said, and from his pocket he produced a square jewellery box.

He sat in beside her and opening the box he handed it to her. Inside on a dark blue silk lining lay a butterfly brooch set with amethyst stones, her birth stone.

"It's beautiful Michael."

"Maureen, this butterfly is a symbol of my freedom. I am acknowledging that I know I am free to go, but I choose to stay with you. It is a declaration of my commitment to you, to us."

"Michael thank you, I don't know what to say."

Relaxing close into him, her physical movements replicated the relaxing of her emotional defenses and he sensing this took control and he was strong and he was tender and it was lovely. It was wonderful.

. . .

Charles was matter of fact and unsentimental about her leaving. He knew she now had a good income from her prints and was happy that he would see her on his return.

In early August, on the day before Charles was due to travel, he asked Maureen to accompany him to the bottom of the garden. "The reason we get along so well Maureen is, I enjoy your sense of drama," he said, keeping in step with her. "I cannot abide people with no sense of drama. I surround myself with people of drama, storytellers, etc. Without a sense of drama there is no life. Oh, by the way, speaking of drama, that friend of yours Faye, she has quite a good voice, I advised her to join a choir. It seems to have worked well for her. A young man is calling, her father tells me."

On the wall outside of the studio hung an object, which was covered with a piece of cloth.

189

They both stopped beneath it.

"Maureen," he said, "I had this plaque made for you to honour your artistic talent and then he reached up and flamboyantly pulled off the cloth and there in all its glory a plaque was revealed which stated:

'Maureen McKinney, Artist and Entrepreneur,
worked here 2005- 2006'

"Maureen I admire your artistic talent. I have no artistic talent whatsoever," he said in a rare moment of petulance.

"Yes you do," Maureen cried. "You excel in the art of persuasion."

"My dear what a lovely thing to say to me," he said.

Then came the moment Maureen had been dreading.

"Goodbye Charles."

"Don't say goodbye," Charles said, "say cheerio. I shall call on you upon my return," and with that promise he bowed slightly towards her and strode up the garden path towards the house repeating to himself, "I excel in the art of persuasion," and gave a hearty laugh.

Maureen examined the detail of the plaque and loved the idea that she was forever linked to this place, to this family, to Charles himself.

. . .

The summer came, the city seemed airless and hot. Maureen's thoughts returned to Wexford. It was important for her to show Michael the birthplace of her inspiration.

"Will you come to Wexford with me?" she asked him one day as they strolled through the city streets. He knew of the cottage and her painting there, but that was all. She had not spoken to him of John and would not. He was in the past locked away and he would stay there.

Some two days later Michael and Maureen drove to Wexford. They deliberately came off the motorway to stop at villages like Ashford and Rathnew which Michael hadn't visited in years.

Michael's tendency was to head west when he wanted a break as he had some family there. The south east was relatively new to him and he was delighted to discover its beauty again. With all their stopping and starting, a journey of two hours took them the whole day and they reached Wexford at six in the evening just as the beaches were emptying.

The cottage was sleepy with disuse, comfortable in its abandonment when Maureen turned the key that evening. Dust lay over the fireplace and lamp table. She opened the windows and gave the place a quick dusting grateful for the lack of furniture. She placed one of Michael's Argentinian throws on the couch to establish their custodianship of the space. As she busied herself settling in, Maureen was worried about the reality of their blending. It was all very well talking about art, but how would they get on in the everyday? Someone constantly wound up busy wouldn't suit her, yet someone slowed to a snail's pace wouldn't suit her either.

Maureen needn't have worried. During the first few tentative days of the holiday they discovered their body clocks were in tune with each other. They were both morning people and developed a natural rhythm of when they wanted to eat and nap. At times they each valued quietness and then simultaneously would feel the need for company again.

He had no aptitude for the garden, but helped and positively glowed from the fresh air and novelty of having a garden. At the end of the first week Michael sat relaxing in the deck chair after some hours working in the garden. Maureen kneeling with a trowel in her hand at the flowerbed, glances towards Michael and he catches the glance. They both beam, their faces flushed in delight, basking in their achievement of harmonious living.

She couldn't imagine life without him. How had she had a life on her own before? That life seemed a prerequisite to this one. From someone who valued her independence, Michael had slipped seamlessly into her life. It was as if he had always been there, travelling alongside her all the while on an invisible carousel only waiting for her to catch up.

. . .

One evening in late August, further along the coast, Tim and Julie walk relaxed down the main street with their arms wrapped around each other. At the bottom of the street they turn onto the quay and Tim sees Kate standing next to a low wall by the water's edge. Her father in his wheelchair sits some feet away from her on the exposed part of the quay. Kate stands in shadow from the evening sun. Tim's mobile phone rings interrupting his gaze.

"Hi Clare," he says and listens for some moments. "Yes, that sounds great," he replies. "I look forward to it."

"It's Clare," he says, turning towards Julie. "She's invited us to visit her and David whenever it suits us. She's looking forward to seeing you again. Will you come?"

"I'd love to," Julie smiles. Tim gives her a generous hug. They kiss and walk on past the quay together.

Maureen is in the cottage on that same summer's evening. The blinds in the front of the cottage are pulled down. In the back the blinds are up, the red setting sun in the west casting ochreous hues in the room. Maureen is dancing a Tango with Michael, blissfully happy. An exotic shawl drapes from her shoulders. All around them on the beaches, in the hotels, cottages and caravans, people are enjoying their holidays.

Families making memories to sustain them against whatever life brings; a well of perfect moments to draw strength from in difficult times; their sanctuary, where love remains alive and faithful, a harbour of shelter in their hearts that anchors them to these golden memories of Wexford.

The End

CIRCULATING STOC_____ PUBLIC LIBRARIES
BLOCK LOAN

F/MAS

#0216 - 220316 - C0 - 229/152/13 - PB - DID1399734